The Bar Where Nothing Works

ADAM GRZESICZAK

The Bar Where Nothing Works
Paperback edition ISBN: 978-1-5272-7879-0
Electronic edition ISBN: 978-1-5272-7722-9

This book was first published on
November 5, 2020.

Copy editor: Anna Bowles
Proof-reader: Amanda Rutter
Cover design: Matthew Revert

Version: 1.1
London 2020

To All

CONTENTS

CHAPTER ONE

The absence of war is just another war. This one started a long time ago – hundreds of years, to be precise and it's still going on. It started long before the LLTS drive was discovered and long before many civilisations came to exist. Those who started it all came from a small satellite galaxy called Tamma IV. This insignificant place had never previously showed any signs of life, and apart from a few natural radio transmissions, it was quiet, empty and isolated. It was a perfect place for them to hide and wait, and sure enough, they did.

Initially, this species came from another galaxy, and only used Tamma IV to refuel and rebuild – and find out everything about us. Their moon-sized monstrosity of a spacecraft suddenly appeared in the power centre of our galaxy's imperial government, destroying it all: planets, moons, space stations and armies, without any warning or apparent reason. It was pure destruction. Then they started to move; system after system, layer after layer, sector after sector, they destroyed everything, and they were not interested in negotiations. For all that time, there was no communication with them, none at all. They just travelled around for centuries destroying everything in their path; planets, moons, asteroids, comets, spaceships, species and civilisations were all wiped out. Most of the galaxy's history disappeared.

The size of their spacecraft was the reason they failed. After taking more and more resources from ruined worlds, the vessel finally collapsed under its own gravity. I guess someone lost their job for wrongly calculating the mass. But this didn't stop the wars; quite the opposite, in fact. After the government failed, everyone started to fight with everyone else, creating war zones, dividing the galaxy back into its original states, and grasping as much power for themselves as they could. The real faces of most of the civilisations were shown, and clearly not everyone liked the central government.

Now, after all that time, we have forgotten why we are fighting. With so many species, no one can get together to talk peace, so the war is still going on. And imagine what the collision will bring.

The more time we have spent watching the cosmos, the more we have realised that there are a lot more galaxies on a collision path with one another than we once thought. After that became known, every single thinking organism wanted just one thing: to escape. The logic was simple: if you stayed, you were likely to die. The collision of those galaxies would bring chaos to an already chaotic world. In peaceful times, the collision of galaxies brings all the worlds together for everyone's benefits, but we are at war, and it's a big one.

* * *

Shan was walking through the dimly lit corridors inside his asteroid garage, passing other crew members' rooms. The dark walls, rounded perfectly into a cylindrical tunnel, had been made with a quantum drill and revealed the polished dark meteorite rock inside, in some places showing beautifully coloured minerals. Below him, the metal floor with built-in gravity, cables, pipes and ventilation was making noises as he walked. Above him, more pipes and ventilation machinery were making noises, too. He didn't hear it anymore, but for any new staff or guest, the first few nights were difficult.

After all, that place isn't a nice quiet hotel, but a cyborg-trying-to-think-asteroid-machine where everything makes noise. Pipes move cold and hot water, and let's be honest; they are not perfectly attached to the rock. The conditioning system makes noises too, pushing the cold and hot air, keeping the corridors and rooms at the right temperature. With a crew of so many different species requiring different environments, life support is complicated. And if you need specialists and experts from all over the galaxy, you'd better keep them happy. Lef and Tix, for example, are brothers or sisters depending on when you talk to them. This is due to their undersea origins. Their bed is hot, their room is hot, and they wear suits everywhere to keep their bodies hot, too. Normally they live on a warm planet where clothes or heaters over their desks are not needed, but here it's a different story.

Here's another room, which belongs to someone from a place where the custom of giving names doesn't exist. Here she's known as Phana, which derives from the place she was born. Her oxygen requirements are somewhat different, so outside of her hermetically sealed room, she wears a mask. Someone with an impossible-to-pronounce name is known as Nailee, which is a shortened form of his real name. His room is, let's say… dark. Other rooms are unique, too. Regarding water pipes, only Goe has an extra one attached to her room, just because she did it herself. It has nothing to do with the requirements of her anatomy, but with being lazy sometimes.

* * *

Shan entered the secondary bridge located on top of the garage where Goe was connecting herself to the computer. It was an elliptical room with windows all around, and it was mainly used for manoeuvring the asteroid and checking for outside ships. From the windows, you could see the surface of the rock covered in spare parts for the most advanced spacecraft imaginable. The bridge was simple with only one seat, a circular sofa in the centre, and controls and consoles all around.

'I thought you'd already connected yourself,' Shan said when he entered the bridge and walked over to one of the windows.

'I did,' Goe answered, 'but there's something wrong with the wireless, so I need a wire. I hid the plug as I never use it.' She was trying to connect a cable to one of the body interfaces inside her arm. She was sitting on the sofa with her right hand on the table revealing the mechanism within. The wire she'd just plugged in caused a little short circuit, sending a few sparks, and a holographic device, normally hidden inside her arm, dropped to the floor. It automatically deployed and started showing images from Goe's youth.

'Is that you?' Shan asked, surprised. He'd never seen her old photographs before.

'Don't look at it!' Goe squeaked, struggling to switch off the hologram.

'Wow, was that a jet engine?' Shan asked. The hologram showed a young Goe wearing a jetpack with two massive engines at each side, clearly home-made.

Shan had hired Goe a long time ago when she came looking for something to do. She was from a species similar to Shan's, with two legs, two arms and a head on a neck, but now her body was so improved with advanced extensions you could mistake her for a robot. Every day you could see some new augmentation sticking out of her somewhere, or she would have a completely new body part. She was an engineer, with not only years of experience but a real passion for machinery and making them work. She had improved the garage a lot since she joined – all thanks to that brain interface Shan envied so much, but was too afraid to use himself. She had quickly become the chief engineer, and was now managing everything.

* * *

Now back to the LLTS drive, also called the low-level transportation system. It allows you to travel through the lower levels of the universe, removing the problem with time dilation, which, by the way, has nothing to do with time in any case. The LLTS drive allows you to travel fast, I mean really fast, not measured by miles per hour, but by time per distance something. Basically, you move way faster than light: LLTS level one equals five thousand times light speed. This conversion doesn't really make sense, but gives you an idea of how fast LLTS is. The first people who tried it killed themselves, which wasn't a great start. You travel fast, but if you don't know where you're going, you can end up going through a star. Stars are fun to be around, but not to be inside, that's for sure.

LLTS blueprints were initially found in a monstrosity of a spacecraft belonging to a species called Besloors. These were the people who started the war, and when their ship broke down, their technology ended up all over the place. Apparently LLTS had been invented by accident, when the Besloors were testing high-energy weapons. During one of the highest-energy tests, they discovered malfunctions. Screens showed no data from any of the sensors, and when the Besloors checked, to their surprise, the core of the newly invented LLTS drive wasn't there. It was found a few hours later, fifty miles south, in the home of some not-very-happy family, sitting there glowing hot in the remains of a smashed jacuzzi. After that, the Besloors discovered the way to travel at low levels.

Once the plans leaked from the wrecked monstrosity spacecraft, governments banned LLTS as it allowed everyone to escape ruined worlds without any control. But it was too late, and it didn't take long for everyone to leave those worlds and spread across the galaxy. Currently, the best LLTS drives operate on level three, and can get you across the galaxy in forty-eight hours, that is, if you have a state-of-the-art power generator, cooling system, and a powerful enough computer to calculate your journey. The robots in Sector Four use it exclusively, but no one else honestly knows how it works, so you can ignore the above sentence. For the rest of us, travelling across the galaxy takes months. Nobody has yet figured out how the robots built this technology, and that's the main reason everyone hates them.

* * *

'Shut up,' Goe continued. 'Yes, it was, and it almost worked, kind of. Why do you think my right arm is artificial? I started when I was five; that's the picture.' Goe showed Shan the photo of her young self wearing an exosuit.

'Argh, this doesn't work.' She unplugged the cable and turned to Shan. 'I feel like something is missing from my body.'

'Try again later,' Shan smiled and looked outside.

'What are you looking at?' Goe asked and walked to the window.

'With the number of clients we have, we'll need another garage,' Shan said, studying the long queue of spacecraft waiting to get their maintenance done.

'With the number of clients we have, we'll need a planet,' Goe replied, chuckling.

'I think I need to talk to our military friends. It's mostly their fault we have so much work. We're the only garage large enough for their battleships, and they won't spare any more resources to build another one.' Shan walked over to the console displaying the map of the galaxy. 'If they did, or if I could find someplace, we could expand. If not here, maybe in another part of the galaxy. Sector Four sounds promising.' He pointed at the map.

'That's where the robots live.' Goe honestly hated robots, at the same time as hugely envying them. 'They have the best technology you can get, and they don't want to share it with anyone. I don't like them; everyone shares technology but not them. They can get across the galaxy in forty-eight hours, and it takes us months, it's ridiculous.'

'Maybe they have a reason,' Shan replied, still browsing the map.

'Yeah right, they've been here so many times and we still don't know how their drive works.' Goe was pacing now. 'They don't even want to escape the collision; they're so stupid.' She sat down on a sofa and started adjusting her left eye lens.

'You've seen their ships. They're so advanced we can't even scan them, but the robots still come here because they can't fix the smallest thing themselves. It's weird.' Shan was annoyed too, but he was also happy as robots paid in good technology. 'Let me speak to the military first. Maybe I can persuade them to give us another asteroid.'

'Fine. But why do you want to expand, and why now? We're all too busy to do anything.' Goe looked at Shan like he'd said something stupid.

'The collision won't happen that quickly anyway, and I have some plans for Sector Four,' Shan replied, walking to the sofa. 'Look at this place,' he continued after a pause. 'I need to think about the expansion; not only expanding here but to another sector.' He sat down and looked at Goe. 'Listen, I am the owner of this garage, and I am responsible for keeping everyone safe, and making sure we fix all those battleships to help the military to stop the war. This garage brings jobs, food and shelter; it helps everyone, and brings us resources. The more resources we have, the easier it will be to escape. This sector is getting worse; the wars and battles are getting out of control. Apart from the robots' planet, the rest of the galaxy is in ruins. Even with a small garage in another sector, we can make a difference. Everyone needs jobs, resources and food, and ironically, the war can provide that. We fix the military's warships, they protect us and provide resources. We don't have much choice; you know that. Robots can help us with protection; that could give us some peace, some normal life for a moment.'

'What do you mean, you're responsible? The war's not your fault, and we're all trying to live and survive.'

'I know, I know.' Shan was quiet again.

'Seriously, Shan, we've been friends for a long time. You can talk to me. Besides, you have no one else to talk to, with your closed personality, trust issues, and general quietness.'

'Thanks.'

'Hey, I tell it like it is. You have nobody, and you're lonely. It is a lonely job being the boss, and if you don't like my honesty, fire me.'

'No, I won't fire you for honesty. I like that, I always did, and that's why I trust you.'

'So you should trust me more.'

'It's not easy, and it might be a while, but I'll try,' Shan said, then took a deep breath. 'I trust nobody; I *am* a nobody who would like to be somebody who could make a difference.'

'What the hell happened in your life to make you like that? I don't know anything about you. You never say anything about your life.' For as long as Goe had known Shan, he'd always avoided talking about his past.

'What happened to you and that jet engine? Why do you enhance your body?' Shan always wanted to know Goe's past, but she always avoided talking about it as well.

'Don't change the subject.'

'I'll tell you everything if you tell me.'

'Fine. The truth is, I'm afraid of dying,' Goe finally admitted.

'That's not a revelation; we all are.'

'Yes, but my fear is exponentially bigger. It started not long after I lost my arm in that jet engine accident. After that, I started to think more, and feel more about myself, and my body, and that I might actually die one day. Thinking that one day I will close my eyes, and I will no longer see my nose, my extensions, and it will be total darkness and quietness… that is causing me actual physical pain. That's why I want to live forever, and not necessarily in my organic body. I can be a robot, a cyborg or even a computer program, but I really want to be immortal. Another reason is to see the future, but for now, that's a secondary problem. Now your turn.'

'Before I opened this garage, I was stupid. I mean, really stupid. Me and my friend back then, we did all sorts of ridiculous things. Our interest in engineering brought us to all those fallen spacecrafts, and they were full of weapons. We'd always dreamed of having our own ship, so we tried to fix them. We took parts from some and tested weapons on others.'

'That's not a revelation. We all did that, come on! Where do you think I got my first enhancement kit?'

'Yes, we did, but I've seen bodies. I've seen what this war has done to us, and what it's still doing. Instead of helping those pilots and those robots, I did nothing. I was so into parts and machinery that I left them there. They were still alive, Goe. Soldiers, war robots, even civilians. I completely ignored them because I was more interested in getting as many parts as I could. It was my drug. Still is, but here I can control it. A drug: taking parts, taking data and more parts, taking and taking and taking. The cost was my health and the life of others, because I left them there to die, and myself to starve.'

'There's more, isn't there? Why didn't you tell me all this before?'

'Closed personality, trust issues, and general quietness. Your words.' Shan smiled.

'Not funny. Continue with the story.'

'I opened this garage with my friend. That's something you didn't know.'

'No, you always said you opened it yourself. What was his name?'

'His name is important to me, and I stopped saying it out loud a long time ago. Anyway, he died shortly after the grand opening. To this day, I don't know who killed him, and I almost died that day as well. Since then I've changed, I think. I started to work so hard, and so much, that the last twenty years have passed as if they were a day. I made myself responsible for his death and the deaths of those I could have helped, so I turned this garage into a place where anyone could come, work and stay. By helping fix those spacecrafts, I could maybe do my part to help the military to stop the war, and help everyone, but I failed. And now it's even worse. The war is worse; pirates are everywhere, in every sector, and on all the planets, and all the civilisations are fighting each other. It's ridiculous, and I'm thinking about a holiday. I feel even worse for thinking that. I need a break while the war is raging, but the war doesn't give you a break.'

'I know the feeling,' Goe said.

Shan continued after a pause, 'I grew up in difficult times – well, we all did, you know that. Times of war and uncertainty, and times hidden beneath the war. Times where we all look for answers, understanding, and ways out. War or not, we all have little wars going on inside us; with ourselves, and with others, about everything and nothing. The war outside changes everyone for the worse, but at the same time makes us better, it's a weird irony. And it's a delicate balance, one usually destroyed by idiots. Good versus bad, them versus us. The war takes away everything and gives you something completely different. It provides you with a survival instinct, which is a good thing, but you have to be careful with it.

'I've never been to war myself, but we've all experienced it. It affected my whole life, my parents, my planet, resources, my toys, food, water and freedom. On one hand, the war was very normal to me. Going to the shop, to the garage, school trips, walks, all the while bombs were falling, soldiers were fighting, guns were firing, spacecrafts were flying around protecting our little world. Maybe because I was an unusual child, I wanted to help others, especially those who were treated differently. I was a kind of refugee myself, I know the pain. Although my life differed from theirs, I think it's ultimately all the same. After the collapse of the government, everyone closed their borders. Everyone from the worlds that had been destroyed tried to escape, but crossing the oceans of the galaxy wasn't an easy task, and it still isn't. I help whenever I can. I hire lots of refugees, different species from all over the galaxy, but now the war is getting worse. You have no idea, Goe. Requests are coming in constantly, from the government, from the military, from everyone, and I can't handle it anymore, but nor can I stop, because then what would you guys do? I was thinking we could expand so I could fulfil all those requests, but am I right or am I kidding myself?'

'Wow, seriously, I don't think you've spoken this much since I met you, and I feel like you need a hug. But anyway, you definitely need a holiday. Everyone takes them, but not you. You don't even do any technical stuff anymore. Every time I see you it's like you're barely here, you're absorbed in that paperwork, and always talking to someone. I haven't seen you in the kitchen for a long time. Go home, go somewhere, take a week off, or two or even more. If you don't, you'll go crazy and then we'll definitely have to close the garage. War or not, you need a break. I've been doing a lot of management here, and with my enhanced body and mind I'll cope. I'm already connected to the garage's system;

I see most of the requests in my head so I can deal with them anytime, anywhere. Lef and Tix will help, they're good engineers. You need to trust us more, seriously.'

'You're right; I need a holiday. I'll think about it. Thank you for that.'

'Any time. You did so much for us; let us do something for you.'

'You know what time it is?'

'I have a built-in clock in my mind; I always know.'

'Then we need to sleep. Don't stay up too late, it's not your shift,' Shan replied, and started walking towards the exit, but after a moment he stopped and said, 'Thank you again.'

He was leaving abruptly, but Goe knew to let him go.

* * *

Shan's garage orbited the primary star between its second and third planet, his home world. The garage was the central hub for repairing spacecraft in this sector. It was also the last one surviving, as it was the largest and the military needed it. Shan, who had lived his whole life in the shadow of the war, had managed to keep the garage operational for the last twenty years. His primary clients were mining and cargo companies, local government and the military. The military took most of the space and time, to his and everyone else's annoyance.

Sector Two, where Shan's garage was located, had used to be the wealthiest place in the galaxy, and it had been the last one to fall after the 'battle of the borders'. Before the war, this sector – which was abundant in resources, asteroids, planets and moons – had boasted the best defences, warships and military schools in the galaxy. It was the place where the central government had been established, before moving later to orbit the central black hole zoo. (Called zoo for its many black holes found in the centre of the galaxy.) The most ambitious projects had started here, and the most powerful weapons been invented. The most prosperous species originated in this sector, and even the poorest here were richer than those in other sectors.

Sector Two had been envied by every other sector and it was under constant criticism for how prosperous and wealthy it was. Then the place was flooded by all those who had harboured dreams of a better future, dreams that had been destroyed by those who were supposed to protect them. Now, Sector Two was like other sectors, in survival mode, and those who had come here now wanted to leave. The great migration continued but crossing the empty oceans of interstellar space had never been easy, and now it was almost impossible. The war, however, doesn't give you much choice. So, they travelled, then and now, on private ships or with smugglers who didn't care about lives, but about resources, as money lost its meaning a long time ago. Smugglers overcrowd their vessels; they don't check maps, they don't cooperate. And they die in sub-quantum nets.

Money is long gone, replaced by a resource, and knowledge-based society. The shift started so far in the past that no one remembers it anymore, but currency on that scale didn't work. It was a slow and painful change, but eliminating money helped with many of its associated problems: greed, power, loans, debts, corruption; all the things that had caused poverty and inflation, destroying communities and economies. Half the civilisations were glad to see it go as they had disliked the concept of money in the first place, some tried to keep it, and the rest had a variety of completely different ideas. Barter was not a solution; it had as many issues as money. But it was decided – money needed to go. The resource and knowledge-based system was introduced, and for many years it was a disaster, but slowly, new generations learned to live without money, and gradually all the other sectors followed. A few of those isolated civilisations that somehow managed to survive decided to keep it, but for the rest, money was something only historians talk about anymore.

* * *

All the rooms were located under the main corridors and near the outside surface. Mainly for easy access to the maintenance floor, but also to keep them far away from noise and vibrations, and to provide natural light. This side of the garage was always turned towards the central star of the solar system, as initially there had been lots of solar panels here. Now it stayed like that so everyone could enjoy the view.

Shan's room had a simple but very comfortable double bed, made by one of the last surviving furniture companies. As payment for fixing their spacecraft, they'd supplied all the wooden equipment for all the staff quarters. In the corner, where there'd used to be a corner sofa, he had a wardrobe, and shelves on one of the walls next to the door were full of things he had collected over the years from all over the galaxy. In recent years, he had been using his quantum drill to slowly expand his room and make space for all the things he was accumulating.

Shan went down to his room. It was either the last or the first, depending on where you started counting from. He closed the metal door and started his after-work routine. The main thing was showering. Space garages get dirty, but no one had ever built a spacecraft-wash. It would be crazy to waste water just to clean ships and those, ironically, don't like water anyway. After his shower, the cook brought him dinner. A long time ago, when the crew was small enough, they'd had breakfast, lunch and dinner together in the main dining room next to the kitchen. Now that was tricky due to the different shifts needed to cover the twenty-four-seven operations of the garage.

'Enjoy: it's the last time you get to eat your favourites,' said Colin, the head chef, entering Shan's room after knocking on the door a couple of times. He put the plate on one of the shelves, which was now functioning as a small table. Shan's main desk was always covered with paperwork, wires, and instruments, so he never ate food there.

'What? Why?' Shan asked, looking up from the bed.

'You forgot again? You need a holiday.' Shan had forgotten a lot of things lately, including new tunnels that were being drilled, and many of the deliveries they'd had in the last few months. 'The last food transports were captured by pirates, or taken down to the main planet,' Colin added. 'We still have food, but you need to do something about it.'

'Oh, yes, sorry. I remember,' Shan answered, and closed his eyes before adding, 'Yes, I need a holiday, and I need sleep, and I need to sort out food.'

'Goodnight, and don't forget: breakfast the day after tomorrow in the small kitchen,' Colin said. He left the room, thinking that Shan probably wouldn't make it.

'Another day, another part,' Shan mumbled to the empty room.

He was working so hard, he never had time to himself. This evening he was falling asleep over his dinner when the screen, attached to a mechanical arm on a wall, started flashing with hundreds of unread messages. *I seriously need some time off from it all*, Shan thought. He was tired of this: he was missing breakfasts and never socialising. Days were long, hard work, but the worst thing was that he was losing his passion for spacecraft, computers and all the engineering he had once loved. Now his job was mostly paperwork and managing the garage, trying to accommodate as many battleships as possible in the shortest amount of time.

He finished his dinner and lay down, thinking about his family and the old days; about friends, and most importantly, about his grandfather. Shan had always been interested in his family history. He didn't know his birth parents and had made it his mission to find out any details he could about his biological family. But even with the most advanced technology and medicine, Shan's DNA tests didn't return much. The only thing he had from his real family was a photograph his foster parents had found when they discovered his cryo-pod. It was a portrait of his family standing on a hill with an unknown city below. He did all sorts of tests on the photo paper, from seeking experts' advice to carrying out sub-quantum analysis, but no origin was ever found. The photograph itself he kept inside a hidden asteroid with all his other valuables.

Shan had appeared one day as a speck of dust on the radar of a family of engineers who were travelling home from the cosmic garage where they worked. The speck was a cryo-capsule, and they had never seen anything like it: sleek and advanced, while the cryo-pods they knew were made of scrap metal, and you prayed to who-knows-which god that they would work at all. Shan looked a bit different to his foster parents, but as they already lived on a planet full of different species, they didn't mind; ironically, the war was bringing diverse cultures together. They took him to their big house full of parts, plans and tools, and it was there that young Shan got interested in engineering: first in breaking whatever he could find, and then in fixing it.

Now Shan moved the screen and brought the keyboard closer to him to type a new message, ignoring all the unread ones. *I know I shouldn't*, he thought. Lacking Goe's body extensions – he had never liked installing things like that, even if he loved them, for fear of developing another addiction – he had to use a regular old-fashioned keyboard. He typed a message in a sub-quantum chat with Eli, a girl he'd met a long time ago, who was now living in the wreckage city on the bar planet. He'd met her when she came to the garage to get one of her science vessels fixed. No reply came now; she was probably sleeping thanks to the difference in time zones. (If you have time zones on one planet, imagine time zones on thousands of planets. Booking meetings was a real pain.)

Shan fell asleep.

* * *

In the morning, the garage floor was busy with two large battleships having maintenance done. The room was enormous: a hole running straight through the asteroid and divided in half with corridors suspended on one side. Lef and Tix were floating around checking the spacecraft when the screen inside their helmets lit up. A message from Shan appeared.

Meeting this afternoon with Goe and me. 3 pm, please.

Shan's office was a small room next to the main bridge, where he could focus on work. There was a simple desk, some shelves, a chair, a wall planner filled with text, and no window, just screens on the walls showing the status of all the garage systems. He was sitting in his chair when Lef and Tix entered the room.

'Have a seat. Goe will be here in a minute,' said Shan, unconsciously checking his internal body temperature. 'Is it really that cold here?' he asked, knowing the answer when his body reported normal operating temperature.

'Well, I guess we can take off the helmets for a moment,' Lef replied. You could see almost everything through his and Tix's skin, as it wasn't designed to operate off their home planet. All their veins, brains and eyes: you could literally see the inner workings of their bodies.

'Might as well start,' said Shan. 'I'm going to travel for a bit. I need a holiday, and I'm going to have to leave the garage for you two to manage. Not sure for how long, but probably a few months.'

Lef and Tix – who were the two core engineers, one for each section of the garage – looked a bit shocked, as Shan never left the asteroid. His devotion to work was legendary.

'I think we should be fine managing it,' Lef replied first, not really knowing what to say.

'That's what we do here every day anyway. We should be fine,' added Tix. 'Excuse our surprise, but you've never left this place, like, since you opened it,' he continued while Shan stood up.

'That was, like… years and years ago. I don't think you've even gone away for a day or two,' Lef added.

'Yes, I know, and that's why I need some time off. Otherwise, I'll go crazy. I've been thinking about this for quite some time, and the best thing to do is just go. Otherwise I'll spend another twenty years here. I don't want that. It's time for a small change, and anyway, I can always come back,' Shan explained as Goe entered the office. 'Goe, I took your advice, I'm going on holiday. The garage is yours, and Lef and Tix will manage each section. You're in charge for the next few months.'

'Wow, finally. Don't get me wrong, though; I'm not trying to get rid of you. You know that, right?' she asked, though she didn't think that he did.

'Yes, I do. After we spoke yesterday, I spent a lot of time thinking. Well, I've been thinking about this for years, actually, and you're right. I need a break. I'll leave some paperwork for you to do for day-to-day stuff. And one more thing, Goe, can you prepare some… brain enhancements I can take with me? Maybe I'll try them during my holiday. You know everyone uses them but me, so I guess it's time.' Shan sat down and started moving some paperwork while Lef and Tix put their helmets on.

'Can we go now? We have some big spacecrafts to finish,' Lef asked, pressurising his helmet and adjusting the internal temperature.

'Yes, sure. I'll send the message to everyone. We'll be in constant communication over a sub-network. You shouldn't have any issues; just keep doing the excellent work you're doing, and if there's anything you can't do, let me know. I'll help remotely,' Shan explained.

'Where are you going, anyway?' Lef asked.

'Hopefully to Igem. They have the best beaches in the whole galaxy, and we don't need to wear any special suits there,' Tix explained. He remembered the last time he'd gone there and started imagining the sun, the ocean, and the freedom of not needing to wear a suit. He thought of his home planet too, which he missed so much.

'Well, that's not my kind of holiday, though I might check the place out. Got other plans,' Shan replied.

'Enjoy, and see you when you get back,' Lef said.

As they both left, Goe sat down and started talking. 'What do you want? I can give you all the extensions you'll ever need. They can connect your mind to AIs and all types of computers. I have mind browsers, uploaders, downloaders, organisers, managers, injectors, modifiers, rootkits, and exploits. I have organ replacements, and…'

Shan interrupted her. 'How many of those do you have?' he was aware of body extensions but not on that scale.

'A lot. And look at me; I mean, I've tried everything, but don't worry, I'll give you the best stuff.' Goe was excited. 'Some of those extensions are a bit illegal but don't worry. In times like this everything and nothing is illegal. I also have muscle, smell and vision enhancers. And I bet you'd like some skin and sensory enhancers, too.' She winked at Shan.

'Goe, I just need simple things for now. This will be my first time using any enhancements, and I don't want to end up in one of those derelict hospitals,' Shan replied, trying to hide his fear.

'OK, sorry. I'll prepare you something simple. Most of them come in pre-packaged boxes with bots. You put one on your skin and the bots do the rest. They're all universal and can talk to each other. Easy-peasy,' Goe replied and started writing something on the screen on her wrist.

'Cool. Leave it in my spacecraft. But I don't know if I trust those things. How do they feel?' Shan asked, trying to imagine the sensation.

'Feel? Oh, umm, did you ever have a blocked ear? Or a blocked nose? Completely blocked?' Goe asked, trying to explain an experience so subjective that she struggled to find the right words.

'Ear, yes, and nose, yes, why?'

'How do you feel when you unblock your ear or nose, and you can hear or smell again?' she asked.

'I don't know… Good, I guess, one of your senses has comes back.'

'Exactly!' Goe shouted, standing up, her heart racing, and her artificial pupils dilating from excitement. 'And that's how it feels, but a million times more amazing. It's like another sense comes to life or like another arm appears on your body. It's incredible. When you connect your brain to the computer for the first time, the entire world opens up, and you can talk to it, travel its interfaces, data and networks. It's seriously awesome, though not easy to use at first. It's not travel in the literal sense, but you feel it, the same as you can feel and travel around your brain to find a memory, for example.'

'OK, I'll try,' Shan replied.

'You seem a bit sad,' Goe said, feeling that something wasn't right.

'No, I'm just tired. I need time off, seriously.'

After knowing Shan for all those years, Goe could guess what was on his mind, and it was better to leave him alone. 'Don't forget the breakfast,' she said, leaving his office.

* * *

In the morning, Goe entered the small kitchen. Breakfast was eaten here as the big kitchen wasn't in use at that time of day. It was located not far from the secondary bridge, and it had small windows in the ceiling as Shan was always careful about having too much glass overhead in space. The little room was filled with the most odd-looking plants, vegetables, fruit, pasta, cheeses, powders, meats and bread. There were even single atoms floating around. At the same time, the appliances made various noises as they prepared meals. The kitchen had to serve many different kinds of food to a variety of species. From Lef and Tix who relied only on vegetables, to the omnivore species Goe and Shan belonged to, to meat-eating Kolubs, to the specially designed artificial diet for drots, to nano and bot species who could only eat food constructed on an atomic level. When food was scarce, you could see the metallic and wooden interiors of the kitchen, and when it was plentiful, it was everywhere. The kitchen was always working; steam was steaming, water boiling, mixers mixing and builders building. In the middle of this was Colin, the head chef. He came from Sector Three, where he wasn't accepted in his society and had been expelled due to his disability.

Interestingly, it was the feature his culture considered a disability that allowed him to become the greatest cook in the sector. On his home world, his big nose and great sense of smell was considered a disability because the whole planet stank. No one knew that but him. He tried to tell everyone about the stinking planet, change the laws and society and even overturn the government, but he lost that battle. After spending years in prison suffering from malnutrition, he learned everything there was to learn about smells and food. He was expelled and put on a military spacecraft to work as a chef. Some good came from his protests when others created an anti-stink underground resistance, to try to fight the smelly regime.

'Another new part? You look like a bloody robot, you know,' Colin said to Goe, who entered while he was preparing food.

'Fuck off, Colin,' Goe snapped. 'I don't like your nose,' she added, while looking for something to eat.

'Oh, come on, you know I was joking,' Colin replied, getting a plate ready for her.

'And I've explained to you so many times that my body extensions are a serious business, and nothing to joke about. They are me, part of me and I treat them as my body,' she explained, looking across the kitchen worktop and trying to grab something to eat.

Colin knew that, but he always teased her anyway. 'All right, I'm sorry. Now wait for your portion,' Colin replied, moving someone else's plate out of Goe's reach.

'What's for breakfast?' Goe asked while playing with her attachments, adjusting them to smell and see better.

'Your favourites. Stones on a wing,' said Colin, giving her a plate. The meal was potatoes with cosmic chicken wings, and Goe loved it. Not because she liked potatoes and chicken but because of the spices and sauce. Colin's unique mixture of flavours, collected during his military travels all over the galaxy and beyond, mixed perfectly. Food was something that kept everyone together, and Colin's food was rather like a drug, like the best pizza, or garlic bread, or seafood, or cheesecake. His excellent sense of smell allowed him to make the greatest spices and sauces with almost sub-quantum precision. Something even Goe's improved artificial nose didn't allow her to do.

'You should start selling your spices, you know,' Goe said between bites of chicken. 'You could open your own restaurant.'

'Bit too late for that,' Colin replied.

'In case you've forgotten, we're at war, and we all need to keep up our morale. Especially soldiers, they need food. Oh, my, I love this stuff,' Goe started cuddling her food, stroking it with her newly implanted touch enhancers like the tongue of a fly.

'It's food, you know. Not a toy… or a lover,' said Colin in amazement.

'It's not just food. I could have a relationship with it,' Goe replied.

'I can see you already have. Do you want to get private with it?' Colin was laughing, seeing Goe's face covered in sauce.

'Shut up. Aaaaah, that smell!' Goe exclaimed, touching the chicken with her nose.

'Is Goe having a good time?' Shan asked when he entered the kitchen.

'As you can see.' Goe was all over her food.

'Stones again?' Shan asked, looking at Goe while she spread the sauce all over her face. 'Won't that sauce break her attachments?' Everyone was looking at her in wonder now.

'Let's leave her alone. Yep. For you guys, only stones left. The last food delivery was captured by pirates,' said Colin. 'That was the tanker-class ship,' he added.

'Shit, seriously?' Shan couldn't remember the last time that had happened. 'Those pirates are getting more and more dangerous. Don't worry, I'll remember to do something about it.'

'We can't even take anything from the main planet; it's stupid. We fix their ships, and for what?' Colin replied, trying to express his anger by throwing the kitchen towel.

'For drives, parts, gravity, shelter...' Shan answered, sitting down with his portion.

'Yeah, yeah, I know. We need to start charging in food,' Colin said.

'You had your portion already,' Shan told Goe, as she was staring at his food as if craving a drug.

Glone, a young engineer who had recently joined Shan's crew, entered the kitchen. 'Stones again? I thought you were the best cook in this galaxy,' he said to Colin, then took his portion and sat down next to Goe.

'I'll have it if you don't want it,' she said, looking at Glone's plate.

'Maybe I'll move over here.' Glone went around to sit opposite Goe, next to Shan.

'Goe, try charging in food,' Shan said to her.

'It'll be my pleasure, but I was telling Colin he should start selling his spices… or even better…' Goe's enhanced eyes went wide as she thought, '…we should open a restaurant on the sunny side of the rock. It would be awesome; everyone queueing for the garage could eat there. I'd call it the Hollow Ship Inn.'

'We don't have enough food for ourselves, so how could we open a restaurant? When we have plenty, then we can do that,' Shan explained, killing her dream. Then he added, 'Colin, how much food do we have?'

'I told you not to worry. We have enough for a year, but it's all stones and wings for you guys. We only have so many because I grow them,' Colin replied.

'Grow? Where?' Shan wondered. He didn't remember having a farm.

'I thought you checked all the requests for expanding the garage?' Colin said.

'Well, I'm busy, I don't remember all the paperwork. And where did you get that salad? I don't recognise this stuff,' Shan observed as he took mouthfuls of green, almost mutated, leaves.

'I built a greenhouse on the solar side of the rock. Got stones there, lots of green stuff, some fruit and veg, and chickens,' Colin announced.

'Please tell me you're joking,' said Shan.

'No?' Colin confirmed with a question.

'Well, as long as the garage is safe, I have no problem with it,' Shan answered.

'I know, you told me that the day you approved it,' Colin added.

'Seriously, where did you get the chickens from?' Glone asked, then bit into a wing.

'Long story short: my friend is a smuggler, he had some chickens on board from somewhere, and he didn't know what to do with them, and I needed some eggs. By the way, tomorrow's breakfast is eggs,' Colin replied, finishing his salad.

'Great. The last thing I want to eat is some unborn chickens.' Goe felt her stomach extensions turning.

'You just ate fully born dead chicken, so don't complain,' Glone said.

'Can you show me that greenhouse you've built?' Shan asked, finishing his stones. 'Might as well see it before I go,' he continued, though only Goe knew he was leaving for a holiday.

'Sure, do you want to look now?' Colin replied, cleaning plates.

'Yes, if you have a minute.'

'Let's go then. Anyone else want to have a tour of the greenhouse?' Colin asked, removing his apron.

'Might as well see that secret garden of yours,' Goe said, standing up. 'Anyone else interested in eggs and chickens?' she asked the other two. Glone decided to come, and the four of them left the kitchen.

* * *

'I forgot how big this place really is,' said Colin, manoeuvring the shuttle between military battleships and floating engineers. The shuttles were a fleet of small spacecraft, used to move quickly between different parts of the garage floor as the over three-kilometre-long rock wasn't designed for walking. 'I really should spend more time here,' he added.

'Yes, it is, but with those two massive ships here, it looks small,' replied Shan, sitting down next to him. 'I remember when I got this asteroid. They put it here in orbit, and we flew into it with our tiny shuttle thinking why the hell would we need a rock that big? And now look at it. Oh, I remember that bit.' Shan pointed at a piece of shiny rock that protruded from the garage wall. 'We had so many problems removing it, and adding those doors was a pain. We had to keep fiddling with the artificial gravity to get it all right. I mean, we had to make a hole in the middle of this huge rock, so it wasn't easy. That was all before any of you came aboard,' Shan explained, remembering the early days.

'Oh, this place is like your child,' Colin remarked, flying them towards the docking port on the other side of the garage floor. The place was busy with engineers repairing the hulls, docking ports, and weapons of badly damaged spaceships, and it took time and skill to manoeuvre safely through it all. 'And here we are,' he said, after docking the shuttle. 'Now we have to walk.' The ports were connected to the tube-like corridors that were suspended on the garage wall, allowing people to walk along the whole length of the garage without the need for special suits.

'This way,' Colin said, and he started walking up the metal stairs from the shuttle port to the main tunnel. After a while, he turned right towards the garden.

'I seriously need to walk more. I don't remember that garden tunnel being here,' said Shan to Colin, trying to remember when he had approved its construction.

'OK, this is the entrance, but we need to be quick going through the door,' said Colin. The dark tunnel ended with a metallic door, and he started entering the code on a wall keypad. 'It's hot inside. I try to keep the perfect temperature, humidity, and pressure for plants and chickens. I want to install double doors but haven't had time yet. Ready?' They all nodded. Colin opened the door, and the hot air struck them like a pancake hitting the pan. 'Get in quick!' said Colin and locked the door behind everyone once they were through.

'Oh, my…' said Goe, trying to breathe. 'My home planet is hot, but not like th… Oh, my….' She was already sweating, and her improved body cooling system started working at full speed.

Meanwhile, Shan and Glone's jaws had dropped.

'Did you build this all by yourself? The forest, the jungle, and the water fountain thing?' Shan asked, looking at the small canal. What Colin called a garden was actually a massive forest inside one of the craters, covered by a glass dome. It was hot inside, the perfect temperature for growing different kinds of plants, and for keeping the tropical cosmic chickens happy.

'Yes.' Colin was proud of his creation.

'Of course, no one else is crazy enough to do it,' said Goe, adjusting her temperature sensors.

'Very funny. And that canal is part of the water system,' Colin answered.

'How can you breathe here? I'm all sweaty,' said Glone. 'It's a jungle.' Palm trees of all types were so densely planted that you couldn't see the far end of the garden. They received light from the star and gave back oxygen, fruit and materials in exchange. The cosmic chickens supplied enough meat and eggs for the whole crew to be temporarily independent of food transports.

'I wish it was bigger.'

'Where did you get all that soil from, and who works here besides you?' Shan asked.

'The soil, well, that was the hard part. It took me some time to collect enough of it from smugglers and your home planet. About two years, I think. Ordering smugglers around wasn't easy. They looked at me funny when I wanted tons of soil, but fortunately they didn't ask many questions. For now, it's mostly me here, but others helped a bit, so you might say it's a community project,' Colin explained. 'I'll be honest with you, I recreated some places on my home planet but a bit hotter. And if you don't like it, I'll tear it down. Just say the word.' Colin was clearly hoping to keep the garden.

'Are you crazy?' Shan said. 'This is amazing. The most amazing place I've ever been. How big is it?' *Years? That only confirms I need a holiday; I have no idea what's going on here anymore.*

I spend too much time on paperwork and other shit I shouldn't be doing. Goe needs to step in.

'About a hundred metres across. So you're happy for me to continue?' Colin asked.

'Yes, but…' Shan looked up. 'Install a double door. If that glass breaks and the field goes, we'll lose the garage. And there are some big craters near here; you could expand into them. Just be careful: bullets and other things fly at high speed.'

'Expand with a restaurant, that would be awesome,' said Goe, displaying a holographic simulation of the restaurant in an attempt to get support for her idea.

'I'm not sure about the restaurant bit yet. But I already have a plan for more craters with different environ…' Colin began.

'OK, where are the chickens?' Glone interrupted, walking off into the small forest.

'There! They went to the veggie section.' Colin saw one and tried to catch it. 'Dammit. I'll find them later. They don't like strangers and they can run fast. Apart from the mechanical chicken and the robots.'

'You have a mechanical chicken and robots?' Goe was incredulous.

'Yes, the chicken monitors and entertains the other chicken. You should be able to connect to it. The robots help to maintain it all while the engineers are busy,' Colin replied.

'OK, I need to leave; it's too humid for me here.' Glone, who came from a cold planet, was all sweaty.

'Yes, let's go. Colin, fantastic job, seriously,' Shan told him. 'Can't wait to see more.'

'You'll be even happier. That place produces oxygen. Not much now, but if I expand it, we won't need to buy so much,' Colin added.

'Great news. I'm sure Goe can connect filters to it. And one more thing before we leave… Sorry, Glone, I'm sure you can wait another minute.' Shan looked at Glone, who was struggling to keep his head dry. 'OK, listen. You're my friends, and you probably know this already, but I'm going on holiday today. Kind of now, actually…' Shan explained.

'What?' Glone was surprised. 'Did you know about this?' he asked the other two.

'Yes,' Goe and Colin answered.

'Why am I the last to know?'

'Glone, I need a holiday,' said Shan. 'You all take them, but not me. I didn't even know about those soil transports, that shows how busy I am. I'm sure you'll all be okay without me for a while. And besides, I have remote access to the garage, and we can always talk, so don't worry,' Shan explained and added, 'OK, let's go. One more minute and Glone will die.'

* * *

Shan's original intention had been to visit his parents and then go to the bar planet to see Eli, but after his discussion with Goe about expanding the garage, he decided to alter his plans. The military planet was nearby, and he wanted to visit the general in search of help with the garage's food problem.

He sat down in his spacecraft and had a long sub-quantum chat with Eli; they decided they would meet in four months at the bar planet, and Shan would ask the general why nothing worked there.

In the meantime, Shan had started changing the flight path in the onboard computer when the message popped up on the screen. He recognised it at once. The sender was encrypted, the message was encrypted, and it was basically garbage. To anyone else, it would just look like an error or spam. Messages like this came from robots, always sent directly to Shan and always encrypted. Usually for no reason. *Another robot's spacecraft needs fixing*, Shan thought. Robots usually came to his garage just to repair the simplest things. Often, the jobs were so simple that Shan could do it in minutes, outside the garage. It was worth it as the robots paid with great technologies and parts.

* * *

Artificial intelligence has always been challenging to build, and AI that could really think on its own never really existed. It kind of did, but never at the level of biological organisms, and when left to itself, it usually came to some final conclusions and died.

One story tells of a guy who tried a different approach. It was simple; like all revolutionary things it was so simple that no one had previously tried it. Or rather, everyone tried what he tried, but he forgot to turn it off. Everyone tried to build AI stage by stage, from recognising images and sounds to avoiding obstacles. His idea was different, but his new algorithm still didn't work. Whatever he did, the output was always the same: garbage. Frustrated, he just left it, forgetting to turn it off. When he came back after two weeks' holiday… guess what, it was still garbage. But this time, he saw words in between the random nonsense. Out of curiosity, he left it running, and after a few more weeks, he saw random images and more words. He looked at the code, and it was gibberish, but somehow something worked. To him, it was garbage, but the machine was learning, living, understanding hardware and interfaces, and creating its own internal world. He had created AI, which is now known officially as femacomputions, a word combining the inventor's name with 'computation'. Unofficially everyone calls them Garbs, short for garbage because if you don't understand them, they sound like a talking garbage can.

In the beginning, communications didn't work well. The guy didn't know machine language and the machine didn't know his. It took a year for the machine to understand who we were, who it was, where it was, and what the universe was.

Now, when robots, or machines as they are also known, come to Shan, they send a message about what they need and what they can offer. This time, the problem was their planet. Shan pressed his fingertip to the DNA reader to decrypt the text.

Our planet is dying. Requesting onsite engineer. Sending new LLTS for your spacecraft. ETA 30 minutes.

Robots were excellent at creating new parts, building, and improving everything, but creativity and fixing things were not their strongest points. Their planet was dying, and they wanted Shan to help. *Requesting onsite engineer? Well, might as well go and see their planet at last. Maybe I won't be needing another rock from the military, after all... Oh, and my holiday plans have changed again.* But when Shan had first contacted the general, he hadn't wanted to tell him many details, only that he needed to discuss the garage, and it would be suspicious if he changed his plans now. The military never trusted anyone, even their own kind, especially these days.

* * *

The military responsible for this sector of the galaxy were based on an ancient planet, located four light years away from Shan's garage. It wasn't a nice-looking place, mostly deserted, dotted with massive craters, with smoke and flashes of light randomly coming out of nowhere, and empty cities now used for weapons testing. Whatever your reason for being there, it was better if the military knew where you were. Getting shot at random by a ballistic missile is never fun, getting randomly nuked even less. This place had used to be an ordinary world, but after many battles, there was more army left than civilians. Not because everyone had been killed but because they'd escaped, and those who stayed joined the armed forces, so they decided to keep the whole planet for themselves. Now it was used for building and testing new technologies and weapons.

Shan set the speed to level two on LLTS, activated the drive, and five minutes later he was in orbit around the military planet. *Four light years in five minutes, that's what I call the need for speed.* He received a message giving him permission to land, along with the coordinates of the hole in the quantum net surrounding the planet. *This world hasn't changed much since the last time I was here*, he thought, watching the grey surface through the windows.

Thanks to its purpose and the army's trust issues, this military world had a quantum net covering the entire planet. The only place you could pass through to the surface was through the hole, whose location had to be agreed in advance. Shan was flying along the virtual corridor projected onto the windows of his spacecraft, guiding him through the hole, going slowly and carefully as even the smallest mistake would cost him his ship. He didn't know the size of the hole, and could only hope it was big enough.

After a few minutes' flying he landed in a sandy desert, in a crater still steaming with smoke after the explosion that had created it. *Should I be here?* he wondered, and was checking the coordinates when suddenly all the systems went down, and he and his spacecraft were being dragged under the surface. Shan didn't panic, as this had happened before when he was here, but this time the crater was new.

A moment later, his spacecraft landed on an underground platform. He went downstairs and exited via the loading bay. He found himself in a room the size of a hangar; dark, with a round roof through which sand was spilling in places. It had only one small door, which had opened when he landed. The faint radiance spilling through it was the only source of light, but before Shan could reach it a soldier entered the room. His body was similar to Shan's but with more arms: he was basically an evolved cockroach, from the same species as the general. The soldier looked at Shan but didn't say a word, just turned around and walked through the door. Shan followed and found himself in another room of similar size.

A massive table was standing in the middle, and the general himself was sitting in a large chair, looking like a king on a throne. Shan tried to come closer, but the soldier waved his arms, warning him to stay behind the table.

'So, you want to expand, my friend?' asked the general in a deep voice, speaking in what had once been the official language of the central government. Shan, like many others, was bilingual, having learned the central government language at school, and even now it was no longer the official language, it was unofficially used by almost everyone, almost everywhere. For that reason, the central government language became the most complex language ever created. Galaxy wide language with endless accents, slangs, gender and non-gender related words, nouns, pronouns, verbs, adjectives and never-ending grammar rules. It was possibly the only language spoken by everyone not mastered by a single person but only by automatic translators.

'Have you seen the queue outside my garage recently?' Shan replied. 'It's pretty long. That's mostly your fault, and it's affecting military warships too, but no one wants to spend any more resources expanding the garage.'

'My fault? Don't blame me for the war,' the general said, his mood changing.

'Of course I don't blame you for the war, I blame you for not wanting to expand the garage. We can't repair your spacecrafts fast enough,' Shan said, trying to be careful with words.

'I don't think you understand the situation. Do you think your garage is some kind of spa and we go there for pleasure?' the general demanded, his voice getting louder and louder with each word. 'Do you think I want to be here? Do you think I want that war? Do you think I want to fix those spacecrafts? Do you think I want you and your garage?'

'I don't want that war either, but we have no choice.'

'I have a choice, and I already chose. For now, no new garage for you. We need all available asteroids to turn into weapons. They provide valuable resources.' The general was famous for having rebuilt the shattered army of this sector, mostly by hiring local companies and mining everything available: asteroids, planets, and even cities and civilian spacecraft, sometimes without even asking. Though his methods were cruel, he'd become very popular by stimulating the local economy.

'Then expect a call from the local government when I say "no" to them.'

'I eat that stupid mayor for breakfast!' the general shouted, hitting his chair with his fists.

'You seriously need to work together.' Shan had stopped being nice.

'Where are you planning to expand?' the general asked, his mood changing again.

'First here, and then Sector Four, where the robots are. They pay in good technology.' The general had always hated robots, but they were good for Shan's business.

'Hmm,' the general replied. Shan could see he was thinking, probably not happy about the idea.

'If that's the case…' He went quiet again. 'You know what those robots have that we don't? I can provide you with a whole planet if you can help me get it. I know they come to you often.' The general had to be referring to the LLTS drive and probably a few other things, Shan reasoned. No one ever beat robots, even the military. The story went that the most advanced and powerful weapon the military had used to attack the robots' planet had done absolutely nothing.

'Yes, I need that too,' Shan replied, standing next to a ridiculously large chair. 'But the robots' spacecrafts cannot be scanned or, to be honest, even understood. They only come to my garage to fix simple things.' Shan was lying, but he reasoned that in these times you couldn't trust anyone.

'Keep trying. When you get what I need, you get your new garage,' the general told him.

'Yeah, thanks for nothing.'

'Careful, my friend.'

'What? Are you going to destroy the only thing that keeps your battleships running? You know my garage is the only one, and I have the best engineers.'

'I know.'

'One more thing. Have you heard of the bar where nothing works? Any idea why nothing works there, or what might? Asking for a friend,' Shan said. The bar where nothing works was located on a lonely planet just outside the galaxy, where Shan's friend Eli was living.

'You're asking the oldest question in the universe, my friend. We've been trying to make things work at that bar since we discovered it, and I don't even know when that was. We've wanted to destroy that place so many times, but it's even more powerful than the robots. And we've held so many negotiations there, trying to stop the war, I've lost count. But no results.'

Shan wanted to say OK, but the general continued, 'One of the first negotiations we had was actually with the robots. I wasn't there at that time, but it's all here in the archives. Those robots were not at all interested in escaping or helping anyone else to escape the collision and the wars. For them, it was illogical to leave, and they had no intention of helping anyone else, they just wanted to improve. Those were the fastest and most logical failed negotiations we ever had. After that, we sent many messages to the robots, but they always come back with the same answers: no escape, improve. Improve! I'm sick of hearing that word.

'After that, they never came back to negotiate. We still have many negotiations there, almost yearly, with different species from various places. In a few months we'll have negotiations with the species that started all those wars. They suddenly appeared not far from here, asking for a meeting. I almost destroyed their small spacecraft, but I was stopped.

The most recent negotiations we had were with a powerful species from Sector One, the Tirans,' the general finished.

'They used to make Tiranian gold, didn't they?' Shan asked.

'Yes, and I'm sure they're still making it, and they control most of Sector One. We control most of Sector Two. We need the Tirans to help fight Shad's army, your crazy cousin. That guy is powerful and has quantum nets all around the galaxy. He demands ridiculous amounts of resources from anyone who wants to escape. And he's almost impossible to destroy.' The general was angry. Shad controlled most of the outer galaxy, and his army was a perfect example of pirates waiting for anyone to try to leave or enter. 'Their nets are everywhere, and we are blind. We have no idea where they are,' the general continued.

Ironically, the pirates were also the ones who protected the galaxy, especially Shad. After the military had expelled him, he set himself up as protector of the galaxy. With all those quantum nets he refused everyone exit unless they paid.

'Can you use Tiranian gold to destroy his army? Or wormholes?' Shan suggested.

'It's not that simple. Shad's army is so spread out; you would need an impossible amount of it, and Tiranian gold in sub-quantum is not stable enough. The robots have LLTS capable of incredible speeds, and I'm sure they have weapons to destroy Shad. Wormholes, yes, we are testing them. The problem is that as LLTS is superior to wormholes, we forgot about them for a long time, and we're only doing more research now. What's your plan for escaping the collision?' the general asked. 'I'm sure you have one.'

'To be honest, I was hoping to escape with you,' Shan answered. *Well, not really, but that's what he wants to hear.* The military needed to think that Shan wanted to escape with them because they provided all the protection he needed. 'I'd love to take the garage with me but it's probably too big.'

'With our current technology, we're grounded the same as you. Not even our best ships can get through the sub-quantum nets and mines. But there are other species much more powerful than we are. Our LLTS is slow; not everyone would survive the trip to another galaxy. If I'm going to escape, your garage is going with me, so don't worry. I cannot lose the only thing keeping my battleships running…'

How ironic, thought Shan.

'Robots could survive that trip,' he pointed out, interrupting the general.

'And now you know why we need it. I'm so angry; you have no idea. I even went to Kreton just to destroy one of the planets. We are so powerful but so weak, and those senseless robots don't even care about any of it.'

'I know, and trust me: every time they come, I do everything I can to find out their technology. So nothing works in this bar, right?' Shan asked again, hiding his anger after hearing what had happened to Kreton.

'Nothing. Absolutely nothing. That's why the robots don't go there. It's my only light in the dark, the only place where machines are weak. What scanner do you use in your garage?'

'Sub-quantum version of ETIN, heavily customised.'

'There's nothing better. Keep trying and let me know.' The general's voice sounded tired now.

'One more thing before I go. Would you help to get us some food, and help with pirates? Our food supplies are running low, pirates are capturing the transports more and more often, and if you're not going to expand our garage that's the least you can do. We can live without expansion, but not without food.' Shan was hoping to get as much as he could from the general.

The tired general opened the screen next to his chair and started pushing buttons.

'It's done. You'll get food and protection. Your spacecraft can fly now. Use the lift,' the general said, and slowly disappeared into the darkness.

* * *

A message from Goe appeared on the screen while Shan was preparing to leave the military planet.

Hi, you've got a delivery. Something I would call a very badly designed package. Basically, a small spaceship that looks like it's from the robots.

'*Shit, thank you. I forgot, be there soon*,' Shan replied, and went back to the garage.

'Hi. I'm outside. Have you seen that package?' he asked Goe over the radio while looking firstly out of the window and secondly at the radar console, trying to locate the package.

'Hi, that was quick,' Goe replied. 'It's outside, next to the docking port. It refused to come inside, whatever it is,' she added, rolling her eyes. Shan couldn't see her, but he recognised the envy in Goe's voice.

OK, the package. Shan found the message it was broadcasting and then was able to spy it through the window. As usual with robot-made ships, it wasn't pretty. It was rectangular, like a box, with all the wires and coils outside, making it look like it had been designed by a drunk person. He opened the loading bay, and the package flew itself inside. Then Shan went down to the bay to look at it – and the box looked back, from two protruding cameras.

Shan came closer, not knowing what to expect, and the box started transforming itself, morphing into something with two legs, two arms and a head with cameras sticking out like a snail's eyes. Then it started walking towards the stairs.

'Hi. I thought they sent the new LLTS drive?' Shan asked, surprised at seeing the robot. It was almost the same design as the ones that came to his garage from the robots' planet.

'Hello. Yes, I am the new drive. I will install myself into your LLTS, and this will temporally improve it to level three. I know how,' the robot explained and continued walking towards the engine.

'How long it will take?' Shan asked, and after a pause he added, 'Wait… level three?'

'Fifteen minutes. Your console will send you a message when it's ready.'

'Awesome… and my plans have changed again,' Shan replied, and went back to the bridge. With the new drive, his three-month trip would now take thirty-nine hours.

CHAPTER TWO

Travelling with LLTS is dangerous for many reasons. Radar can't be used in sub-quantum space, so you're blind, which means you could hit another spacecraft, or a ghost, or pirates, or smugglers, or sub-quantum nets. Nets are designed and built by pirates. They're like real nets in the ocean but hidden in sub-quantum space under quarks. If you hit one, it will enclose you like a fly-eating plant and you will die from starvation, unable ever to escape its grip. Or it may damage your spacecraft, or even destroy it completely. If you hit another ship, you will most likely die, but when you hit a ghost, it will put your LLTS drive out of balance. Ghosts are strange; no one knows what they are. The theory is that they're made by a species who somehow manages to live in sub-quantum space. Once you hit them in the sub-network, you hear weird sounds and see nonsense messages on your screen.

* * *

Shan was speeding along below the quarks in sub-quantum space, towards the robots' planet. Particles were moving aside, pushed by the enormous power of the forces within them. Outside was total darkness, as sub-quantum space is not the place where light can easily hang out.

For a while he stood next to his chair, looking outside, seeing flashes of energy. Then he sat down in front of the screen, enjoying the sub-quantum ride, forgetting the space beyond the windows, when suddenly everything went red on the screen, white outside, and shaky and spinning inside. Shan's ship was no longer in sub-quantum space, and Shan himself was under his chair trying to hold onto something. The spacecraft was spinning, Shan was spinning, and it was only thanks to the spinning that everything was still more or less where it should be. The power went down and the emergency lights came up, but that didn't help Shan, who was now glued to the floor.

He knew exactly what had happened; he'd hit a quantum net. Thanks to G-force the blood was draining from his head and he started losing consciousness. Then a moment later the spacecraft slowed its spin. That wasn't good either: something must be controlling it. 'Shit, shit, shit, pirates!' he snarled.

The ship slowed down to the point where Shan could float. He pushed himself up and started pounding the auto-balance button like crazy, but nothing worked. Looking behind him, he heard noises, and knew exactly what they meant. Whoever it was, they had brought his vessel in to dock. He could only hope that they would let him go free – after stripping his spacecraft of anything and everything valuable. Shan floated down to the docking bay below the shuttle's garage, pushing away the objects that were now bobbing around in zero gravity. He heard the docking mechanism being unlocked, and managed to hide behind some boxes near the ceiling. Suddenly a group of creatures flew into the docking bay with an auto-capture net. A minute later, the net found Shan's body heat and trapped him. Shan was trying to break free when he heard one of the creatures saying, 'I know that voice.' A pirate Shan recognised flew towards him.

'Shan? Seriously?' The creature shook his massive torso, looking at Shan. 'You stayed so long with the military you forgot about the war? You shouldn't travel on your own like that.'

'Nice to see you too, Shad. Now let me out!' Shan demanded from inside the net, floating around the loading bay like a ball. Shad was an idiot, a powerful idiot, that was the problem. He was Shan's cousin, but from a different species, more closely related to the general's cockroach species than Shan's two-leg, two-arm body type. Shan had used to fix his spacecraft, but when the military got involved, he had to stop, and Shad had to leave. 'What do you want, Shad? And why are you here? I thought you had soldiers to do your dirty work,' Shan said, trying to free his hands.

'Funny how our names are similar,' Shad said, and all his pirates attached themselves to the floor. One of them switched the gravity back on, causing Shan to drop to the ground like a stone, breaking his gun as it got trapped underneath him. Shad started to walk around the loading bay, checking everything as he went. 'Sorry, did that hurt?' he asked, not even looking at Shan, who was now on the floor trying not to scream from the pain. 'Nice spacecraft you have here. Hopefully I didn't damage it much, as we'll need it. Where are you going, anyway?' he looked at Shan.

'The robots' planet,' Shan answered, still trapped inside the net. There was no point in lying. It would be easy for Shad to find out where he was going.

'Fucking Garbs. I hate them,' Shad said, finishing the sentence in Bemoorung language.

'Me too, but they pay, so what can I do?' Shan replied, now freed from the net but still held down by pirates.

'True… How are your parents, and mine, by the way? I haven't talked to them for a while,' Shad asked, examining something he'd found in the loading bay.

'What, now you're interested in the family? After all these years?' Shan snapped.

'Well, you know, I'm busy protecting the galaxy.'

'And killing it from the inside at the same time, you idiot,' Shan shouted.

'Oh, come on, you know the story. Don't blame me. The whole galaxy is at war, and you know who with? Not with the idiots who started the war. With ourselves now! And a bit with another galaxy, too.' Shad was so angry he threw the object he'd been holding across the loading bay. 'It's civil war; we're killing our own people. It wasn't like that before.'

'Not that you remember before, but you're right...' Shan couldn't have agreed more.

'And you know what? Since the day the war started... When was that? Oh, yeah, it was so long ago no one fucking remembers anymore. Since the day it started, we can't get it right; no one can make peace. How fucked up is that? All those fucked-up politicians and leaders and fuck knows who, they've got no fucking idea what to do. And then you have the extremists and other idiots and everyone else, they're all fucked up as well. It's all fucked up.' Shad was furious.

'True... but the military...' Shan tried to say, but Shad interrupted.

'Oh, for fuck's sake, seriously, don't be delusional. The military, what do they do? That stupid general should take control and fix things. Exactly like I did.'

'You fixed things? Are you fucking mad? Well, I agree with you about the general, but don't say you fixed things!'

'I did, kind of. I protect you all from the aliens...'

'Killing us at the same time.' Now Shan interrupted him.

'Well, I need resources to protect and fight those idiots, don't I?'

'It's not easy, this whole thing,' Shan said quietly.

'No, it is easy, but no one understands. That's part of my plan,' Shad announced.

'Should I ask about your plan?' Shan remembered the not-so-great-plans they'd had when they were young.

'I'm planning to extend my nets and weapons all around the galaxy, to make it like an impenetrable ball,' Shad exclaimed.

'Seriously? I've got a better plan. No one talks to anyone anymore, and as you can see this galaxy can't exist without a central government. So why don't you create one? Why don't you get all your resources and nets and your army, and force everyone to work together for once at least? This would, let's say, unite everyone.' *I just came up with that, and it's not a bad idea.*

'That would work, too…'

'I'll talk to the general about this plan and about you. Get off me!' Shan stood up, shaking off the pirates. 'We need to stop this fighting, or we're going to wreck this galaxy.'

Shan was right, the galaxy was in bad shape. Most, if not all, species and planets were at war with someone. Even the rule of protecting less developed systems had been broken a long time ago.

'You forgot about the collision.'

'Don't worry about it,' Shan replied like it was nothing.

'Don't worry about it?' said Shad, surprised. 'You're talking like the robots, you idiot.'

'What do you want me to do? Disappear? Go to another galaxy? I live, and I need to live. I provide food and shelter, resources and services to everyone. The collision will bring all the galaxies together, and if you stop the war before that, it will be the greatest thing that ever happened to us. Imagine all those species together; imagine the economy, imagine you yourself.' Talking directly to Shad's ego had always been an effective way to make him do things when they were kids.

'Me?' Shad looked confused.

'You, as the one who started and finished it all, you'll be a hero. You'll be remembered until the end of the universe for winning the war and uniting the galaxy again. You will become the real emperor of this place. You will build a new central government.' Shan had a lot of experience with Shad, gained over the years.

'I like the sound of that… But!' Shad started to think, and Shan could see his eyes moving around as if they were following a fly. 'I tell you what.' He looked at Shan. 'I will let you go.'

When one of the pirates said something in Bemoorung language about not being happy with Shad's decision, he continued to Shan, 'I will let you go because you're my cousin, and because on the way back from the robots' planet you will bring me something… And because of the emperor thing, too…'

'Bring you what?' Shan asked, suspicious.

'LLTS, *or* Tiranian gold, *or* their quantum nets. Your choice,' Shad replied, accenting each *or*.

At least I'll be able to keep my ship, thought Shan.

'LLTS is not possible, trust me,' he said. 'You're not the only one interested in that. Every time they come to my garage, I try to find out about it. Tiranian gold? Seriously, even you are not that stupid.' One of the pirates hit Shan for saying that, but he continued, 'They have way more powerful stuff than that. Quantum nets; I'll find out about them.'

'I'll need insurance,' Shad insisted.

'You can take something from the ship. And by the way, I'll speak to the general.'

'No, no, no, that would be too easy. We stopped taking things a long time ago. Now we're giving you something.' One of the alien pirates brought over a small cage. 'That.' Shad pointed to a maintenance spider-bot inside.

'What the hell is that?' Shan demanded, looking at the bot as it ran around the metal cage trying to escape. It was round, with lots of different-shaped legs. He knew exactly what it was, but preferred to pretend he didn't.

'It's a fascinating bot, a fascinating creature. It will integrate itself into your spacecraft so completely that you won't be able to remove it.' Shad opened the cage, and the bot ran to the nearest network junction box and connected its legs to all the cables, becoming part of the spacecraft's system.

Those bots were available in many flea markets throughout the galaxy. They were originally built for maintenance work, but were often hacked and sold for quite a different purpose. 'I will monitor your progress, so don't do anything stupid. Let's go!' Shad said and left, followed by his guards.

Shan was left alone sitting on the floor of the loading bay. He was glad the conversation was over, and that he had only been captured by Shad. If it had been any other pirate group, he would most likely have ended up in some deserted scrapyard trying to find a way home. *Shad was right, I did forget the war, and I'm not a soldier. The war has always been normal for me, but I shouldn't be travelling like this on my own. I was stupid… Wait a minute!*

Shan stood up and almost ran to the bridge, which was only lit by the emergency lights. He tried to open the map, but there was no power. Apart from the essential systems, everything was down. He checked the damage by looking at the status lights under the floor hatch. *It's not that bad. I hope it's only a fuse, please be the fuse.* Shan walked back to the main engine room where the primary power source was located, along with all the fuses, then opened the cabinet. To his surprise, the bot Shad had left was running between junction boxes, replacing fried fuses and wires, and testing systems. *Well, I guess maintenance is still its basic instinct.*

He went back to the bridge, sat down, and started thinking again. *What's Shad doing here? Isn't he supposed to be running his galaxy-edge empire? But he's here, and going by my calculations, we're between sectors. Yes! Exactly between sectors.*

It was well-known that no rules applied in the space between sectors. It was the grey area, the DMZ, the no-man's land, and it had been claimed by so many civilisations and pirate groups that now it was filled with endless nets and interstellar mines. Most were forgotten and abandoned, only waiting for someone to hit them. Crossing those borders was something only fools did – or Shan, who was so tired and inured to them he forgot all about them.

An hour later, everything lit up. *The bot's fixed it!* On a freshly booted console, Shan found a map. He started looking at his current position and the closest systems. Nothing. *Why would Shad build nets here? No sane person crosses those borders unless they're hiding something.*

* * *

Shan spent most of the day cleaning and securing everything while his spacecraft travelled towards the robots' planet. The autopilot stopped the ship in orbit and gave Shan a loud message over the PA system, signalling its arrival. Shan looked at the console, which was displaying the flight path sent earlier by the robots, and let the autopilot finish its job.

From the orbit of the main planet, the robots' planet was the most ridiculously green place Shan had ever seen. The clouds, oceans, lands, deserts, and mountain ranges looked a lot more greenish than usual, but, Shan reasoned, with all those millions of solar systems in the galaxy it wasn't surprising to find one world that looked green. *I don't see this world dying at all; quite the opposite.*

From overhead, while landing, he could see roads, pavements, skyscrapers, cars, spaceships, trains, trees, and everything else you would expect from a typical planet in peacetime. That was the difference; the war had never come here. OK, it had, but even the monstrosity ship hadn't been able to destroy the robots, and the robots hadn't seen any logic in retaliating, or helping anyone else. That was just another reason everyone hated them.

The autopilot followed the virtual path and landed the spacecraft on a round pad with lights and markings in an unknown language. The landing pad was entirely covered in grass, and one of the robots was cutting it with an inbuilt lawnmower. Shan walked to the console and checked the atmosphere; it was perfect for him. He was even more amazed when the console showed that the air had been deliberately optimised for his body. After a lifetime spent living in the atmosphere of the garage and his adopted planet, his body was used to a different type of air. *Are they so advanced they can control the environment?*

He went down to the loading bay and lowered the ramp. One of the robots came over. It was small, half Shan's height, and partially covered in flowers that grew from all the points where soil could lodge on its body. It floated in the air, and it had antennae, cameras and arms ending in tools that were designed for catching and holding. It wasn't pretty, it was functional.

'Hi, robot,' Shan said, using central government language. He'd never liked calling them Garbs, and since their first visit in his garage he had called them robots. 'Do you have a name?' None of the robots he met in his garage stayed long enough to give their names.

'Hello, Shan. We don't have names, we have internal IDs,' the robot replied.

'OK, you float; can I call you Floaty?' Shan asked, only to regret this decision a moment later when he realised there were lots of floating robots around.

'Yes. Follow me,' Floaty said and hovered down the ramp. Shan walked, and Floaty floated, through a perfect, windless summer's day. They went down to the surface, and along a road in the middle of a city. A city with tall buildings, streets, cars, tunnels and shops all lit up and in perfect condition, but with no one here to use them except robots. After a few minutes of walking, Shan saw the problem.

'So… what's the problem with your planet?' he asked Floatie. *I imagined this planet entirely differently.*

'We improved nature to the point that we cannot control it, even with our improved tools. Nature is everywhere now, and it's disturbing our existence.' Machines had no concept of breaking things, only improving them, so when they were left alone they fixed and improved everything they could find.

'Yeah, I can see that everything is green. I thought that was how it's supposed to be. What would you like to do about nature?' Shan asked.

There was a little pause as Floaty communicated with someone in charge.

'We want to improve our existence, our machines and nature.'

Well, that was a revelation, Shan thought, rolling his eyes.

'I think you have no trouble with that. I think you need to *stop* improving.'

'If you save our planet, we will build a planet for you.' Yeah, Shan heard that too.

'Sorry… What are you going to do?' Shan stopped, Floaty stopped, and the robot turned his way as the wind blew past them.

'We will build a planet for you. We calculated that reasonable payment for saving our planet was the offer of another planet.' Floaty spoke without any emotion.

'I didn't know you can build planets.' Shan was a bit surprised.

'To a design, yes.' Robot's logic was famous across the galaxy as the simplest you could get. IF, THEN, ELSE statements. And he didn't have to ask if they had any planets to spare for his garage.

'OK, well, I need to analyse the problem, read about nature here and what you did to it. I'll need to check your world, and I require freedom to move around.' Shan's logical mind started analysing the issue, but at the same time he wanted to explore. A moment later, through the cars on the busy road and the spaceships overhead, he saw a yellow vehicle flying his way. It landed in a parking space next to the pavement where Shan was standing.

'You can travel anywhere you want in this car,' said Floaty. 'All your questions will be answered.' And the robot left.

'Hi,' Shan said to a second robot, which was sitting in the car. This car hadn't been designed for robots, that was for sure. It had seats like the one Shan had in his spacecraft, and all the controls were designed for biological species similar to his.

'Hello. Where would you like to go?' asked the robot. It was rectangular, with two long stick-like legs and antennae, wires, cameras, plants and flowers sticking out of it like a hairy spider.

'I would like to walk first and then we can use the car,' said Shan. 'Would you like to join me?' *I've spent enough time sitting in my ship.*

'I will stay with you all the time, and I can answer all your questions.'

'Can I call you Spidey? You remind me of a cartoon character I liked when I was a kid.' *Floaty, Spidey, I'm greaty at naming robots.*

'Yes, you can,' Spidey replied.

They walked away from the car and the landing pad, passing what would have generally been considered an ordinary but overly green city. Shan could see the problem. Robots were repetitively cutting trees and grass, but everything was growing back so quickly that their improved tools couldn't cut fast enough. Offices, buildings, roads, houses, blocks of flats, cars, spacecraft, robots, walls and everything else on this world was covered in foliage.

'What did you do to those plants?' Shan pointed to a flowerpot on the pavement. The flower was continually growing, as a specialised robot tried to cut it back.

'We improved them,' Spidey replied, standing next to the plant.

'Yes, I know that, but how?' Shan asked again, watching the garden robot struggling with the single flower.

'We started at the biological level. We improved DNA and RNA and then cells to have a better growth rate and better water, mineral, and gas management. The last thing we did was on a mechanical and AI level,' Spidey explained.

'AI?' Shan asked, surprised. He tried to look closer at the plant and understand what the robots had done to it.

'We added nanobots to the cells, so they could use other minerals to build their structure. Trees can grow taller now and give more wood. Flowers are bigger and more colourful. All the plants can now make use of titanium and other materials in their structure.'

'What about the AI?' Shan asked again.

'We only added it to one flower, but it was transported to other plants via bees, which we improved, too. Bees can give better honey now.'

'How did you implant AI into plants?' Shan asked again, trying to get some answers.

'We can build specialised nano-robots. We injected them into plant cells to help with making decisions about water, minerals, predators and genetics.'

'Genetics?' *Should I be surprised?*

'Robots inside the cells helps to make sure the DNA is free from damage and chooses the best mutation possible. After that, the plants evolved, and now they need nanobots less and less.' *Brilliant. So the robots injected themselves into nature.*

'What about animals?' Shan asked, moving off.

'We did the same for all animals,' Spidey replied, walking next to him.

'Seriously? Anyway, can you prepare some historical data disks with all the details, so I can read them in my ship?' Shan asked, as he needed some time to think about this problem. For some reason, the robots believed that if Shan could fix their spaceships, he could fix nature, too.

'Yes, this is now in progress.'

After a few more hours of walking and examining the improved plants that covered parks, coasts, buildings, shops and blocks of flats, Shan and Spidey arrived back in the city centre. Walking down the main avenue, Shan saw a camera in a shop window. He recognised it as being similar to the one his foster parents owned. He couldn't read any of the text on the sign next to it, but even so it was interesting.

He'd always liked history, and he'd always wondered what would happen to the robots' planet, to all the planets and species, after the collapse of the civilisations, and the eventual end of the universe. One day, he thought, he might open a cosmic museum, and was always collecting objects and data for it. He wanted to preserve everything, forever. But he even wondered about the afterlife, what would come after the universe, what lay beyond the universe, and all the things that were without explanation. He always wanted an answer for everything. Even when he was little, he'd asked a lot of questions. How that works, why this floats, why you look different, why there is war, why this and that. His parents were patient with him; Shad wasn't.

'You know, Spidey, I have a photograph of my grandfather,' Shan said now. 'Not digital but paper-based film. Not that you're interested in my family, of course. But I wonder if they sell film cameras here.'

Spidey may or may not have been looking at him with amazement, as the robot didn't have any facial expressions.

'Yes, your grandfather bought his camera in this shop,' Spidey said after a moment of silence.

'What?' Shan almost screamed.

'Yes, your grandfather bought his camera in this shop. It's the largest and most famous camera store in the city. They've been making cameras since…' Spidey replied, but Shan interrupted.

'How, where, how do you know that? Have you met my grandfather?' Shan started asking a lot of questions, thinking this was some kind of joke.

'He was the last of our creator's kind, and left for the stars. He left you a message in the photograph you had in your cryo-pod,' Spidey replied.

'What message? How do you know about the cryo-pod?' Shan was lost now.

'We built it,' Spidey replied after its circuits calculated the logical response.

'What?' Shan almost screamed again.

'We built it. We didn't detect any hearing problems when we scanned your body, but...' Spidey was evidently trying to find an explanation for Shan's repeated questions.

'I can hear you, all right? What do you mean, you built it? Tell me the whole story! The whole story of my biological family, the cryo-pod and everything,' Shan yelled at the robot, shaking its body.

'Your biological family goes back to a time before our solar system was properly formed. Life started when two comets from another galaxy hit our planet. Those comets were carrying the DNA information needed to start life. Your grandfather was an expert in genetics, and he left for the stars to look for the origins of life. The origins of our creators, your biological family and comets,' Spidey explained.

'Wait a minute. Comets can't travel between galaxies.' Shan's analytical mind was taking over, after the initial shock of learning first about the nature problem and then about his family.

'The comets we found were made from a material unknown to us, that did not come from any of the systems in our galaxy. They have undeciphered inscriptions on them that survive to this day. We calculated that they came from somewhere in 3704 Solarii, one of the oldest galaxies in the known universe,' Spidey replied.

Shan sighed and sat down on the pavement. 'Can you sit down here with me? Somehow?' he asked. Spidey's legs shortened and it lowered its body.

'So my grandfather was born here?' Shan asked, looking down, trying to fully comprehend the new facts about his family.

Spidey paused to search its knowledge base. 'No, his kind left this planet hundreds of years ago, but his family were genetics experts, and he inherited all their research. He decided to search for the origins of his species.'

'Do you know where he went?'

'Towards the galaxy 3704 Solarii,' Spidey said again.

'How far is it?' Shan asked. He'd never heard of the place.

'Three hundred and twenty megaparsecs from here,' Spidey calculated swiftly.

'Do you know where my grandfather lived before he went to the stars?'

'No, he decided not to reveal his location, but he left you a message with all the details in the photograph,' Spidey replied.

'What about my father and mother?' Shan asked. *They're probably long gone, or maybe they died when I was young. That'll be why my grandfather took care of me.*

'You don't have a father or a mother,' said Spidey, after checking the knowledge base.

'What? What do you mean, I don't have parents?' That was another shock.

'You were organically built by your grandfather with help from our genetic centre. Your grandfather designed you based on his DNA.'

'What? Show me proof, now,' Shan demanded. 'This is getting ridiculous. Take me to my grandfather's office!' he stood up as his mind spun. Not only from the sudden blood pressure change, but from the release of buried emotions.

Spidey took Shan to the main genetic research centre, which was located west of the city. The journey took a while, but to Shan, who spent most of it thinking and staring into nothing, little time seemed to pass.

The small – almost tiny – building did not look like much, but it had a huge parking lot with cars and spacecraft everywhere. Shan and Spidey landed not far from the building and started to walk towards it.

'Is that where I was built?' Shan asked. *What a ridiculous-sounding thing to say!* Now he had calmed down a little, he was able to process all the new facts.

'Yes.' The robot walked in front of Shan towards the door.

'It's not very big,' Shan commented, pointing at the insignificant little building that looked more like a small roadside diner.

'Most of the rooms are located underground.'

They went through the main door, and a voice said, 'Welcome home, Shan.'

'That's weird and a bit… awkward,' Shan said to Spidey.

Inside the diner-like building, all the walls were so perfectly white that you couldn't see the joins

'Why is this place so bright and white? Why no colours?' Shan asked, looking at the interior walls. It was so perfectly white in here that he couldn't see any edges or shadows. It was challenging to walk around when you couldn't see where the floor ended and the walls or stairs began.

'Originally the building was a nuclear shelter with a hospital, then it became a genetic research station. At that time, almost everything was white. We improved it, removing all the shadows and making the white whiter. We have individual lights that automatically adjust so you don't have shadows. It's almost impossible to create a shadow here. Even under your shoes, there are no shadows,' Spidey explained.

They went over to something that looked like an elevator, but after the door closed behind them, the one in front of them opened almost immediately. The cathedral-like primary research building was large, with a long corridor containing pillars, desks, chairs, computer equipment, terminals, running holographic simulations, beds, pencils, paper, pens, books, models and of course, robots in white lab coats doing research. It was so huge Shan couldn't see the far end.

'Whoa, wait a minute. This place wasn't that big outside, we didn't even go down,' Shan protested, trying to understand what had just happened.

'We did,' Spidey replied.

'When?' Shan asked in surprise, looking back at the lift.

'In the telelift.'

'What's a telelift?'

'It's a lift,' Spidey replied, logically.

'So why didn't it move down or up?' Shan's curiosity about technology made him demand an explanation.

'The lift doesn't move, we do.'

'There wasn't any lift!' Shan was a bit annoyed now.

'The lift didn't move; we did.'

'Listen to me, robot: just tell me how the lift works, OK?' Shan demanded.

'The lift uses a teleport. We have been teleported to the lower floor.' Spidey finally found the right answer.

'I have no more questions,' Shan replied, and followed Spidey.

They walked down the corridor between the busy robots for a few minutes before coming to a door. When they passed through to the room beyond, the same voice as before said, 'Welcome home, Shan.'

'Who said that?' Shan asked.

'The AI that takes care of this building. This is your grandfather's office.' Spidey said, entering the small, white room.

'It's empty,' Shan said. There was nothing here but a single terminal.

'Yes.'

'Why?' Shan asked. He had expected his grandfather's office to be fully equipped.

'Your grandfather took most of the equipment and data when he left.'

'But surely you have some data here about me?'

'That's the only terminal left.' Spidey pointed at the small computer in the corner.

Shan spent the rest of the day reading the data Spidey gave him, but there wasn't much about him specifically. It was full of details about DNA, history, researchers, and some projects, but lots of records were missing. After the discovery of DNA, researchers had aimed for the ultimate goal of designing and building a life. That failed horribly, but overall they improved the lives of many. When they left the planet, they told the robots to continue their research but forbade them to build life. They could only simulate it.

Shan was tired after all these revelations, and he needed to be alone, but Spidey had other ideas. Nature was still more important to robots than Shan's family was, so Spidey took him on a trip. The spacecraft flew above the land, lakes, oceans, and mountains, and everywhere robots were trying to cut quickly growing flora. There were farmer robots, war robots, science robots, and every other kind of robot who could help. Nature was out of balance and even the oceans were no longer blue, nor the mountains white, as it was all covered in foliage. Shan looked down, trying to think about the nature problem but it wasn't easy as thoughts about his origins kept coming. His long-earned holiday had become a mission, a mission to finally find out the truth about his family. He started asking Spidey questions to take his mind off things, 'How many planets do you have?'

'Fifteen main planets and millions of other objects; mostly asteroids and moons but also machines built by our creators and ourselves.'

'Are the other planets habitable, or covered in foliage?' Shan asked.

'This is the only planet in the habitable zone of our star. But our creators built colonies on the other planets. We are improving all of them.'

Of course you are. Shan started to think again. On the way back, he didn't look at the green planet below, but stared at the glass of a window. *Fuck, I need time to think. These robots have no idea what's going on. My grandfather hid everything about me, but why? What is wrong with me? Well, apart from the fact that I was never born. I need to get the photograph.*

'My spacecraft isn't fast enough, and I need time to analyse the data you gave me,' Shan said to Spidey when they landed. 'I may have to ask my friend about it. I'll be back in a few months.' *That should give me enough time.* He was exhausted, and after a full day of walking, inspecting nature and finding out he was a robot he needed to be alone, and to look for answers.

Spidey went quiet, this time for a bit longer.

'We will improve the LLTS drive in your spacecraft so you can come back faster,' Spidey replied after a few minutes, and landed the yellow car near Shan's spacecraft.

'OK, whatever, tomorrow. I need to sleep. Goodnight,' Shan replied, and went to his spacecraft. He lay down on his bed and started to think again. This whole thing was chaos, and completely ridiculous. It was hard. Robots had been coming to his garage for years, and they'd never said a word. He'd never asked. *Why would I?* They'd never said anything. *Why would they? Now I know why they came only to me and why they invited me here. They only trust me. Or is it trust? Is it that I'm one of them?* His whole life had changed today. He'd finally found his home, *kind of*, but discovering that he didn't have parents was a shock. *Am I a machine?* All those years of looking for clues and finding nothing… *No wonder the DNA tests hadn't found anything.* He'd been designed and created with the improved version of their DNA. *Am I a machine?*

I don't know how other creatures or machines think or feel. This is me. I think, I see, I dream, I imagine. I am biological. My body is. I've never looked inside my body, and even the doctors who checked it when I was ill said it was OK. I guess they just assumed I'm from a different species. It was normal on my planet, and doctors had a tough time helping everyone when each species was unique. I look up. I see a ceiling. I close my eyes. I open them a bit, and the ceiling is still there, my nose is still there. I am inside. I am my consciousness; my consciousness is in my body, this body. Is it? Does this mean anything? Is everyone like that? Every species? How do robots see and feel? Do they see some status messages in their eyes or cameras? How much of my DNA is from their original creators? I'm falling asleep... Shan closed his eyes, and for the first time in years, he fell asleep without taking a shower first. New dreams came... or were they memories? Visions of his day started randomly appearing. The final image was the photograph; he was looking at his grandfather holding him, and the camera was taking a photo.

He woke up in the morning thirsty and hungry, thinking again about yesterday's revelations. First things first though: shower, then breakfast. It was porridge with dried fruit, and coffee from Kreton, the most straightforward food to transport, to keep for years, and to prepare for consumption. It was worth it, and it was something to celebrate. *But is it? Should I even eat this? Do I need to eat? Oh, for fuck's sake, stop thinking!* After breakfast, Shan watched some general news, ignoring all messages, then lowered the loading bay door. Outside, he saw a few robots waiting for him. *Them again,* he thought.

'Hello, Shan,' one of the robots said. This was definitely not Spidey or Floaty, but a tank. A robot on caterpillar tracks.

'Hello, robot,' Shan replied, walking down the platform. He wasn't going to bother naming them anymore.

'We came to upgrade and install an LLTS drive and a cube reader, and do general upgrades and maintenance of your spacecraft,' the caterpillar robot said.

'There's nothing wrong with my spacecraft. Can you do this quickly?'

'Yes,' said the caterpillar robot, and scanned Shan's possessions. 'We detected that most items need repair, and everything needs improvements.'

'Everything? Fine, just don't break anything.' As robots started to enter the spacecraft, Shan added, 'And one more thing. Can you leave a list of stuff you did after you finish, please?'

'Yes,' the caterpillar robot answered.

Shan took his bag and went for a walk, as there was nothing else he could do while robots were upgrading his ship. It was about ten am on the robots' planet, which corresponded precisely with the time in his garage. It was Shan's thing: wherever he went, he always tried to land on a planet at the right time by his internal schedule. He achieved this mostly by controlling his LLTS speed, but sometimes by waiting in the orbit of the planet. He did the same here. It was easier to schedule everything, and he didn't have to worry about space lag. First, he decided to go back to the photography shop to find out how his family photograph had been made.

The streets were busy with robot cars, robot cyclists, robot rubbish collectors, robot street vendors, robot office workers on the way to work, robot night workers coming home, robot cleaners, robot plumbers, robot teachers, robot police and of course improved traffic lights and improved traffic. Shan was trying to find his way through all this when the robot guide came to help him. After a brief conversation, he started following the robot, which was trying to entertain him with some historical details. After smelling some improved almond croissants, Shan bought one and walked towards the photography shop, smiling. *At least it will be something different to eat.*

The store was quiet at this time of day.

'Hello, Shan,' the robot trader said as he entered. *I really should get used to the way they all know my name.*

'Hi.' *I can't be bothered naming them all.* 'Nice shop you have. It doesn't look that big from the outside.' Shan tried to mentally calculate the distance to the back wall. 'Can you explain to me how the photograph I had in my cryo-pod contains a message? I checked that picture in the most advanced scanners we had, and I didn't detect anything.' *I assume they all know me and my story.*

'The photograph was taken using one of the sub-quantum cameras you can see here.' The robot pointed at one of the shelves. 'They can take a photo and at the same time embed a unique code, which matches another code in sub-quantum space. When this code is activated, the message is streamed directly from sub-quantum storage.'

Shan didn't answer, but as he was interested in technology he went further into the shop to browse different models of camera. The latest were at the front. The best of them operated entirely in sub-quantum space, which removed the need for lenses and storage. These were still there but only as accessories. Connecting directly to the fabric of the universe allowed the cameras to take a photograph or video of any place in real-life resolution and store it directly as sub-quantum particles. Older models had lenses and memory cards. Lenses with titanium-net quantum glass and improved sensors allowed them to see at any distance and in any wavelength. Memory cards with almost unlimited storage could store real-life resolutions of any image or video. At the back of the shop, the oldest improved cameras were to be found, some still with the film.

Unmotivated and not really knowing what to do till the robots had finished improving his spacecraft, Shan spent some time wandering around the castle on the hill, which had been recommended by another robot guide. He went there by a cable car that was pulled by improved ropes on improved slopes. He passed old improved shops in old improved buildings, trying to both think and not think. He visited stores and museums; he went to the downtown area and some neighbouring villages to see farms and their improved animals, tractors and local pubs, and to see robots taking part in agro-tourism.

Later that day he went down to the beach. He asked for a chair, and sat down to look at the sea. All around were boats, ships, robots, palm trees, sand, stones, waves, and more robots. Robots on windsurfing boards, on jet skis, fishing, walking, kitesurfing, flying, making cocktails, and doing all the robotic things robots do. Shan was constantly thinking about how he was from this place, this was his planet, his parents were robots. *Weird*, he thought, and weird it was. It's not often you find out the truth about yourself, especially not that kind of truth.

What to do next? Should I stay here, should I go back to the garage, should I go to find my grandfather? So many questions and destinations and thoughts. The collision was a priority, and with the new LLTS he could go to another galaxy. It wouldn't take that long. He could find some civilisations, get contacts, and prepare for people to move there. But the collision could wait: for now the photo was the most important thing in his life. *That's where I'll go next, to the black hole zoo. It needs to be done.* That was where he'd hidden the photograph and other valuable things. The place was so dangerous that even the species who had come in the monstrosity ship didn't go there, although there were civilisations who lived there together with refugees from other places. *Eli came from there.* That was the next thing on his list: the bar and Eli. Shan had wanted for a long time to be with her, that one friend who he could talk to about anything, but there was always something stopping him, mainly work and fear. He needed her now more than ever, to help with the robots' problem and with his own life. He was confused, desperate for answers to all his questions.

It took the robots all day to install the drive and repair and improve everything there was to improve on Shan's ship. He was approaching the spacecraft when suddenly something dropped to the ground in front of him. It was the bot Shad had installed. Shan looked at it, then looked up.

'What did you do to my ship?' he started shouting at the robots, angry that the improvements weren't what he had thought they would be. The robots had rebuilt most of the systems, keeping the craft functional but not sleek. Coils, wires, hydraulics, and even the door locks and the water tank had been moved outside, for reasons known only to them.

'We fixed and improved everything, including that.' A robot pointed at the bot Shad had installed, now lying on the ground fixed and awaiting further instructions.

'Yes, thank you, but my ship looks completely different now!' Shan was pacing around and inspecting all the cables and pipes on the outside of his ship. 'Can you please make the exterior look like it did before? I mean, hide all that stuff somewhere. And what is that thing all around it?'

'They are the new LLTS coils. We cannot hide them,' the robot replied

'Hide them somehow, or at least try to hide everything else so it'll look like it was before, please.'

'But that won't be an improvement,' one of the robots replied.

'Yes, it will. Just do it and put back one of the original kettles, the original shower and a toilet,' Shan demanded, looking at the pile of equipment that had been removed from his spacecraft.

* * *

Many hours later, when he came back from a forced walk, he tried to say goodbye to the robots, but they had already left. He went inside his ship and locked the door, which wasn't that easy with the robots' improved locks and hinge mechanisms. He sat down in his now amazingly enhanced comfortable chair on the bridge and looked at what the robots had done.

They had installed additional consoles, one of them to read the data cube that robots have left, and they changed most of the interior, although they had evidently tried to restore the original design after Shan had complained. The chairs were different, as was the kitchen – even the kettle – and one of the toilets, too. It was so seriously advanced that Shan was scared to use it, as it looked like a kettle turned inside out. *Ehh, I'll check the rest of it later.*

He activated the central console, and was amazed by what he saw. 'Wow, what did they do to it?' he said to himself, looking at the vast amount of detail about the ship and the new interfaces, windows and graphs. 'This looks amazing, but all the buttons are missing.' Then he understood that the whole console was now a touch-screen. 'Cool! Wow, how did that happen?'

The console switched to show the status of the engine, then changed to that of the communications. Whatever Shan thought about, the console responded. He said aloud, 'So it's not only a touch-screen, but also a thoughts-screen… OK, enough of robots, time to go to the bar. Though what am I talking about? Not the bar, my holiday plan has changed again… and who am I talking to anyway?'

Shan put his head down on the console, closing his eyes. He started to think, crying at the same time. The truth about his past was too much. He didn't have parents. Robots had built him, his grandfather had left him to look for the origins of life, and now he was here, on the planet where he been made – practically 3D-printed. *My whole childhood made no sense. OK, where is the manual?*

Shan stopped thinking, stood up and was walking around the bridge looking for his spacecraft manual when one of the consoles lit up with the word 'manual'. *Yeah, the thought control thing.* He sat down and started to read, scrolling the alphabetically arranged pages. He moved to the letter L – LLTS.

LLTS – Improved from version two to version three and prototype version five – use with care.

'That's it? No more details?' Shan said to himself. The manual was not what he had expected. He moved to the next console along, which lit up with an image of the galaxy. No, image was the wrong word. It was a holographic 3D presentation you could touch. *Cool view.* After a moment looking at the controls, Shan pressed the sub-quantum view on the panel, and his eyes widened. *Seriously, fuck! That's what I call improvement.* What he was seeing was beyond his imagination and anyone else's, as nobody had access to that kind of technology. Everything was lit up in blue, red, yellow, white and orange. Some lines and blurred objects also appeared. Spacecraft and their flight paths, nets set by pirates, and even ghosts appeared on the screen. All the unknown elements that everyone thought were impossible to detect. Basically, it was a sub-quantum radar on a galactic scale and beyond.

Shan kept shifting his gaze between different objects with amazement but no understanding of their purpose when finally he spotted the place where he had ended up in Shad's net. The in-between space and no-man's land. He looked at it in shock. The sheer number of quantum nets out there was staggering, not only at the place where Shan met Shad but at all the borders between sectors. *How did I not die? It was a miracle!* Unattended nets had been left like landmines after forgotten wars.

Shan was looking at a live view of the galaxy, and he was again in shock. Watching species die on the TV news was one thing, watching them fly into traps in real time and not be able to do anything about it was another. He saw a small spacecraft, probably containing refugees trying to get from one sector to another, explode in seconds. One turn left between the nets, and they would have survived. A few minutes later another one, in another sector, and so on. *Another reason to hate the robots. Or is it? On the one hand, they stay away from all this, and they have since the beginning. The moral question is: if you have the technology to help, should you be required to help?*

This one small piece of equipment could save millions from death, but to the robots it was just another piece of improved technology. Shan moved away from the console with the live map as he couldn't look at it anymore. He set the destination on his light drive to the bar, to see how fast he could get there. It showed four hundred thousand years at half the speed of light. LLTS calculations showed forty years on LLTS 1, a hundred and twelve days on LLTS 2, two days on LLTS 3 and forty minutes on LLTS 5.

'We've come a long way to achieve this… Well, the robots did,' Shan said aloud, then started to walk in circles again. *The problem with robots is, they don't suspect anything, I could give this to everyone, and the robots could do nothing about it. I must be careful. No one needs to know… But what am I saying? Nobody can know, I'll be dead if anyone finds out. The whole galaxy would chase me for this technology. What? The thought control, so the robots already know what I'm thinking. Well, never mind.*

He walked to the kitchen, drank some water, and returned to the console, where he turned on LLTS level five and said, 'Yeah, right. Would be good to know the meaning of "use with care" first.' Then he switched to the sub-quantum chat and sent a message to Eli. He didn't want her to suspect anything so he said he would get to her in four months as planned. The reply came almost instantly.

I wish you could be here now.

He didn't know what to say to that, so he sent a universal reply: a smiley face and a 'goodnight'. *We're friends; I don't want to destroy that.* Those thoughts had been in his mind since he met her all those years ago. It had never been anything more than friendship, and his trust issues weren't helping. Looking completely different to everyone else in your family is not fun. Shad had always made fun of him, and so did the others in school.

Another message appeared on the console screen:

I don't know how you removed the bot, but I will find out!

It was from Shad, who had found out he was no longer able to monitor Shan.

Don't worry. I will still talk to the general about the plan. Forget the robots' technology, Shan replied.

I'll find you anyway!

Good luck ;)

Shan set the autopilot to head for the black hole zoo, the sector in the exact centre of the galaxy, where he kept the storage asteroid. LLTS 5 would get him there in forty minutes, but he didn't want to test the 'use with care' warning, so he limited himself to LLTS 3. The next day, the spacecraft was still travelling when Shan checked the progress on the screen in his bedroom: twelve hours left. He put some music on and made himself a coffee and some kind of breakfast food with a thick consistency like porridge.

After breakfast, Shan loaded the new sub-quantum dishwasher and rechecked his course. The spacecraft was passing stars, planets, other ships and nets. He moved to another chair to check the cube the robots had given him. Inspecting its surface, he found it to be flawlessly smooth and unmarked. He inserted it into the reader, and the screen lit up. The interface was simple, and all the data was translated into central government language.

Records revealed that, hundreds of years ago, the species that created the robots had escaped their planet, which was dying after they had released too much carbon dioxide into the atmosphere. They had established two colonies on other planets, but they mostly relied on the central world for resources, especially water and food. Although the colonies would have been able support themselves, the robots' creators still left, leaving the robots with a final order to take care of the planet and to improve everything. *And they sure did.* A summary of the data showed the incredible history of this species, one of the most advanced in the galaxy at that time. Thousands of years of history, wars, peace, languages, culture, innovation and creativity preserved by the robots. *Another irony.* Even more ironic was the fact that robots had restored nature, removed the CO2, and made all the planets habitable again.

The cube contained much more data; all the knowledge of the creator species, from the very beginning of the planet's existence to the present time. Millions of years of knowledge, texts, images, videos, smells and 3D holograms. Shan was amazed again, though nothing was really a surprise anymore. He scrolled through some images of the creator species, seeing that they looked like him: two legs, two arms, a torso, two eyes, and five fingers on each hand. *Well, no wonder they look like I do. Or rather, I look like them. The only other person who looks almost like me is Eli.*

Then a minor thought occurred to him. He'd told the robots he needed all the historical data they had, and that was precisely what they had given him. It did not include any information about what the robots were doing to nature. *That's a secondary problem for now. I've had enough of those robots after hearing the truth about myself.*

* * *

The spacecraft calculated the optimal path between black holes, then entered the asteroid's orbit where Shan took control. The autopilot worked perfectly, but flying was Shan's second favourite thing. He manoeuvred the spacecraft between asteroids, and after a few minutes, his own rock appeared, spinning out of control.

What the hell? Shan thought. When he'd first found the place, he'd set it up to rotate at a precise speed, but now it was spinning in all directions. *Probably something's hit it, but it's not that bad.* He matched the spacecraft's pace to that of the asteroid and managed to slow the spin by using a tractor beam. He entered the tunnel that led inside the rock, and –

What the fuck? The container that had been attached to the wall wasn't there. Instead, he saw the rods and holes where someone had ripped the box off the wall.

'No, no no no!' Shan couldn't believe what he saw. 'All my stuff's gone! Drives, weapons, parts!' *Fuck the stuff, the photograph! How could I be so stupid? Not even the black hole protects things against people who are desperate enough. I don't even know when it was stolen. Why didn't I set the alarm or the beacon?*

Shan stopped the asteroid from spinning, the debris inside starting to float around. He collected most of it and put it on the loading bay floor: there were ropes, hooks and sheets of metal from his container but also parts from another spacecraft. *What probably happened is the raiders couldn't cut all the rods, so they just pulled the rest, and when they snapped, the broken parts hit the tunnel walls. That would explain the asteroid's rotation and all these parts floating around.* Shan analysed some of the parts he found, and one of them pointed to a class of spacecraft he had seen years ago when Eli visited him

OK, the map. Shan went to the bridge, opened the galaxy radar and seeing the vast number of black holes together with their gravity forces that slowed everything, he located Eli's home star system. He threw himself into the pilot's chair, pushed the thrust lever to start the engines and headed for the only inhabited planet he'd found. The autopilot plotted the course between black holes, making sure not to stray into their gravity fields, and an hour later, he was at the planet. *Cold, and a perfect place to hide.* The planet's surface was featureless, white, icy, and covered in snow that stretched away to the horizon.

How the hell am I supposed to find a small container that could be anywhere on this whole planet? Shan was pacing again, criticising himself for his stupidity. *Wait a minute, the radar!* The sub-quantum view of the planet showed a perfectly intact surface under all that ice, unlike other worlds that had been destroyed by wars. *Most probably due to the black holes; it would be suicide for even the monstrosity ship to try to get here.* He tried to keep his cool, but something snapped, and he started imagining what would happen if he met the thieves who had stolen his container; anything from asking them politely for its return to nuking the place.

Flying above the frozen desert and watching the radar, he found a network of caves and a large square structure inside one of the tunnels. It was set at the crossroads of many smaller tunnels, which created an underground motorway. The radar showed brick-like segments stacked in endless rows and columns, some near the centre stack and some set at a distance. Apart from a single enormous cargo spacecraft parked in the middle of it all, the traffic was scarce, almost non-existent. *So that's where they load and sell those containers.* Shan continued to fly above the planet's frozen surface towards a tunnel entry leading to a central cargo hub. He went to fly inside, but a small spacecraft was blocking the tunnel. Seeing someone standing next to it and waving at him, Shan landed in front of it. He saw that the spacecraft was damaged, missing the very piece he had found in his asteroid. He went outside, wearing warm clothes, and keeping his distance, he shouted, 'I'll get straight to the point. My container has been stolen, I need it back, and I can see your spacecraft is missing a part. I found it where my container used to be,' Shan said, holding up the missing part.

'They all say that,' the pilot of the spacecraft replied through its speakers.

'I don't care what other people say, but I advise you to give my container back. It's a standard-sized box with markings like this all over it.' Shan displayed a holographic image of his container from the screen on his wrist.

'We are gatherers. We find things to sell or use,' the man standing outside the spacecraft replied.

'Sounds like stealing to me. If you'd just found it, you wouldn't have had to rip it off a wall,' Shan replied. *They just confirmed they found my container.*

'It wasn't guarded; we found it.'

'Stole it.'

'Found it.'

'Call it whatever you want; it's mine.'

'I don't think so, and even if that was true, it's ours now.'

'It's more valuable to me than to you, and I can see you don't have many weapons on this ship.'

'You're right, but those caves...' the pilot standing outside said, looking at the ceiling. 'It would be a shame if that ice dropped on you,' he finished, and ran inside the small spacecraft, which fired rockets at the ceiling of the cave at the same time as flying off. Shan decided to jump under his ship as massive chunks of ice started falling everywhere. He lay between the LLTS coils and the underside of the ship as everything shook under the falling ice. He managed to crawl to the loading bay, which was partially blocked by ice, and after moving some chunks of the stuff, he managed to get inside.

'Status report!' he almost screamed. 'I won't let those bastards take the most important thing in my life!' The computer showed the status of all systems in subtle green colours, unbothered by the sheer pressure of the frozen earth laying on top of Shan's spacecraft.

'Full steam ahead!' Shan moved the engine lever full ahead but that only caused more ice to fall. *Shit. I don't think standard engines and weapons will work here, and if I shoot, it'll just bring down more ice. It looks like it's time to try the forbidden part of LLTS.* He opened the radar to see a mile-thick ice sheet on top of his spacecraft and pirates flying towards the other side of the planet with what looked like a container. The map showed only one exit, and that was where Shan programmed the computer to stop, on LLTS 1. *This is it; either it works or I'll become part of the ice.* An instant later, he ended up outside the tunnel on the far side of the planet, which looked quite different. *What is wrong with this place, seriously?* The ship's sensors were reporting that the temperature outside was over forty degrees Celsius when he landed on the sand next to the exit of the cave. *Now, how do I get the container back?* I think I know how. He flew into the cave, blocking it completely. *We'll see what they say to that!*

An hour later, the pirates' spacecraft showed up in the tunnel.

'How did you escape?' came over the radio.

'That's no concern of yours. And you might not be so lucky this time when I blow up this cave, so please hand me the container.' A few moments of silence later, the container dropped in front of Shan's ship. 'Thank you. It wasn't that difficult, was it?'

'No, but it will be for all the families we could feed from selling that.'

'What are you talking about? What about all those huge containers and a massive cargo ship I saw?'

'Go and check again. They're mostly empty. Leftovers from our golden age. From the time when we used to export a by-product of those black holes. The war destroyed our customers, and that destroyed us,' one of the pilots explained over the radio.

'How do I know you're not lying?'

'Really? Our tiny spacecraft, against yours? We're desperate. We have nothing. We're completely isolated on this forgotten doomed planet. Yes, we're protected by black holes but we have no resources. We are dying, our children are dying; no one comes here anymore, and we can't grow any plants. We survive on mushrooms and anything else that doesn't need much light. We live like ants, and we're slowly moving towards the mantle as the surface is no longer suitable for living. One day we will perish, becoming one with the planet. So no, I am not lying.'

Shan felt uneasy. *Maybe he isn't lying, and perhaps I can help. Somehow.*

'OK, listen, I need a few things from this container and you can have the rest. How's that?'

'Why would you do that?' the pilot was clearly as confused as hell. No sane person would help another species, especially here, especially now.

'Because I'm just a guy who can help. I'm nobody, OK? I'm not a soldier, a pirate, or anything like that. I fix spacecrafts. I have my own garage, and that's what I do. I'm just lucky I was raised somewhere we had food, that's all. I'll check the container and leave what I don't need.' Shan flew towards the container, then took it outside the cave with him. It was too big to take on board, so he docked next to it and went inside. *Do I really need all this?* he thought while browsing through everything he'd collected. *I had all those parts and weapons for years and never used them once. Oh, fuck it, I only need my memorabilia, these things are worthless to them but priceless to me. And maybe I'll keep a few of those guns.*

After an hour of browsing and moving things back to his spacecraft, he undocked the container and quietly left, placing the box on the sand for the two pilots to take. He quickly grabbed the photograph and put it on the console next to the cube, hoping it would work. The picture disappeared, to be replaced by a simple holographic image of Shan's grandfather, who said:

'Hello, Shan.

'First, let me apologise for everything you've had to go through, as I am responsible for it. I'm sorry. I'm sure you've already found out most of the details about yourself, and I understand it must have been hard.' Shan's grandfather paused for a moment.

'I think every advanced civilisation is looking to answer the same questions: what's next, what's there, what's behind this and that? What's beyond the universe? Another universe? A brick wall? Is it infinite? The problem is that researching this is a tremendous responsibility and requires lots of compromises and sacrifices. My sacrifice was that I had to leave you. At that time, our technology was advanced, but I could only afford to take one robot with me. Trust me,

I wanted to take you, but in the big picture, it was a better decision.' He paused again.

'You have no idea how much I want to see you; I hope that you are well and healthy, and that one day with the help of the robots' technology you will find me. Or if not me you will discover what I hope to discover: the origins of our kind.

'I created you for many reasons. One is that my son died, and you are like a son to me, but the second reason is more important. You see, our kind is gone, long gone. There are a few of us left, and they will soon die. After stupidly destroying our planet, we destroyed ourselves. You are the first, and you are the proof we can recreate our kind. You are the one who can tell the robots to start Project S84N. They will only listen to you.

'I'm sure you have many questions, but rest assured that they will all be answered by the data contained in the photograph. Again, I hope you are well, and that one day you will find me. The photograph will show you the way.'

The video ended.

'That's it?' Shan said to himself. 'The first time I see him, and he just talks about recreating his kind? *He doesn't talk much. Same as the robots, I guess. What do I do now? Start the S84N project? What is it anyway? Why didn't he say his name?* Having a million thoughts at once was kind of the new normal for Shan these days.

After the message finished, the console displayed lots of data; everything his grandfather was working on, and where he was going. From the discovery of the DNA to the death of his son to blueprints of Shan, and Project S84N. This project goal was to recreate their kind and repopulate the robots' planet.

I cannot do this, Shan thought. *If I repopulate this world with my kind, they'll destroy it again. Or maybe I'm wrong? Who am I to make this decision? On the other hand, what if I can find an empty system and start again?* After some more reading, he set the autopilot to take him to the bar, and disappeared under the shadow of quarks.

CHAPTER THREE

The bar. The most famous place in the galaxy. It was built on an interesting planet orbiting a peculiar, lonely star, located just outside the galaxy. It is a place where you have to expect things not to work. Once you get within a certain distance of the bar planet, no device will function correctly. That includes spacecraft, guns, computers, and even your laces and shirt buttons. For that reason, your landing isn't really a landing but kind of a blind drop, and the landing strip is strewn with wreckage, enough of it to constitute a separate city. To land successfully, you have to perfectly set the speed and the angle, and brake with your landing pads. It works if you're lucky; if not, your ship becomes part of the ever-expanding landscape of wreckage city. Watching spaceships arrive is one of the locals' favourite things to do, and the landing schedule is usually found on the local computer network.

The bar isn't, well, clean but it isn't really dirty either, it's just that in this place even a mop or bucket won't really work. The only things that work perfectly are those that were made when the bar was built: coffee makers, alcohol dispensers, clocks, cash points, tables, chairs, the roof, heating, windows, stairs, beds, lights, radios, glasses, plates, dust and everything else you would expect from a bar with rooms, including a newspaper: *Interesting Galaxy Times*. It's entirely recyclable, made not from paper, but from a particular kind of almost two-and-a-half-dimensional material to help with the dynamic content, which includes texts, videos, sounds, music and even movable parts. Originally written as a news bulletin, the *Times* gradually became a full newspaper with the latest news from the whole galaxy and beyond.

Why would anyone come here, you ask? Just imagine the possibilities. It's the perfect place to hide, or to hold negotiations. Nothing works here, and no weapon could ever function. Someone even tried to nuke the place, but the rockets broke just above the planet and dropped from the sky like anvils. No one worried about the radiation from the missiles as even that wouldn't cause you any harm. Others tried to destroy the place, using the most powerful weapons ever created, but they had no effect. Many spent centuries trying to determine the rules of physics that applied on the bar planet, but everyone failed, and apart from Eli, no one bothered anymore.

Even before the wars and negotiations, everyone met there for a bit of peace and, obviously, to drink alcohol. No one knows when the bar was built or who by, but the current owner remembers the previous one, who joined the wreckage city after a not so perfect landing. Over the years, it's been possible to find people from many worlds here. They come, sit, drink, talk, negotiate, sleep, pay, leave, or sometimes live, wasting, or not, their whole lives. For some, it's a place to hide, to survive, and for others a place to thrive.

* * *

Only an hour away from the bar planet, Shan slowed down to LLTS 1, and sent a message to Eli, the girl who was famous galaxy-wide. She had featured in the news as the youngest scientist to ever get a PhD in the low levels of the universe. She was called a genius after she improved the original LLTS, reducing the time it took to get across the galaxy from decades to months. Some tried to steal her plans, others to keep them secret, but it was too late as she broadcast them all over the galaxy. Anyone who had access to sub-quantum communications got them. After that incident, she went from genius to hero. Finally she ended up at the bar, not as a bartender, but trying to solve the unsolvable. Why nothing worked there: it was her personal challenge. She thought there was nothing else to discover. How wrong she was.

'You're already here? You're supposed to be here in four months!' Eli replied to Shan in the sub-quantum chat, adding some happy and panic emojis.

'My plans changed, so I came early,' Shan replied.

'Your plans always change.' Eli was right. Even when Shan had worked in the garage, he couldn't keep his wall planner straight, sometimes literally.

'Are you ready to travel?'

'Ready to travel? I thought I had four months to pack, not four hours!'

'Don't worry, I'm on holiday, so no rush. I'll be landing in one hour.' On hearing that, Eli went into a bit of a panic, declaring that her flat was not the cleanest place.

Shan needed to calm his mind. His holiday, his work, the war, Shad and the general could wait. He needed to think about something else; he needed a distraction, he needed a friend.

He went to the shuttle that was kept docked above the loading bay at the back of his spacecraft. He was still having some difficulties with thought control and almost closed the shuttle door before he entered, but he managed to get in and sat down in the pilot's chair. The shuttle's systems went online, the inner door sealed automatically and the external door, exposed to the cosmos, opened with a familiar sound of escaping air.

Shan felt something was missing from this experience. He loved switches, buttons and joysticks. Thought control worked excellently, but it took away some of the joy of operating the ship manually. He activated the autopilot and slowly flew out of the shuttle bay before turning the shuttle towards the planet and following the virtual path projected onto the front window.

Seen from above, the bar world was big, but really it was the size of a moon rather than a planet. *And here things get interesting. Seatbelt on, eyes closed, and hold onto something.* The landing sequence was pre-configured and available to download from the bar network. You could do it manually, but that wasn't a good idea, unless you wanted to test 'spacecraft ground/atmosphere disintegration'.

Landing on a planet usually involves calculating all the variables, and continuously adjusting them, but here it's pure ballistics. The only thing the computer does is set the initial speed and angle, and hope-for-the-best. Hope-for-the-best is one of the useless settings in the config file, which was added to the calculations at the request of pilots. You can set it to whatever number you want, but even setting hope to one million per cent makes no difference. Once you pass the breakpoint, you can't change anything even by adjusting the balance, as the balance system will not work. If you activate it, you will get out of balance. Balance is good, burning and falling at the same time is not.

The entry itself takes about five minutes, during which time you are surrounded by hot plasma, which may or may not show up, may or may not be hot, and may or may not be actual plasma. Then the tarmac. Here things get interesting again. The landing strip is long, wide and positioned on the massive slope of a mountain. The landing pads hit first, then sparks fly and the ship comes to a sudden stop, hopefully before hitting the wall at the end of the runway. It's never pretty, especially for large spaceships, but those are rarely seen here these days.

* * *

Shan's landing was very ordinary, as his ship's improved pads did most of the job. The crowd wasn't entertained and gave him zero points. Then the spacecraft was transported to a parking spot where it would wait for a launch window.

When Shan tried to open the shuttle hatch, it stuck. He attempted to use a hammer, but its handle broke. Finally, he kicked the door, at which point his belt broke and guess what happened to his trousers. Eli was waiting outside, laughing. Being from a similar species to Shan's made it easy for her to find clothes for her two legs, two arms and single-headed body. She was wearing slightly overlong trousers with custom-made tools and monitoring equipment attached to her belt. Her shirt had a hidden mechanism to keep her clothes in place as buttons would not keep anything together here.

'Why are you laughing?' Shan asked, stepping out onto the moving platform where the shuttle was standing.

'I'm sorry, but I love to watch landings here. Your clothes are funny too.' She hadn't laughed so much for a long time. Neither had the others who were watching.

'If everything worked here, they would look normal. How do you keep looking so great?' Shan asked. Eli's clothes were perfect, which you couldn't say about those of the people around them.

'After ten years, I've learned how to keep everything tight.'

'Time flies, right?' They hugged and started to walk towards Eli's flat.

'Time doesn't fly. Anyway, you're too early,' Eli said, remembering how many things she still needed to do.

'Sorry... and wow, that place has changed.' Shan was looking at the city, which had so many new structures he didn't know where he was. The end of the landing strip and the parking lot marked the start of a now-expanded city. Hundreds of spaceships joined together made the new spaceport district, at the edge of which Eli's flat was located.

'Yes, it has changed. I remember when we first came here. This was all empty, and my ship was in the middle of nowhere. Fields mainly,' Eli said, thinking about all the years she had spent here.

'You haven't moved?' Shan asked, remembering where her flat was.

'No, I've been too busy doing research, and the closer you get to the city centre, the louder it gets.'

Eli was living in her old spacecraft, which she had connected to a few more, left by other scientists, creating lots of room. It was easy for her to detach her ship if she needed to escape, but for the last ten years, there had been no reason to.

They walked between the landing gear and pads of other ships until she turned left and pulled the rope to open the ramp on her own ship. It dropped almost like an anvil, but without behaving like one. They walked across a metal floor covered in tiles that transformed into carpet further inside the ship. The main cargo bay they entered was full of boxes stretching all the way up to the ceiling. They were full of paperwork, data drives, tools, books, curtains, newspapers, decorations, and everything else she had collected over the years. Not that she liked collecting clutter, but the city market wasn't a place you could buy the same thing twice, and it was good to pick up something useful when you saw it. Eli closed the ramp behind her, and they went up to the main corridor that connected all the rooms. The bedroom, bathroom, and other smaller rooms were filled with equipment, too.

'You've made a lovely home from this place,' Shan said, following Eli upstairs. The living room was big and comfortable, and was the only place without any scientific equipment. To make it more like home, she had covered the metallic walls using fabrics bought from the market.

'Thanks. I like keeping the living room free of any work-related stuff, although that's sometimes difficult, as you can see.' She pointed at some boxes lying on the floor. 'Please excuse the mess, as I didn't have time to clean.' Eli left her bag on a chair and went to boil the water. 'Tea, coffee?' she asked. 'Sorry about the kettle, it takes a few minutes to boil the water. I'm afraid the new instant makers won't work here.'

'Maybe tea, thanks, I just had coffee. Probably the last one, anyway. Is that all we need to take?' Shan asked, pointing to some boxes on a trolley.

'Before you came, I thought about taking everything with me and leaving this place, but the truth is, I don't need any of this. I can take just the essentials as I have nothing to do here anymore,' she replied, waiting for the water to boil.

'I'm sure you can leave this flat here for a while,' Shan said, looking out of the window. 'What do you mean, you've got nothing to do here anymore? Shouldn't you be solving the unsolvable?'

'I've lost hope that I can solve the bar problem. But anyway, what do you have for me? Tell me,' she urged, sitting down with the tea.

'Regarding the bar, not much. I did ask, but it's beyond me and beyond the military. They tried to find out why nothing works here, perhaps hoping to use it as a weapon, but they got nowhere,' Shan explained, drinking tea.

'Yes, I've seen them a few times. They come here, full of excitement and thinking they know everything, but at the end, they leave with nothing,' Eli replied, remembering many negotiations she'd seen.

'Can we go to the market, and to the bar for a moment? I haven't had that famous beer for a long time. What's it called? The Fallen Spider? And I would like to take some with me.'

'It's called the Smelly Bee now. They change the name too often. Drink? Yes. Take away with you? Not really, as it will disintegrate if you take it off the planet. Should we take a walk first? It's not often someone comes here to visit, and my friends don't really enjoy walking.'

* * *

One advantage of having a flat near the landing strip was that Eli had easy access to new parts if she wanted to expand her living space. The disadvantage was the noise from ships landing, including occasional crashes and screams.

When she'd first come to the bar, the surrounding area had been mostly empty space only taken by a few scientists. At that time, they were sure they could solve the bar problem and leave, so they stayed near the landing strip. Some remained longer than others. Many departed after a year, and some left their research spaceships behind.

'You have a scratch studio?' Shan asked, walking past one of the ships. Set into its side was a drive-in scratching machine that took prepaid cards, a popular way to pay for things here. They had been installed at the beginning to solve the problems with barter in a place where most things did not work. You could get a card by providing some resources to top it up with credit. The prepaid card was much easier to use than paying for a bus ticket with a diode or a bag of potatoes, although some drivers would still only accept resources, depending on what they needed that day.

'We also have other businesses,' Eli replied, then added, 'hotels, B&Bs, useless repair shops, travel agencies and cafes where you can buy delicious soup and excellent coffee. We even have a software company someone opened by mistake.'

'You don't open a business by mistake.'

'Here you do. A few friends bet that they could write a fully – or fully to a point this planet will allow – functional text editor adhering to the latest best practice but with as many bugs in it as possible. It worked, and it's still being developed here as an open-source project. They write other software, too.'

* * *

The wreckage city is not easy to describe. Imagine a thousand spaceships of different sizes dropped in one place, and then turned into living space. That's a lot of metal – well, most of it is metal – and it's actually beautiful if you like metal. It looks wonderful during the night when all the lights are on, and in the sunset and sunrise when you can't yet see the chaos but only the golden shimmer of the titanium. During the day, it really is chaos. There are some sort-of streets, along with tunnels, and lots of bridges connecting different flats, or rather ships. You walk mostly under their hulls, between their landing gears and pads, and sometimes through whatever is left of their interiors. There is no city centre, but a few large civilian spaceships sit in the middle of it all. That's where you'll find the main market, but be careful, as most of the stuff on sale either won't work here or won't work anywhere except here. Basically, you need to know what you're buying. The market is bustling, crowded and fascinating, and although making anything work here is a challenge, the market manages it. In this place, some items are sold by the ton, or gram, or litre, or the amount of damage they can cause. For example, you could pick any ingredient and add it to your tea, or drink it straight, and you would be perfectly fine. There is an actual food market, but if you have a weak stomach, don't try it. Still, you will be OK eating anything, as even raw meat or pure plutonium can't do you any harm here. You can buy anything you want. From clothes, food and home appliances to the most powerful and deadly weapons, poisons and hazardous materials ever created.

Despite all that, it's the safest place in the entire galaxy. You won't be mugged or murdered, and no one cares where you're from, what you wear, what you think, how you look, or what you say. There are no courts, laws or justice system, just everyone living in peace. Here wars, negotiations, plans, reports, weapons, laws, courts, shops, notepads, pencils, water, alcohol, food, thoughts, ideas, and everything else you can think of have difficulty even existing properly. For some, it's a paradise, for others not so much, but for most, it's just a nice place to live. There are buses, space shuttles and trains, and everyone has chaotic cars made from whatever they could find. The buses don't have a schedule, nor the trains, and no one knows when or where they go. That's another mystery to solve.

* * *

The city tour was quick as Eli avoided the centre to get to the nearby hill. It had benches, trees, lots of green spaces and a magnificent view of the city. As it was situated opposite the landing strip, you could enjoy watching spaceships land, without having to listen to the loud bangs, crashes, and screams. Many came there to get away from the chaos, racket and general annoyances of the city. You could lie on the grass, not worrying if something was going to drop from your ceiling, or the ceiling itself drop on your head.

'Amazing view, I must say,' Shan told Eli, looking at the city. 'There's tons of metal just lying here, but it's kind of alive with all those residents, and the lights and noises of everyday life.'

'It's a beautiful place,' Eli replied, sitting down on a bench that looked more like a bunch of random parts glued together.

'Sometimes I miss the city, and it reminds me of this place.' Shan took out the photo of his granddad on a hill, and showed it to Eli.

'You showed me that before, online. It couldn't have been taken here,' she replied.

'I know, but the place looks kind of similar.' Shan studied the photo, thinking about the last few days.

'You'll find your family, don't worry,' Eli told him.

I'm a robot, thought Shan. *Well, I'm not as such, but that's not easy to forget. Should I tell her? No, I need to stop thinking about this at least for today.*

'Will it crash?' Eli asked, watching a spacecraft land.

'Doesn't look like it,' Shan replied, watching the sky.

'Yes, it will.'

'How do you know?' Shan asked, as nothing seemed to be going wrong with the landing.

'Experience. If you don't recognise the spacecraft, that means it's someone new. The pilot will panic at the last moment trying to steer the ship, not trusting a ballistic trajectory,' Eli explained, and added after a moment, 'I was right.'

'Yep. Will it survive?' Shan asked, watching the falling parts.

'Of course. Even death doesn't work properly here, and again, no one knows why. So you'd better not get burned during entry. You'll be kind of burning *and* falling, breaking your bones at the same time, and trust me, it's torture. In this place, your head might even explode, but you'd still be alive,' Eli joked.

'In this place, I'm not even sure if that's a joke. Anyway, did you get anywhere with your research? Into why nothing works here? You mentioned you have nothing to do.'

'I haven't, I'm afraid. I've used all the knowledge, devices, simulations and computers I have. I've even used dirt, but nothing. It must be something in sub-quantum space, but I can't access it, and without proper funds I'm stuck. I need a break from this place, so the quicker we leave, the better.'

'I understand. I needed the same from my garage. Breaks are good; I've got results already.'

'Results?'

'I've stopped worrying about things – spacecrafts, wars, the military, paperwork – but I think I'm cursed.'

'What do you mean?' Eli wondered.

'When I worked in the garage, I could never keep my diary straight, and I could never keep appointments. There was always something. I'm not working there now, but it's the same. I wanted to see my parents, and I went to see the general instead. Next, the robots invited me to their planet, and my plans changed again. After that visit, *everything* changed. Now I want to find my grandfather, but again, something's come up.' *My mind came up. There's a blockage stopping me from talking about what I think and feel.*

'What changed after you visited the robots?'

'It's not easy to talk about this.'

'Listen, I'll help you with your diary, and you'll help me to get away from this place, and we don't have to talk about it now.'

* * *

The bar, located on the far side of the wreckage city and thousands, or even tens of thousands, of years old, was still in perfect condition. From its mechanical interior with pipes, to all the mechanisms outside the walls, to the wooden pillars holding up the ceiling, it looked ancient and enchanting. Inside, the wooden walls were covered with photographs taken over the centuries, and the pipes and clockwork mechanisms added up to give an impression of beautiful chaos. Wooden pillars kept the ceiling and the roof stable, and the windows kept noises and light inside. The wood was still original, as even bark beetles couldn't do their job here.

As Shan and Eli entered through the wooden doorway, they were welcomed by the smell of age, and of course, food, alcohol and most importantly the aroma of all the species of this galaxy and beyond. The bar itself was packed, as, according to the archives, it always had been. Not with travellers, who only came here for the experience of the non-working planet, but with locals, who considered it the planet's main attraction.

The first floor provided rooms with beds, and the cellar was used for storage. Eli sat in her favourite seat, next to the wall in the corner, joined by Shan. The table only had two chairs, and after ten years, everyone knew it was Eli's preferred spot. It was reserved for her most of the time, as she came here almost every day for dinner. Sometimes for lunch, too, if she wasn't in the mood for cooking or getting a takeaway, which required some serious handling skills. In the beginning, everything here had been exciting for her; now she'd seen it all.

'I love this table. I can watch everyone from here and stay hidden,' she said, then seemed to drift into thought.

'Hey,' Shan said to her at last, 'you look like you're somewhere else.'

'Sorry.' She took the menu, an interactive book with text and pictures of the various options.

'You need to help me. A lot has changed since the last time I was here,' Shan said, trying to decide what to eat.

'Luminous sea crab for a starter to share and then Beguilian beef for you and Crystalline bird with noodle soup for me. And cold local beer,' Eli replied quickly.

'Sounds good,' Shan replied, and the waiter took their order. 'Wait, they serve Calczoid here?' Shan asked, reading the menu. 'It's one of the most poisonous substances in history. I assumed it was banned.'

'Yeah, but you can eat it safely here, and I hear it's trendy outside the bar, too.'

'Trendy? You can't eat Calczoid,' Shan objected. 'That stuff caused the death of a few civilisations.'

'Here you can eat anything, but in some places outside the bar it's only available as a takeaway, and you must hold it perfectly still and flat, otherwise the poison will touch your food. Once you open the box, you can remove it. It's mostly popular with couples who each prove their trust in the other by accepting the food from them,' Eli explained. 'At least the service is fast here,' she commented as the waitress brought their meal.

'Seriously. Anyway, have you ever seen negotiations taking place here?' Shan asked, watching the crowd. In most places such a crowd would be weird or even appalling, but not here. All those multiple eyes, heads, arms, legs or sometimes a complete lack of those things on creatures that were hairy translucent jelly torsos with cybernetic extensions and inside-out organs, which here became a form of art, and complete normality just trying to keep their clothes together.

'Yes, a few times. They're interesting. Sometimes people try to argue and fight, but even that doesn't work here. I don't think this war will ever end,' Eli replied, then started to eat before adding, 'This place used to be exciting and amazing, but now I've seen everything. I mean, it's still exciting, but after ten years... Look over there.' Eli pointed at the other end of the bar. 'Those two ladies are always there, chatting, drinking coffee, and later they'll spend hours talking to everyone via a ham radio. That painter who just came in works in the wreckage city, painting everything she can. Her clothes used to be black, and now they're white from the paint. That creature, at the middle table, is something, it can drink a lot of alcohol, and nothing. No wonder it is almost made of it. That group next to the bar is always here; they're funny and they drink a lot. They'll do karaoke later. I've joined them a few times, it's fun. That cleaner has been here since forever, and whenever I speak to him, he says he wants to leave this place. He said he used to have a dream, but lost it. And that girl in the corner – no one knows who she is.

'You see how boring this place has become? It's all the same, I know everyone and everything here. Nothing's happening; it's the only place in the galaxy that never changes. Never. I mean, nothing's changed here since it was built. Imagine that: everything you see in this bar is original, and thousands of years old. No one knows how old anymore. It could be millions.'

'I don't know; I like this place. No one's here to judge anyone else, no one cares how you look, where you're from, or what you think. I'm glad nothing changes here. We need one place we can rely on. The outside world changes too much, especially now.'

'Yes, I know, my home planet isn't like that. Everyone hates each other in the part where I live, and then we also hate the other side of the planet. How stupid is that? Don't get me wrong; I like this bar and this world, I really do. It's just a bit boring now, and at the same time it's kind of perfect. The planet, the bar, the city, everything and everyone. It's like an entity no one is able to touch. You know I come here every day? I meet so many different species, drink so many different teas, coffees, alcohols, juices and cocktails from all over the galaxy, and sometimes from other galaxies. Sometimes, I don't even know what I'm eating or drinking. I've tried everything, even petrol, liquid oxygen and nitrogen and liquid helium cooled to almost zero – it was leaking through my skin. All the poisons. Even paint and plutonium. I've tried it all. I always wanted to taste everything. Don't ask why, I know it's weird, but this is the only place where you can do that.

'I've seen so many things: weird weapons and devices, cars, planes, species and even ideas. I've seen many planets in my life, but this place is beyond imagination and description, and at the same time, it's so simple, like any other planet with a bar. It's simultaneously magical and average.

You see the bar, and it looks so normal. Parking lot, sign, doors, chairs, stairs, stage, floor, everyone enjoying themselves, music. Drinking cocktails, talking, sleeping, or being drunk. I told you I like to watch spacecraft landing, but the people here are even funnier. You don't need to be drunk to look ridiculous, because your clothes will look baggy, loose, oversized or very tight, and if you don't find a clever way to fasten them, they'll fall off immediately. At the same time, everything looks so ordinary. The bar has two floors, a basement, a roof, nice rooms upstairs, double beds and even TV and radio, which connects to the LLTS now. Visitors come here, but they never stay. Only the military come here for negotiations, less and less often now. I think after all these years they've realised no one wants to negotiate.' Eli paused and seemed to be thinking again, rolling her eyes, making faces and calculating something in her head as usual.

'You OK?' Shan asked after a minute.

'It's nothing, sorry. Anyway, the wreckage city has been my home for the last ten years. I've seen the whole planet during that time. It's not that big, anyway. I've been in the tunnels, mines and caves, and even in the basement of this bar. The rest of the planet is either deserted or is waiting for development. I like this place, and I get a bit sentimental about it. At the same time, I kind of hate it. Ten years and nothing. Absolutely nothing. I've met so many scientists who come to do their research, and most leave after a year. I was the only one stupid enough to stay, and for what? I need to go through the data again. Sorry, I'm talking too much.'

'Maybe, like you said, it is magic.'

'Maybe I just need to find the right spell.'

They had only just finished their dinner when somebody entered and seemed to recognise Shan. He came over to their table, took another chair, and sat down without saying a word. That behaviour wasn't rude; it was the custom in the Bolenga system.

Shan had met him many years ago, right here, when they'd spent a whole night discussing everything from the economy and intergalactic issues, to gods or the lack of them, to what type of beer is the best. His name was unpronounceable, but everyone called him Beadon, the name of the city he came from. If anyone else had come from the same town, people would have had to use the unpronounceable name. He was smaller than Shan and Eli, but from a similar species, and was wearing a big grey suit covered with random bits of fabric. A gas mask, with a flexible pipe protruding from one side and connected to a bag on his belt, merged strangely into his face.

'Even after twenty years, you're still wearing that mask?' Shan asked, looking at Beadon, remembering he'd been wearing the same clothes the first time they'd met.

'If I get used to this atmosphere, I won't be able to survive on my home planet. And you remember my people's custom dictates that I can't show my body here. Besides, my skin won't like the weird air on this planet,' Beadon said, then looked at Eli. 'Can we trust her?'

'Hey,' Eli snapped, then her frown faded. 'Well, at least something interesting is happening. I've seen you here a few times.'

'Of course you can trust her. Why?' Shan asked him.

'You are the only one I can trust. I've been here for years waiting for you, and today you've come. My species is looking for a place to escape to. Can you take our civilisation with you?' he was very close to Shan, speaking very quietly.

'I remember we talked about this years ago… but take a whole civilisation with me? Why me? How do you know I want to escape?' Shan was a bit confused.

'You told me all those years ago, so I've been waiting.'

'It won't be easy, but I have some ideas. How can I find you or contact you?' Shan asked. You had to play things straight with Beadon's species. He'd learned that many years ago when he'd spent too much time in this place, mostly drinking, being too honest and making bad jokes.

'Those are my details.' Beadon touched Shan's hand. It was an old Bolenga trick – well, some see it as a trick, but for them, it's just a regular everyday data transfer. They have the ability to carry data, thoughts and ideas in their bodies, and can transfer them to other compatible organisms. Once the data was in the cells of Shan's hand, it would be replicated all around his body.

'Once I know something, I'll tell you, trust me on this, but I need something. Do you know anyone here who would be able to get me some Tiranian gold?' Shan asked, thinking, *There's no point in small talk with him – might as well use his contacts.* Tiranian gold was officially forbidden everywhere in this galaxy, and, it seemed, in some others nearby. It had nothing in common with real gold, apart from its colour. People often said: 'Tiranian gold is easy to transport, and hard to make. It tastes like oranges, and destroys everything', and yes, you can actually eat it.

'Yes, I know, it's still only made in one place in Sector One, but there's a dealer not far from here. Give me your hand.' Beadon transferred the number of the market stall, leaving a mark on Shan's skin for the seller. Then he stood up abruptly and left. He was always like that: straight to the point. Their whole civilisation has quite different customs to most others. They don't do small talk, and don't knock on doors, even when entering offices or government buildings. You can just go in and talk to anyone anytime. There is internal security, but that only applies to foreigners. They don't check each other even if someone is going to the president's bedroom in the middle of the night to talk to him about issues with garbage on the streets. Their whole species is genetically programmed not to harm their own kind, and they cannot break that rule. It's also difficult to tell them one from another, as they all look almost exactly the same. They've managed to build an advanced civilisation on a couple of planets, and on a few more they mine rare elements, which help them with their economy. They have an army and powerful weapons, but they are weak in the area of strategy. Lack of instinct or logic is bad for fighting wars.

'Why the hell do you need that gold? You know it's forbidden,' Eli whispered.

'I know, and I will explain properly later, but I met my crazy cousin recently and I might need it one day just in case.' There was no knowing what he might encounter in the galaxy he was heading for, and Shad being Shad it was better to have some.

'All right, I don't want to know,' Eli said. 'Just be careful. That stuff destroys planets.' Then she added, 'Now I'm thinking. Would it work here?'

* * *

The next morning Shan woke up in the room Eli had prepared for him and immediately fell out of the bed, causing a bit of chaos. Eli had moved a lot of clutter to make space for his bed, and now it all landed on top of him.

Eli came in quickly, hearing all the noise, and tried to find Shan under all the books, boxes, cups, gravity detectors and everything else she hadn't moved to other rooms. 'Shit, sorry. Hope you're OK.'

'I'm OK, and yeah, this was an unexpected wake-up call,' Shan joked, standing up.

'Breakfast?' Eli laughed.

'Yes, please,' Shan replied, and after spending some time in the bathroom trying to use equipment that wasn't working properly, he came to the kitchen. 'Yeah, I forgot how this place works... or doesn't.'

'I should have explained the bathroom, shouldn't I? I'm also tired of this place, to be honest. Nothing works here, and after ten years, I just want to go someplace where it does. So, if we could leave as soon as possible?' Eli repeated herself. 'You used the fork and knife yesterday, so you should be okay. Be careful with that tea; it's hot, and holding a cup in a place where there's issues with friction might not be a very good idea.'

'Yes, I experienced that yesterday. Anyway, what's the plan for today? I can leave anytime, so it's up to you,' Shan said, trying to eat breakfast.

'Well, you can help me clean and pack. Later we can go to the market to find your gold. I also invited a few friends to the bar to say goodbye this evening, and we can leave tomorrow morning.'

'Good plan.'

* * *

Later that afternoon they were on their way to the market. It was a few minutes' walk from Eli's flat to the south-west of the city. Quite enjoyable, if you like walking under metal. Metal filled with flats, cargo bays, docking ports, landing pads, engines, exhaust pipes, weapons and businesses of all different kinds. The city centre was busy as usual, crowded and very noisy. Merchants from all parts of the galaxy had little shops here, built from all kinds of scrap and held together by just about everything except nails, which didn't work in this place. Some traders were shouting out the latest deals, sales and deliveries, but others were sleeping, not trying to sell anything.

They passed crowds of different species wearing everything, from traditional clothes to their bare skin, while dust from all those feet and wheels and pads made its way to the nostrils of everyone who had them. Stalls were filled with everything from toilets and plumbing tools to car and spacecraft parts to mini nuclear bombs and warheads. Data drives filled with stolen personal records and enterprise information, exploits, passwords and viruses were lying around for those interested in hacking sub-quantum networks. Amongst all this were small food stalls, and in the centre was the big food market. The smell was amazing;

steam rose from boiling water, and meat, vegetables, and anything else you could ever imagine was cooking.

Shan saw in his mind the information Beadon had transferred, and slowly made his way to the stall in question. It didn't look like much, being randomly built and located between long rows of other stands. The seller was sleeping in the corner with bags of clothes covering his, her or its body. The stall was full of antiques, which were the seller's speciality. Shan was examining an old-looking content reader when the seller woke up.

'It won't work here,' the seller said. 'If you're interested, I know someone who can get you a working version.' She spoke in the official bar language, which was the one that had been used by the defunct central government.

'Nothing works here, so how can it?' Eli, the expert here, replied, looking at the seller's products.

'It's one of the originals,' the seller responded.

'Oh, yes, I forgot about them. Those are expensive. Where did you get it from?' she asked, examining other items.

'I have the best prices as always, especially for you. I dig them out, usually. After all those years this soil is a gold mine. Although the ground scanners have issues, so it's back to basic metal detectors,' the seller replied.

'Maybe later. Right now, I'm looking for number eighty-six in your catalogue,' Shan said, and showed his arm to the seller, pointing at the little mark Beadon had left.

'Oh, that. It's popular. I don't keep any of it here; it goes too quick. The mines are constantly being moved, so it's increasingly difficult to find. Give me your hand.' The seller touched Shan's arm and left the details of the Tiranian gold mine, currently located between Sectors One and Four.

'Who else knows about this place?' Shan asked. *Now I understand. Shad is between sectors for the gold, and if he finds it, this galaxy will be gone. Him and the gold is a bad combination. It'll make him so powerful no one will be able to stop him. I guess my plans have changed again.*

'Just a few or everyone, depending on who you ask. No one truly knows what's going on between sectors, and there are no maps. A bit of advice: don't go there, or at least don't tell anyone you're going. Here, you're safe; there, you're dead,' the seller explained and then added, 'May I interest you in these old players, or some data drives?'

'No, thank you,' Eli replied, pulling Shan away, knowing his data addiction.

'Hey, I wanted to check those drives,' Shan protested.

'I've got copies of them all.'

* * *

The next morning, they arrived at the shuttle, ready to go. After Eli had held a small leaving party at the bar last night they hadn't slept much, and they were still a bit drunk.

The ground crew started to move the shuttle to the catapult. For a small spacecraft it was easy, but not so for the large ones, and often they got stuck there forever. One of the many remarkable things about the bar was that you could get seriously drunk there and then still use the catapult. It sounds disgusting, but here's why: your stomach is trying to vomit inwards, pulled by the G-forces, your head is spinning, and then you pass the breakpoint, and it all disappears, making you sober instantly. And that's exactly what happened.

Shan docked the shuttle at the main spacecraft, locked the doors, and they both started moving boxes out to the loading bay.

'So where are we going?' Eli asked.

'It's a surprise.'

'I'm intrigued,' she replied.

'It'll take a while to get there, so after we unpack, I've got some films if you want to take your mind off the bar and everything.'

'That would be nice. New films don't work in the wreckage city, so I imagine I have lots of catching up to do.'

CHAPTER FOUR

Over the years, Shan's internal clock had set itself to wake him up at six am garage time. It was helpful. He didn't like to sleep late, and the earlier you wake up, the more day you have, especially in a busy garage. He didn't like to waste time, although in practice he did waste a lot of it on various things.

This morning he read the news until half past six. It was full of war, war and more war, with additional news about pirates, smugglers, and of course, the war. The war news these days was mostly from the front line. Holograms and virtual reality feeds were the worst, although the video feeds weren't nice either. Shan had never understood the point of showing death everywhere: spaceships with holes in their hulls and bodies floating around, frozen, with hope for a better afterlife.

He spent the next half an hour browsing the latest offers in the spare parts market, his favourite. Finally, he decided to get out of bed. He changed his clothes and went to the main bridge. It was a single room, containing living space and a kitchen. Shan took two cups, put them on a table and waited for the kitchen's built-in kettle to prepare some water. He was still using the old one. He liked the traditional model, and he couldn't be bothered to learn how to use the robots' kettle yet, especially as it didn't seem to come with instructions. Well, that was a lie, the thought control worked perfectly.

What am I supposed to do with all that automation? I like making coffee, preparing breakfast. I don't want that replaced. While the kettle was boiling, he took the Kreton coffee from the box and put four spoonfuls into the coffee press. *I know, I know. I should keep it for later, but it's such a good coffee.* The kettle got louder, letting everyone know the water was ready. It was preprogrammed to boil it to the perfect temperature as specified by the coffee association on Kreton.

Eli came up the stairs yawning. 'Sorry.'

Shan poured coffee into both cups and put them on a small tray. 'Did you sleep well? Coffee?'

'Yes, please,' she sat down and started reading a book Shan had left on the table yesterday. After reading the back cover for a minute, she said, 'It's too quiet, it's weird. The wreckage city is way too loud. Everyone just talks and talks and talks. Then there are ships landing, crashes, grinding metal, screams, and the music from the bar every weekend. Anyway, I couldn't sleep for the last hour, so I came here. It's the time difference for me, and that bed in my room, oh my, it's seriously comfortable. And your spacecraft looks seriously weird inside, what did you do to it?'

'I'll explain about the interior later, and that's a good book.' Shan put the coffee on the table. 'Do you want to eat? Breakfast is almost ready.'

'Sure,' Eli replied, then the light from the window caught her eye. She turned and saw a planet lit up by a nearby star. 'Where are we?' she asked.

Shan, who was now making breakfast, answered casually, 'The robots' planet.'

'You are fucking kidding me!' Her eyes widened and her jaw dropped as she calculated the distance they had just travelled. 'That's impossible, unless...' she looked at Shan as he washed tomatoes, '...the robots gave you their technology, and you didn't tell me!' She pointed at him.

'I had reasons for that.' Shan put two plates on the table. 'Breakfast is ready.'

'Breakfast shmekfast! How did they solve the problem of heat and power and coils and structural integration?' she pressed her face to the glass window. 'I didn't feel anything. It's more advanced than I expected!' She turned to Shan, who had sat down and started eating bread. 'What about pressure and quantum forces?'

'That's why I needed you here. I have no idea how all this works, and at the garage I was too busy with other things to even ask.' He put the sandwich on a plate. 'Just before I left, I received a message from the robots. They asked for help because their planet is dying.' Shan took a sip of coffee and started to eat again. 'Eat,' he urged Eli.

'Dying? How?' Eli sat down and started drinking coffee, curiosity overcoming her initial shock.

'You know how…' he paused to chew bread, '…they like to improve everything. I went there to check, and basically, they've improved nature so much it became so powerful that they can't control the trees and plants or even the grass anymore. They've improved animals, too. They upgraded my LLTS drive and thousands of other things on this ship, so I could return quicker after reading their data about nature. That's why your bed is so comfortable. I haven't checked all the data yet, but I think the only thing they can do is stop improving what they've created and destroy it, unless you have other ideas.'

'I'll have to go through the data to find out. Any other surprises?' Eli asked.

'Well.' Shan smiled, put his sandwich away and walked to the centre of the bridge, taking his coffee with him. 'Look here.' The map of the galaxy was displayed on the interactive table.

'Nice map. We built a similar one.'

'No, you haven't,' Shan replied and switched to the sub-quantum view. Eli's eyes and mouth went wide again.

'That's impossible in sub-quantum, even you know that.' Eli couldn't stop looking at the map.

'One thing I've learned recently: something's only impossible until robots do it.' Shan was switching between different views.

'Seriously, how? Are those spaceships? Nets, stars, planets, and what's that?' she was pointing to all the dots on the map in turn.

'I don't know what some of it is.'

'I know what this one is,' she pointed to a long thick blurred braid-like line coming out of the centre of the galaxy. 'It's confirmation of our theories. We detected these centuries ago. They're passages of some kind, or waves of energy in sub-quantum, connecting all the galaxies, and it's not gravity. We can control gravity easily, but we have no control over this. We can detect it, kind of measure it, but whatever energy we use, it doesn't affect it at all. I have a theory about it all, but that's for another time.'

'I also have a copy of all the robots' data.' Shan gave her the tiny cube.

'Wait, I need a cold shower to help me think after all those revelations,' Eli replied and went to her room to cool down, taking the cube with her.

* * *

A couple of hours later, Shan saw light coming from the status console; it was signalling someone was in the engine room. *Eli?* He went to the loading bay where part of the LLTS drive was located.

'Are you OK?' Shan asked, walking in and seeing Eli sitting on the floor.

'Oh, hi, sorry, yes.' Eli was surprised and confused at seeing him.

'What are you doing, and why is the engine open?' Shan sat down next to her, looking at the drive.

'Well, I was curious how they achieved the higher speed, and I think I know how.' Eli pointed at the drive.

'I've seen it before, in the garage when I was fixing their crafts, but we could never find out how it works,' Shan said.

Eli was unusually quiet. 'Are you OK?' he asked again.

'Yes, sorry, just thinking. Basically, there are no parts here,' Eli told Shan. The drive looked mostly white, showing bands of shimmering.

'No parts? It needs to work somehow,' Shan replied, trying to understand.

'Yes, exactly that.' Eli's reply wasn't what Shan was expecting.

'I don't understand.' He was even more confused now.

'OK, I think what you see here is an atomic-level – our-level – physical representation of the LLTS drive that's actually built in sub-quantum space. So that drive exists on both levels, ours – the atomic – and the quantum level,' Eli explained.

'Seriously what?'

'I know it's not easy to understand...'

'Explain it to me like I'm five.'

'You want me to explain the sub-quantum mechanics like you are five years old?' she looked at Shan, thinking. 'OK... See this wrench?' Eli picked up a wrench that had been lying on the floor.

'Yes,' Shan smiled, knowing what a wrench was.

'To you, it's a wrench, but if you look very closely, it's just a bunch of atoms put together. From another atom's perspective, it's a bunch of atoms, or actually, just atoms, cause if you were an atom you'd see atoms next to you everywhere, so you wouldn't even know that atom next to you is part of something or not.' Eli tried to be as simple as possible.

'I already understand that.'

'Wait. Now, if you are that atom and you want to make a tool, like a wrench, you need to make it using something smaller than yourself. Quarks, for example. And at the same time if you are a quark and you need a wrench, it needs to be made from something smaller, like sub-quantum particles. Now, if I put lots of wrenches made of sub-quantum particles here on this floor, like loads of them, you wouldn't see wrenches, but that.' She pointed to the LLTS drive. 'So, for you, those wrenches would be too small to use, but they are there, so it's the same with the LLTS drive. It is there; its parts are made from sub-quantum particles working together to achieve LLTS 3. How? No idea yet, I couldn't find the data in that cube you gave me, but I know robots can build in sub-quantum space,' Eli explained.

'…and five,' Shan said, as if finishing a sentence.

'What five?' Eli asked, trying to find the context.

'They improved this drive to achieve LLTS 3 and LLTS 5,' Shan explained.

Eli closed her eyes, trying not to think. This was a bit too much for her. She who had known it all now didn't know anything anymore.

'How?' she asked quietly.

'Easy,' Shan replied.

'No, it's not easy, Shan. We cannot build at a smaller scale than atoms; we cannot even think on the atomic level. If we put many atoms together, they won't work on that level; you have to zoom out to see the final product. What the robots have achieved is a final product built and working in sub-quantum: that's why I'm so confused and amazed and shocked and sad and confused again. The deeper you go, the more interesting it gets. If you could be a thinking atom, you could build a wrench out of quarks and use it in your tiny atom world. If you could be a thinking and walking quark, you could create a wrench out of sub-quantum forces and particles, and use it there in quantum space, the same as you use a wrench made of atoms here,' Eli continued, gesticulating. 'But this… This is something. This is impossible, unexplainably impossible.'

'You see how much there is still to explore?'

'Yes,' Eli replied, standing up, and added, 'there is, and I need to read more of this data from the cube.' And she went back to her room.

Shan closed the engine and went to his room to read as well. He knew Eli enough to tell when he should leave her alone, especially when she'd discovered something new to learn.

* * *

All the rooms were directly below the bridge. Having four bedrooms, together with a living room, gave Shan something like his own home, which he'd never had before. It was quite the opposite of his parents' house: a simple design, perfectly clean, and everything had its place.

In the afternoon, garage time, Shan went to check on Eli and asked what she would like to eat. He knocked on the door, and she invited him inside, where she was sitting on the chair, eating snacks from the fridge, and reading data on the screen.

'Have you spent all day reading that?' he asked, entering the room, knowing the answer.

'Yes, it's so interesting. It's not easy to find such a complete record of a civilisation. The robots' creators went through a lot: wars, dark ages, revolutions, innovations, and at the end, they almost killed themselves by killing their planet. At that time they believed that time exists, dimensions, multiverses and even the big bang. They did get the maths right, but for the wrong ideas. They were blinded by their ignorance and fear.

'They were right about gravity, though. One thing that's weird here: there are lots of missing and redacted records, like they wanted to hide something from everyone. Anyway, after they left the dying planet, the robots took over and carried out their makers' one last order: to improve. We used to be like them. Most species were. We used to believe in all that, too. We actually proved it mathematically, then disproved it.' She stopped and turned to Shan, who was now sitting on her bed.

'You realise it all happened hundreds of years ago, thousands, even? And how do you know we're right?'

'I don't, but as far as we know we are. Every so often we hear from scientists that this or that shouldn't happen, but it is happening, and then we need to explain it somehow. At the same time, a couple of hundred years from now, someone might prove our theories completely wrong.' She turned back to the screen and pointed at something. 'The last entries are a bit sad. They left because they almost killed their planet. They built lots of colonies on some other worlds, but they couldn't live without the support of the main one. They tried to terraform another planet, but that didn't go as planned. Before they had to leave, they were living in a golden era and didn't even realise. They took what they wanted from their planet without thinking. Without realising nothing is forever, and resources are finite. Millions died from diseases, poverty, lack of clean air, water and food. Actually, you remember Kroni VII?'

'The place where everyone died in one day?' Shan replied, looking at a book he'd found on Eli's bed.

'No, that's Dofloos. Anyway, something similar happened on Kroni VII.'

'I remember Dofloos, terrible things happened there. Everyone died almost instantly. After that, the central government closed the planet to all traffic. Pirates still went there for resources, but they all died,' Shan replied, and Eli changed the screen to a view of the star, accompanied by all its data.

'There's another issue here. The robots' star is dying.' She pointed at the screen.

'What? What do you mean, their star is dying?' Shan stood up to look at the screen.

'I wonder how you even got here; their star is marked with a warning on all the maps. It's going to become a red giant at some point.' Eli showed the forecast of the expanding star, with the habitable zone slowly moving outwards.

'When?'

'Not easy to say, that process is slow. The star is slowly expanding, and they're on the edge of the current habitable zone. In many years' time, that planet will turn into a desert with machines on it. How come the robots don't know about it?' Eli was surprised as they were supposed to have super-advanced technology.

'This wasn't on my map, but I haven't updated it yet. The robots only think about improving everything, not fixing their star.'

'Maps are updated automatically. Why did you change to manual?'

'The last time they updated, I had to change the whole navigation system. The software had a bug.'

'Anyway, we need to tell the robots about this. There's no point in fixing nature on their planet if their star is dying,' said Eli, watching the screen.

'They need to move, but if they can build planets, they should be fine,' Shan replied, sitting back down on the bed.

'I asked you earlier if you have any other surprises. Build a planet?' Eli looked at Shan.

'You remember I wanted to expand my garage?' he asked, and continued after Eli nodded, 'I wanted to ask the robots if they had a planet to spare.'

'A planet to spare? What kind of question is that? No one has spare planets, especially now when we have so many wars.' Eli wasn't convinced.

'The military has. They'll give me one if I give them the robots' technology.'

'Will you?'

'Of course not. The robots said that if I save their planet, they will build a planet for me.'

'I shouldn't be surprised anymore, should I? Although that seems to be the new normal for me.'

'If they can build planets, maybe they can fix their star, or find a new one. It only takes forty-eight hours for them to get across the galaxy.' Shan was thinking aloud.

'For a spacecraft! But moving the whole planet? Planets are big, Shan, huge, and stars are even bigger. They are so big, and huge, and gigantic, colossal, enormous, and massive, it's beyond your imagination. And you want to move one?' At this point, Eli became lost for words.

'No, they'd have to move all the planets. They have colonies there,' Shan calmly explained.

'This is ridiculous. Should I take another shower? I'm sorry, but they can't build planets, or move them, and they definitely can't move whole solar systems. Are you crazy?'

'Eli, they can fly across the galaxy in forty-eight hours – well, actually in forty minutes with LLTS 5. They can see in real time what's going on in this galaxy, which yesterday you thought was impossible. It might work. Let's talk to them.' Shan was trying to keep her calm.

'Shan, if they can do all this, I will burn my PhD. We know nothing, I know nothing anymore. We know so much, but still nothing. We haven't even explored our local group of galaxies properly... What am I talking about, we haven't even explored the galaxy next to us! It would be easier to live on a flat planet protected by gods, not knowing we're part of that mind-blowingly gigantic universe. We can't even imagine that; we can't imagine infinity. We have this amazing technology, and still for the last ten years I've been stuck in that stupid bar trying to find something, and nothing, and for what? Now I'm here trying to be a fucking biologist helping robots, how stupid is that?' Eli lay on her bed, crying.

'Yeah, I wanted to tell you something about that bar.'

'What? Now you're smarter than me, are you?' Eli snapped.

'Come on, don't be upset. Look here.' Shan moved to her chair and switched to the view of the galaxy.

'And? What? I've seen it.' Eli looked at it with one eye.

'Look now.' He switched to the LLTS view and pointed at the bar.

'The bar exists in sub-quantum space. Which means you can go there in LLTS and just land.' Eli was trying to understand how and why the bar planet was different to other planets.

'I didn't want to do it. First, I didn't know what would happen, and second, I didn't want to show everyone that I have the new drive. One more reason: I can't fly slowly in LLTS, and landing at that speed is not advisable.'

'Well, that doesn't solve the problem of why nothing works there. I've exhausted all my scientific ideas, and I don't have to go back there. I have no purpose.' Eli lay there, covering her eyes with her hands. She was trying not to think; she wanted to disappear.

'Yes, you do. We need to help the robots – they asked for help – and we need to escape the collision and wars. Imagine the possibilities; imagine what else there is to discover. Besides, there's another surprise, kind of a big one.'

Eli looked at him. 'Please don't kill me with another surprise,' she said quietly.

'This time it's about me,' said Shan, looking calmly at her. She sat up, listening. 'You know how I always wanted to find my real family and the only thing I had was the photograph?' Eli nodded. 'I did find my family.'

'That's amazing!' Eli's mood changed.

'Wait till you hear the rest. I wasn't born, I was made. By machines. Those robots built me.'

'Robots? How? What are you talking about?' Eli was confused again.

'It's a long story, but basically I came here before, to check their planet, and they told me I had been built. I was designed and made by my grandfather as a test to prove that they can recreate their kind. Don't get me wrong, I'm not a robot. My body is organic, with organs, there's DNA and everything.

'They're all dead, Eli, everyone from this planet is dead, and now the robots can recreate them. I am proof of that. My grandfather left for the stars to look for the origins of his kind, and of my kind. Now I don't know what to do. There's the collision, my garage, my family, my grandfather, the robots, you, and I don't know what's more important now. Should I stay here, or maybe look for my grandfather, or move to another galaxy? I need your help.' Finally, Shan was opening up.

'Hey, it's OK.' Eli hugged him. 'Listen, I'm here, I'm your friend, we'll figure something out. We're both in this together; we're here for each other.'

* * *

Eli and Shan were standing on the bridge, looking at the robots' planet. It was partly blue, but mostly green. They could see spaceships coming and going, with many in orbit around the planet. Shan, in his mind, asked for permission to land. There was no reply, but his spacecraft started to move.

'Did they just take control?' Eli asked, feeling the movement.

'Looks like it,' Shan replied and went to drink some water.

'What do they look like? How do we talk to them?' Eli was glued to the window, admiring the planet below.

'I've seen many types of robots here.' He took the glass of water and walked back to Eli. 'They aren't all the same. Some have two legs, some have four, some have wheels, some fly and some have tools. They all have antennae, cameras, cables, wires, a power source, and a computer. They are very specialised; each one is different and designed to do a specific task. They all speak our language, but sometimes it takes them a few minutes to come up with the answers, so be patient. Oh, and they're generally small. Half our height, unless they fly or walk like spiders. I named some of them, too.'

The spaceship landed in the middle of a city centre, on the same pad used by Shan previously. It was almost entirely covered in grass and flowers.

'You ready?' Shan asked Eli, waiting to leave the ship.

'Sure, I already have experience talking to robots. I just met one called Shan.' Eli was joking. 'He's OK, I guess,' she added and started walking.

'Very funny,' Shan replied, opening the ramp.

Outside, a single robot was floating, waiting for them. It wasn't pretty, but it was functional. It was mostly cuboid, or more precisely it looked like a rectangular box. Mostly black, with some of its internal workings outside, mainly cables. It did have two cameras, two antennae and different arms, wires, and pipes all around it. It was also covered in ivy.

'Hi, Floaty,' Shan said.

'Floaty?' Eli asked.

'I kind of named two of them, mostly for fun but it helps when you're talking to them. Anyway… Floaty, this is my friend Eli; she's helping me to help you. Where would you like to talk?'

'Here,' answered Floaty, who clearly knew nothing about good manners.

'OK. The only thing you can do is analyse nature on your planet, find its weak points and destroy it. We need to check the information you have about it, and what you did to it exactly. The cube you provided didn't have many details,' Shan explained.

'Follow me. We will provide everything you need to stop nature,' Floaty replied. Then it turned around and started moving towards a small spacecraft parked on the road.

'Wait!' Eli almost screamed. 'There's another issue we need to talk about.'

'What is the issue?' Floaty asked.

Eli took a deep breath and said, 'Your star is dying. It's becoming a red giant. This planet will be a desert, and eventually it will be completely destroyed.'

It took an unusually long time to reply, presumably communicating silently with other robots.

'Do you think it's broken?' Eli asked Shan.

'No, I think it's just checking and analysing the issue,' Shan replied, sitting down on a loading ramp.

While Floaty was thinking, Shan and Eli spent the next ten minutes admiring the robots' city.

'Do you think it's broken?' Eli asked Shan again, as Floaty was still unresponsive.

'No, it's just thinking about a very big issue.'

'This is a beautiful city, but a bit too green to be honest,' Eli started saying when Floaty suddenly replied, 'Correct. We need you to help us fix our star.'

'Told you they're very logical,' Shan said to Eli.

'A bit too logical,' Eli replied. 'Can we sit down somewhere and discuss this?' she wasn't used to standing on a landing pad discussing the future of civilisation.

'Follow me,' Floaty said and started moving towards the flying car, which was parked nearby.

Eli and Shan followed. The journey took about five minutes, until they landed on a roof of a skyscraper. The robot led them to a big meeting room, where about ten more robots were waiting.

'Can you help us fix the star?' one asked.

'Well, we discussed this,' Shan said, looking at Eli. 'One solution is for you all to move to another system. Is that something you would consider?'

'No,' another robot replied.

'OK. What about moving your planets?'

The robots went quiet for a bit, then one of them replied, 'You can use our technology. Details will be provided. We will offer you planets in return for saving our planets, and a star for saving our star.'

The robots started to leave, but Shan asked, 'What do you mean, you can offer a star? Can you build stars?'

'To a design, yes,' Floaty replied logically.

Eli didn't believe him, but she asked, 'How can we access your technology and documentation, so we can find a solution?'

'Take this cube. Access it in your spacecraft,' Floaty replied. A data cube appeared on its arm and the robot handed it to Eli. Then the robots began leaving the room.

'Are they fucking kidding me? Building LLTS is one thing, but building a planet and a star? Shall I laugh or cry or just jump out of the window?'

'Let's go back and check the cube. Shall we walk?' Shan replied and headed for the door.

'Sure, I like walking. Jumping out of the window would be quicker, though. And why did we come all the way here? That robot could have told us the same thing back at the pad. I thought we were going to meet some robot leader or something,' Eli said, walking down the corridor towards the elevator.

'Who knows how they think and why they needed a meeting? I don't think there's one leader here, I believe they work together, and each robot communicates with all the others,' Shan replied as they waited for the lift.

The express elevator took them all the way down. The weather outside was perfect, not too hot, not too cold, just a lovely summer's day. The road was clean, the pavement was clean, the palm trees were green, and the robots were busy doing their thing. Which these days mostly meant cutting back plants. Most of the buildings were covered in some kind of improved flora, with improved fauna buzzing around. All the businesses were open: clothes shops, electronics stores, restaurants, camera shops, car shops, spaceship shops and finally coffee shops.

'So, you think they sell coffee here?' Shan asked as they passed one.

'Looks like a coffee shop to me. Let's ask,' Eli replied.

When they entered the coffee shop, it looked magical, not because that was its theme but because of the greenery that grew everywhere. Grass was growing from the improved, and now invisible, floor. Climbing flowers were hanging over the tables, and the unseen walls and ceiling were covered in climbing plants. Shan and Eli spotted a robot through a small hole cut from the vines that hung above the counter, and they ordered coffee, which was collected, dried and ground right in front of them. Then they continued walking for many hours, enjoying the best food and drinks, including more coffee, as well as watching the robots trying to control the plants. They continued discussing nature on this planet, the star, and a good deal about robots until they finally arrived at the spacecraft. 'Can we stay here? Forever?' Eli asked. 'There's no one around, they have the best food, it's clean, it's safe, everything is working properly and there's this amazing sunset and weather. With all the technology and knowledge, it's an overgrown paradise.'

'We need to help them, or there won't be any paradise left,' Shan replied, killing the mood. 'They can improve everything, so I don't really understand why they can't fix anything.'

* * *

After spending most of the day and night reading and analysing the robots' data, Eli concluded it would be best to replace the star. She was sitting in her room watching the simulation, with Shan next to her.

'It would be *easier* to build a star, but it would take too long. Replacing the star is easy theoretically – well, it's not easy, but doable with the robots' technology.' Eli stood up and started walking in circles. 'We cannot simply move the star away as all the planets would move or get ejected from their orbits. We need to remove the original star and replace it almost immediately with a new one. Mathematically it works. Practically it's an engineering problem. The robots will have to use a wormhole, a seriously advanced wormhole. LLTS would be better, but we won't be able to control the movement of the star precisely enough, it's too big and wobbly. It's like trying to move a nuclear explosion at the speed of light and suddenly stop it. The wormhole will simply move the whole star without the star even realising. The wormhole generator will need to be enormous, but if they can build stars and planets, they can probably do that, too.' She switched the simulation to images of nature. 'Regarding the problems with nature, they've built themselves into everything organic. I'll have to find a weak point in their design.'

'Can they really build planets and stars?' Shan was puzzled.

'Yes, from what I've read, they can. I don't want to believe it, but it's science, so it's true. I mean, theoretically, it's always been possible. We've known how to do it for ages, we just haven't had the technology. I mean, it's not a piece of cake to build a star, and why do it anyway? Although when I think about it, I can find a few reasons. Anyway, for the robots this technology is just a by-product of their innovations and improvements. They've improved LLTS so much it allows them to do it. You know how we can build everything from atoms up?'

'Yes.'

'It's the same thing, but they can do it on a lower level. You remember how I explained the new LLTS engine you have in your spacecraft.'

'Why do we never use wormholes if they can move stars?' Shan asked. 'They would be faster than LLTS.'

'You've spent too much time using LLTS, you've forgotten about wormholes. Yes, wormholes would be faster. We've tried. The issue is, the further you go, and the more massive the object you want to move, the more energy is required. To send a spacecraft across the galaxy it's still easier to use LLTS than to build wormholes, unless you're desperate, because with wormholes, you don't fly, but just appear at the destination, which comes with other issues. Imagine you're bending the fabric of space: it disturbs everything around itself, and you don't want that if you're going near other objects. Then there's another problem: it's not that easy to make sure you end up where you want to end up.'

* * *

The next day Eli and Shan sent both proposals to the robots and, as they lay on the best beach either of them had visited in a long time, a robot came and told them the robots were going to design and build a wormhole generator.

'Wait!' Eli called after the robot. 'I want to be involved in this project.'

The robot agreed and left them on the beach. It was a long strip of improved golden sand, with seaweed trying to take it over. The dying sun was shining, roaring waves were hitting the shore, and palm trees provided shade. In the distance, cargo and fishing vessels were busy with their work, and overhead birds cried through their improved beaks.

Shan was lying on a deck chair next to Eli with his eyes closed. It looked like he was sleeping, but actually he was thinking. Finally he said aloud, 'You can learn a lot here, but I need to go.'

Eli opened her eyes, not believing her ears. 'You aren't going to stay?'

'No, but I'll be back in four months to see the star replacement. You don't really need me here, and you can learn a lot from the robots' technology. I need to get ready to find my grandfather and look for a new home. Even with the improved LLTS drive, it will take me about a month to get there.' Shan knew this would upset Eli, but being alone and preparing to find his grandfather was more important to him. 'You know I need to go. This has to be done, I need to find my grandfather, and this is the first step.'

Eli tried to control her anger. 'I know. We've just been so busy I forgot about it. I'll stay here with the robots. It's going to be weird, but I might learn something new.'

'I'm going for the same reasons. Almost.'

After a few minutes of silence, Eli couldn't hold onto her temper any longer. 'We see each other once every few years or sometimes decades, and you always have to leave! Why? Why can't we spend some time together?' she sat forward in her deck chair and almost screamed.

Shan didn't know what to say. His life hadn't been easy as an adopted child. Shad had always been difficult, and his foster parents were from another species and felt love differently, so hugs were non-existent. Add to that his anxiety, and you end up with Shan's character. He thought he loved Eli, but he wasn't sure as he'd never really known what love was.

'Do you want to see the other side of this planet? I don't have to leave now,' Shan answered, trying to make her feel better, but Eli was quiet.

'No, go now, and we'll travel when you come back. You're right, this is more important, and it seems we both need some time off from each other again.' She needed time to think, and she hoped they could be together one day, but having spent her whole life lonely wasn't helping.

* * *

Shan hugged Eli, entered his ship and took off without looking back. *OK. Let's go to that galaxy, but first to the garage.*

No, not the garage, Shad and the gold mine. My plans have changed again… Shan set the destination to the Tiranian gold mine and LLTS did the rest.

Sitting in his chair on the bridge, Shan opened the map and took a deep breath. 'This will be a long trip.' He still had some time, so he decided to check the intergalactic journey. Galaxies were everywhere, and on the map the journey looked easy, but the reality was different. The distances were vast. The first galaxy he looked at was the closest one to him. It was called 6598, a catalogue number rather than a name. It would take him twenty-three days at LLTS 3 to get there, or about four hours at LLTS 5. The next galaxy, numbered 5512, was much further away, a year's journey at full speed. Other galaxies were much further away, and they were something for the future. Maybe Eli would join him to go to his grandfather, but that would involve LLTS 5.

He was speeding through sub-quantum space, at the same time watching the radar. He switched from the galaxy map to the grey area map, that showed the space between sectors. Specifically, he was looking for a giant asteroid where Tiranian gold was made. According to the details given to him by the seller, it had been moved from Sector One, where long ago it had been part of a network of asteroid mines throughout every sector. Pirates had used to capture people to work in those mines and factories in appalling conditions, paying them very little or nothing at all. Recently they had started 'hiring' refugees, especially those captured in the nets between sectors. Migrants illegally crossing borders, unmonitored by anyone, were an easy target. They were on no lists, and perfect for running the mining business. Another sad irony, people moving from one war zone to another.

Shan kept checking the map, zooming in and out, but the vast number of rocks that weren't officially mapped didn't help. The coordinates the seller had given Shan pointed to empty space between asteroids. He was moving from one end of the sector to the other, to the place the asteroid was supposed to be. It wasn't there, and he found what was in its place worrying. Quantum nets were everywhere, from the edges to the centre of the galaxy, in all the grey areas. The images of spaceships crossing borders came back on screen. *Hold on a second. I can't give this technology to everyone, but I can definitely use it to help them.* The robots' technology was too important to spread, it would cause another revolution and probably chaos on an unprecedented scale, but he could use it to help a bit.

He couldn't watch the screen anymore – live-action death, how ironic. *I have to check all the sector borders to find that rock, so I might as well do some good on the way.*

After spending all day searching through the endless light-years of stars, planets, asteroids and nets, he finally found all the mines and created a simple map of the grey areas, giving coordinates of the gaps in the quantum nets. Later he would publish it in some dark corner of the sub-quantum network for someone to find and broadcast everywhere. *It will help people crossing the borders.*

* * *

Shan rested that night, and the next day his spaceship was a few light years away from the asteroid mine. It wasn't visible through the window, but showed as a dot on the radar. In reality, it was a huge and perfectly round piece of rock, almost the size of one of the moons orbiting Shan's home planet. Quantum nets were all around it, and apart from Shad's army patrolling the space nearby in search of this mine, there were no other spacecraft anywhere in the vicinity. *With such a big army, it won't take them long to find it.* Shan had a considerable advantage thanks to LLTS 3, and a big reason for wanting to get there first. His cousin getting a Tiranian gold production line would mean an end to this galaxy – or a beginning. With that amount of gold powder, he could destroy everything. Not only that, he would have the power to become sole ruler of the galaxy. It would be bad, although he would probably end the wars – by creating new ones.

Shan came closer to the asteroid mine. He could almost touch the nets that were suspended a mile above the surface, but removing them would not be an easy task. All the net generators, the devices powering and controlling them, were hidden behind the nets themselves, and someone had done a really good job of hiding and protecting this place. The generators looked like flat panels, taking power from sub-quantum space and distributing it to the nets. They were designed like bombs: any unusual activity, and the nets would be triggered to enclose you. Shan used his radar to zoom in and study every point, but there were no gaps.

A moment later Shad saw Shan's ship on his radar. He flew closer and said over the radio, 'Good to see you, cousin. You can move over, I know how to open the nets.'

'How do you know that?' Shan asked

'Let's say I met the owner of this mine and he told me,' Shad answered.

'Yeah, I'm sure he did. Anyway, go ahead,' Shan said, monitoring everything on the console. He could see Shad's spacecraft and his crew, and when he zoomed in, he saw exactly what they were doing. Shad quickly flew his spacecraft around the rock, finally stopping between two nets, knowing the exact spot. 'I wouldn't do that,' Shan said over the radio, seeing Shad trying to disarm the net using remotely controlled robotic arms.

'Go away, I know what I'm doing,' Shad replied sharply.

'Same as you knew the time we found that bomb near the desert?' Shan replied, seeing the generator behind the net activate. What happened a moment later was exactly what everyone apart from Shad had expected. His spacecraft was trapped in the net like a fly in a carnivorous flower. Getting caught in the net would normally mean death, but now Shad was in Shan's hands. 'So... How's it going, cousin?' Shan asked, quickly manoeuvring his spacecraft towards the asteroid's surface through the hole that had formed when the net enclosed Shad.

'How did you get in there, you little bastard?'

'I think I'll ask the questions at this point. So... What are you doing here?'

'None of your business! When we get out, I'll kill you!' Shad was angry, pushing his engines to the limit to force the net open.

'Oh, you wouldn't kill your own cousin.'

'You're not my cousin; you never were. You came into my life like an annoying fly, buzzing around, destroying my perfect childhood and my plans to dominate the family. You were always the smart one. Everyone hated you, and they hate you now!'

At that point, Shan blocked the radio signal, ignoring Shad's messages. Then, using manual control, he flew closer to the rocky moon and entered the cave system.

Flying a spacecraft for miles down narrow passages was not easy. Tunnels barely larger than the ship itself challenged Shan's flying skills. Neither the cameras all around the ship, nor the map the seller had given him were great either, but with the help of his sub-quantum radar, he managed to get through with only a few scratches to the hull. The end of the tunnel had a few docking ports with an emergency spacecraft attached to one of them. Shan docked at a port deep inside the cave and opened the door. The air was breathable, but the dark corridor was filled with a horrible stench similar to a dying tropical cow. Shan was forced to go back and put on a helmet. The seller's map ended at this point, but the sensor map in his goggles showed a vast network of caves, all converging on a few large chambers deep inside the rock. The problem was, all the corridors were sealed off for miles around.

'There you are!' Shad said, appearing and pointing a gun at Shan.

'You again. Why don't you just stay in that impenetrable little ball you're supposed to be building? How did you escape that net, anyway?' Shan asked.

'My army destroyed it, and a few more. What are you doing here? Why are you interested in gold?' Shad asked suspiciously.

'I need it, just in case. Why do you need it? Do you have a planet to destroy?'

'This is the first mine I've found, but I need all of them. I have plans.' That didn't sound good. Shad's plans usually involved destroying and blowing things up, and his indiscriminate hatred meant he would destroy everything and everybody. 'Forget about helping this galaxy; it's already finished. With all the gold from all the mines, I will become emperor myself; no one will stop me. Now go home and never come back. We'll start drilling,' he said to his crew, then went on, 'Listen, Shan, I don't like you, and I'm ready to kill you, but because of the family, I'll give you one chance. Go home and forget about this place, now!'

Shad's tone was so serious that, for the first time in years, Shan began to be afraid of him, and decided to retreat, thinking, *Seriously, what an idiot. I need to stop him; he's dangerous. The easiest way would be to destroy these corridors, but that would kill him, and as much as I hate him, I don't want to do that. I need to come up with something else, so I can destroy this mine and all the rest. The gold has already caused too much suffering.*

Shan was back in his spacecraft, and started watching Shad's army. They flew off to look for the rest of the mines, leaving Shad with his small crew and the quantum drill. Shan changed the map so that he was looking at the mine itself. All the corridors had been destroyed. *Someone really wanted to keep that rock from being found.*

The primary mining operations were located in the main hall, which was a bit larger than Shan's ship. The source material for the gold would then be transported to smaller rooms for production. *If I could only somehow appear in that cave,*

Shan was thinking. *Wait a minute, I can! The problem is that the first rule of LLTS is: never go through planets, moons, or anything else solid. I already did that, sort of, but only through that thin plate of ice. This is a moon, a rock, more massive than the ice plate so it might affect a spacecraft.*

Shad and his crew were making progress with the power drill. They would finish soon, getting inside the main chamber. Shan would have to get there first, and somehow destroy the mine.

He slowly flew outside the cave, trying not to attract the attention of Shad's crew, and continued just above the surface of the asteroid but below the nets. He parked on the other side of the moon, thinking, *I am the expert here… Or am I? I fix those LLTS engines and spacecrafts in my garage, and I've seen the damage, and repaired them after they've been through small asteroids. I haven't inspected any significantly damaged ones. But still, I don't see any other way. I hope the robots have improved this spacecraft enough for that trip. The problem is mass: during normal LLTS operation the spacecraft travels deep below our normal levels, and the hull is designed to withstand those normal forces. When the spacecraft has to pass through some object, its mass causes the particles to accumulate that may cause the hull to break. Going through black holes or neutrino stars must be fun.*

Shan calculated his trajectory, LLTS speed, and the hull's strength by relying on his instincts, as calculating this would require data from the robots which he didn't have. What Shan was thinking was simple. His spacecraft would enter LLTS above the asteroid and stop in the largest cave inside it. The pressure change caused by his ship appearing in that cave could damage all the tunnels, hopefully without killing Shad. But the truth was, he didn't have a clue what was going to happen once he was inside.

He manoeuvred his ship as far as possible from the rock, but still between the nets and the surface, and activated the sequence. Shad and his crew, unaware of what Shan was doing, continued drilling.

'Boss, we're getting closer, I can feel it,' one of Shad's crew said.

'Good jo…'

Shad didn't finish his sentence because the tunnel blew up, sending them all flying half a mile away from where they'd started. It was Shan's spacecraft appearing inside the main chamber, pushing the air out, and sending the seismic wave through the asteroid that started to break it apart.

Shan's ship had attached itself to the rock, close to the small chamber where the gold was supposed to be, and now Shan was running like hell. He was pulling his portable tractor-beam trolley behind him, almost damaging it. The cave was shaking when Shad's voice appeared in Shan's helmet.

'What the hell are you doing?' Shad screamed.

'Oh, hi, Shad, I'm kind of busy, you know. Sorry about your tunnel, but I think I helped you finish it. I would suggest you escape as this mine is collapsing in on itself.' Shan was running, at the same time trying to collect as much gold as possible from one of the storage chambers.

'What the fuck did you do to it?' Shad screamed over the radio, while trying to get out from under some rocks.

'Oh, nothing, my quantum drill is just a bit more powerful than yours, I guess. I'm just inside collecting some gold, so busy, busy…'

The storage chamber wasn't big, it was massive. There was enough gold here to destroy solar systems, civilisations, and even black holes under the right conditions. While Shan collected more and more boxes, and threw them into his loading bay, the asteroid was getting increasingly unstable. Rocks and stones were falling, and the walls started collapsing. 'Shad, if you're still here you haven't got much time before this place collapses, and with that amount of gold mixed with the lava below, it will be a pretty big explosion,' Shan said over the radio. *Shit, I wanted to kill him, and now I'm trying to save him. Eh, family.*

'You destroyed the tunnel; I'm stuck here, you idiot.' Shad had found his drill and switched it to full power. He started walking towards the main chamber, crushing the rocks before him.

'I think we're both idiots, so I suggest you make it over here somehow, and I'll give you a ride.' *Well, that didn't go as planned.* Shan was still collecting boxes, wondering how not to get killed by Shad and the collapsing mine, when one of the walls fell, blocking him from getting any more gold. He rushed back to his spacecraft, where he found Shad standing in the loading bay. 'Strap in; it'll be a marvel if we survive this!' Shan ran to the bridge, followed by Shad, locked all the doors, and tried to load the automatic escape sequence, when everything went from shaky and loud to complete silence and whiteness outside.

'Are we dead?' Shad was surprised too, staring into the emptiness of space beyond the window.

'I hope not, but this is weird,' Shan said, looking at the radar. 'The mine has disappeared.'

'What do you mean, it has disappeared, it was huge,' Shad replied. Only distant stars were visible through the window.

I think I know what happened, but how? 'I haven't activated the LLTS yet, so we're still at the same point in space, which used to be inside the asteroid. Look here.' Shan pointed to a map of the local system showing a ring of dust around what had used to be the asteroid. 'This is a cloud of stuff from the destroyed rock. The mine collapsed and the gold and the core of the rock mixed together, causing a massive explosion. It destroyed the whole asteroid.'

'You know how many people you killed?'

'Not intentionally! And most of your army weren't here, anyway.'

'Yeah, right, and I don't know how we survived. Nothing can survive Tiraniain gold. You realise how much gold there was? You could destroy black holes with it, so how we are still alive?' Shad was pacing and shouting now.

'I don't know, but my plan kind of worked. Destroying the gold was part of it, so you wouldn't get hold of it. You're crazy, and stupid. Destroying worlds and civilisations? What's wrong with you? There's already enough death; you're supposed to be helping to stop it, not encourage it. In all these years, you've learned nothing,' Shan accused Shad.

'There you go again. You think you're perfect?'

'I saved your life.'

'For that, I will let you live. For destroying the mine, I will hunt you down.'

'Anyway, where would you like to go?' Shan asked, ignoring Shad's words and watching the map. 'Looks like your army is coming here.'

Shad looked at his arm with the screen attached, and sent a message to his crew. 'They'll dock, I remember where the shuttle bay is. And don't think I didn't see the gold you took. Keep it, you'll need it when I get *all* the mines with all the gold.' Shad said, putting his helmet back on, and a few minutes later he left with his crew.

Shan was trying to understand why the explosion hadn't vaporised everything, but the spacecraft didn't have any logs. No information on what the defence system was doing or had done. Everything was happening automatically, but Shan hadn't expected to survive that kind of explosion. *I guess the robots have improved this ship beyond my understanding.* He couldn't believe what had happened with the mine, but he could understand why Shad wasn't interested in the gold Shan had collected. Shad's ego trumped his logic as it had done all those years before, when they were both teenagers. He was so upset that Shan had beat him he couldn't bear to be beholden to him for anything, especially help. *I need to make sure I destroy the rest of the mines before he finds them.*

* * *

Shan spent the rest of the day travelling back to his garage, and when he finally arrived, he saw the long queue of spaceships waiting to be repaired. He flew around the garage, and... *What the fuck?* he thought, looking at the spot on the surface where Colin's greenhouse had been. The glass dome had been destroyed, leaving an empty crater. He quickly docked and went straight to the bridge.

'I knew I would find you here,' he said to Goe, who was watching one of the console screens. It was her and Shan's favourite place. For a reason. It was a private viewing room – small, with a sofa bed, table and chairs. But the most important part was the ceiling, which was transparent, so that you could see all the spaceships flying around, stars, planets and the river-like line that was the galaxy. In ancient times people had truly believed it to be a magic river that slowly carried souls to reincarnation somewhere else.

'Hi, it's a surprise to see you,' Goe replied and walked towards Shan to hug him. 'How was your holiday?'

'I'm more surprised about that big hole in our garage. Colin's chickens revolted?' Shan joked.

'Well, no... or kind of. The mechanical chicken did. It got some virus from the sub-quantum network and became conscious. Then Colin got involved, but it was already too late as the mechanical chicken was holding the other chickens' hostage, and finally it jumped out of the window. The pressure did the rest, sucking everything out and destroying the glass ceiling.'

'What happened to the field that was supposed to protect the garage?' Shan asked, trying to believe that a mechanical chicken had achieved consciousness.

'The chicken hacked our systems, locked the door and disabled the field, but I managed to stop it from doing any further damage. Don't worry, the chicken is gone, and I upgraded the garage system so it should be protected against any future hacks.'

'Colin is OK? Did you install some additional stuff in your head again?' Shan asked, seeing new parts on Goe's body.

'Yes, the latest models, so now I can connect to all systems. You should do it; it would be easier to get the data from those old spacecrafts you like so much. Here, take this box. I have plenty more,' Goe took a box with brain attachments she had prepared earlier and gave it to Shan. 'And Colin? Yes, he's fine. He's already got a plan for an improved version of the garden, so I guess the explosion was an opportunity. I also managed to convince him to build a restaurant. Awesome, right?'

'How did you do that?'

'That's a long story for another time. Anyway, we're being paid in food now, so it's OK, we've got plenty. Did you find another asteroid?'

'Yes, kind of. But not yet. Come with me to my ship. So, not much changed while I was away?'

'Not really, but the queue's got a bit longer,' Goe replied, walking towards the docking port. After a few minutes, they entered Shan's ship.

'You really have upgraded this place,' Goe said in wonder. She started touching everything and inspecting it with her improved eyes.

'Kind of, and we need to talk. What's your plan to escape the collision?'

The question took Goe by surprise, as she had already told Shan that her only choice was to escape with him. 'I was hoping I could escape with you. I wanted to talk to you about that,' she said. Of course, her Plan B was to become a robot and move into sub-quantum space, and travel for aeons and never die.

'That's why I need you here to manage everything. I'm travelling around trying to find a place to escape to. I'm thinking of installing LLTS in the garage and taking it to the nearest galaxy, 6598.' Shan said.

'That's pretty far, but still the closest to us.'

'Yes, it's the only place for now. I'll be away for a while; I need to find out if we can move there. I'm sure we're not the only ones with the same plan, so it's not easy, and it takes time. There are so many new bands of pirates, and so many nets – I ended up in one. The general has agreed to help us with food and protection, but I'm not sure how long the military can hold pirates away, especially Shad. He hates me even more now. So drill holes, build rooms and the restaurant and a garden. Hire more staff if you have to. I have enough resources to install LLTS in the garage, so don't worry about that. I did think this war is close to ending, but I don't see it happening right now. We need to leave, the sooner the better.'

'When will you come back?' Goe asked, already knowing the answer.

'I don't know, but I will be in contact, so please tell me if anything happens. OK?'

'OK, will do. Before you go, though: everyone's started wondering where you are. They want to know if they can escape with you as well.'

'I know. But the collision is still far away so I don't think we should tell anyone about our idea yet. The official plan is to escape with the military, so let's keep it that way. They need to think we're with them. I asked them to send some additional patrols, so if you have any problems, contact them.'

'You won't be back for years, you know that,' Goe said, unaware of the improved LLTS drive.

'Yes, I know.' Shan shook his head, showing Goe that he was lying but she should keep it secret. After years of working with him, she understood.

'I'll leave this place in your capable hands,' Shan replied, then added, 'Sorry for dropping the management of the garage on you like this, but you're the only one I can trust.'

'I understand, don't worry,' Goe replied.

'Thanks. Then it's time to go. I don't want to stay, because I might change my mind about my holiday.'

'Good luck and be careful,' Goe said and left the spacecraft.

Shan flew one last time around the garage and disappeared into sub-quantum space.

THE SELLER
SHORT STORY

A seller has a difficult life. It's a profession everyone needs, and also one that everyone hates, at least in this part of the cosmos. He always wore the same clothes, old, and cheap, and dirty. And this market in the middle of nowhere where he worked, hardly anyone visited. Occasionally people came, but he always looked sad or distracted, so they didn't go over to him. He wasn't sad, just didn't have enough resources to pay for travel and was not brave enough to hitchhike; he was just fed up with being stuck in this place. Like everyone else, he had a plan to escape, of course; to leave and never come back.

One morning he woke up from a beautiful, vivid dream. *I don't often have those*, he thought, then spoke aloud to himself, 'Why did I wake up? Well, another day, another part, I guess. Maybe I can find something useful to sell today.'

He got up and went out in his shabby clothes, pulling an old floating trolley. For the first time in a month, he found an interesting part near the hill of scrap metal. A place where old spaceships ended up. 'Wow, nice drive! Those are expensive, I wonder why no one's picked it up yet?' he said, surprised and happy. The further he went, the more advanced the parts were that he found. Now he was nervous, as he always was when things might go wrong.

'Wow,' he said again, standing on a pile of rubbish, looking at one of the wrecked spaceships. He started to run down the hill of junk so fast he lost the floating trolley. He was thinking about nothing except her. She was lying unconscious next to the wreckage. He didn't know what he was getting into, and right then he didn't think about it. He tried to talk to her, check if she was alive.

She was.

She opened her eyes, looking scared.

'What happened? Who are you?' she asked, surprised at seeing someone, trying to remember what had happened.

'You had an accident; your transport crash-landed. Are you OK?' the seller asked, trying to help her to stand.

'Yes, but my head hurts. Hold on!' She was looking all around.

'What's wrong?' he asked.

'Let's go.' She pulled him into the wreckage, and they went running through the trashed corridors.

'Where are we going?' the seller asked, running behind her. They reached the loading bay and entered a small shuttle.

'I hope you know how to fly one of these,' she said, pushing him inside.

'Yes, but first tell me who you are,' he persisted, confused.

'Just fly, and I'll explain.'

He took off, and the shuttle left the spacecraft through the wrecked loading bay doors. They flew above the hill of scrap metal, where they collected his floating trolley. Then, to her protests, the seller landed next to his shed and quickly ran inside to take some of his personal belongings. When he came back, she told him to fly upwards, anywhere, as far from this place as possible. Finally she explained who she was, why she had run away, and where from. She needed his help, and he finally escaped.

King Tiranian, as his name suggests, was a tyrant. Everybody hated him, and at the same time loved him. He killed many and united even more. Born two hundred years ago, to a family of slaves on Argus V, he quickly became known for inciting revolution, first in his local community and then in his district. He became the leader of the colonies, and under his rule crime dropped to zero and the economy prospered beyond imagination. The former was mostly because he executed all criminals, whatever their crime, and the latter because he eliminated money altogether, and replaced it with a knowledge and resource-based society – in a day. Those who didn't like it either escaped or were killed.

Years later the whole planet was under his control, and his species had invested in technology that gave him the most advanced transports and weapons anyone could imagine. He quickly used this to wipe out crime from every planet in three systems, becoming ruler of them all. He was big, with four arms, two legs and no neck, and his diet consisted mostly of sticky green fluffy stuff that was high in proteins and produced in easy-to-transport bars. By everyone else's standards, his species was hideous, as were their ships. They were ugly but advanced, and this was more important than any design.

One day King Tiranian was sitting on his throne, and he was angry, but you wouldn't have known it. His species showed no emotions, just because nature had designed their bodies that way. His wife had escaped, and when no one could find her he obliterated the entire colony of criminals. The only things he wanted now were to bring her home and unite the galaxy. It was his long-held dream to become ruler of the universe.

Now, the seller, knowing the best place to hide, flew towards a ring of wreckage – chunks of smashed spacecraft orbiting all three stars. The shuttle would not be able to go any further – they would have to go back eventually – but it was the perfect place to hide and talk. The girl explained that she was the king's wife, but she hated him, and there was nothing for her to go home to.

Then the shuttle's radar picked up some life signs.

'A single person, here? That's impossible!' the princess said, looking at the radar.

'Maybe they're hiding like we are? Let's ask!' the seller replied, looking out of the window.

'Are you crazy? It might be one of them!' the princess said. After her escape, she was scared and suspicious of everything.

'No one comes here. It must be a survivor from one of the crashes. Maybe they need our help,' the seller replied.

CHAPTER FIVE

After fifteen days spent locked in a spacecraft travelling towards the 6598 galaxy, Shan couldn't take it any longer. He missed the outside world: the stars, the planets, and having someone to talk to. He'd wanted to get away from that, but now he missed it.

He switched off the LLTS and stopped, relatively. Looking out of the window, he couldn't see much so he put on his suit, connected himself to the spacecraft with a rope, and to pipes providing him with oxygen and removing CO_2, and went outside. This was something he shouldn't have done, especially in a place where no one could hear him. *The chances of getting hit by a rock between galaxies are slim, so I should be fine.*

Using his wrist control, he switched off all external lights and everything went dark. The kind of dark where he couldn't even see his hand in front of him. He was standing on the hull waiting for his eyes to adjust when he remembered they had already adjusted. He looked left and right, and there they were. Two galaxies. The most magnificent view anyone could imagine. It was indescribable, and he would never forget it. Two gigantic titans of the universe opposite each other, waiting to fight, with many small soldiers waiting for their turn to join in. The giants had a speck of life between them: Shan. Protected only by the metal hull of his spaceship, and right now by the suit alone. *I could just open my helmet, and I would be gone. The universe would still be here, and I would wake up somewhere else, as someone else, taken by the river.* When Shan lay down, he could see both galaxies in his field of view. It was like seeing the curvature of a planet for the first time, or feeling G-forces for the first time, or reading your favourite book for the first time, or eating your favourite pizza for the first time. You could spend your life here just watching it. Just as ancient philosophers could look up and think and never get tired of it. He fell asleep.

* * *

Eight days later, autopilot stopped the spaceship in the night, by garage time, not far from a solar system Shan had selected earlier. He woke up when the alarm rang in his room, and the light slowly increased, simulating daylight. For a moment he switched it off to look outside, but there wasn't much to see. Just stars, stars and more stars. He was in another galaxy.

Shit, I am really quite far from home!

He had never heard of anyone coming here, and knowing he was the first was very exciting. He put the lights back on, changed his clothes and walked to the kitchen. The floor and stairs had used to be metallic and noisy but now, improved by the robots, they had the most comfortable surface to walk on. He was excited, but didn't want to rush anything – the universe wasn't going anywhere, and Shan had enough food for a year of exploration if he decided to stay that long.

To celebrate his arrival, he made his favourite meal, porridge with loads of mixed fruit. The fruit had been given to him by Colin, which as you can expect, was not something to rush but enjoy. Eating breakfast, he almost turned the radio on, to a familiar station, but then changed his mind. *No more war news for a while. I'm in another galaxy, so let's hear it.* He used his mind to tune the analogue radio and scanned across a few random frequencies and modulations. *Interesting.* The voices, sounds and music he was hearing were similar to those he was used to, but he couldn't understand the languages, and after listening for a few minutes, he switched the radio off.

He watched his favourite TV show, almost finishing another season. It helped to switch off his thoughts, even for a moment. He had been thinking too much recently and watching TV shows was something he missed in a busy garage. He finished his breakfast and left the dishes in the sub-quantum dishwasher. When he looked at the radar, the sub-quantum view was empty. No one here had developed LLTS yet. That was one of Shan's ideas for when he moved. Open a garage and help the locals to advance. They need to be prepared if they were to accept a whole galaxy of different species. *Shit, this is ridiculous,* he thought. *My entire galaxy, and maybe two more, will try to get here. It's going to be a big surprise, and the place could get a bit packed. Imagine that, a queue to enter a galaxy.*

He detected a lonely spaceship on his radar and flew closer to start a conversation. When he did a scan, he found to his surprise that the spacecraft seemed to be from his own galaxy. Taking a closer look, he saw it was damaged. Shan decided to check the emergency channel, which for some reason his improved spacecraft decided to ignore, and then he heard it. The translator detected the language, and Shan replied.

'Hi, this is Shan, can you hear me?' he sent a message while the translator was doing its job.

'Shan! Shan, yes I can hear you. Help me, I have no food, and my drive has been damaged!' The voice was weak and desperate. Or not the original voice, but rather the translator. Knowing not only the language itself, but how each species conveyed emotions, the translator could simulate those too.

'Seriously, how the fuck did you get here? How long did it take? Are you crazy?' Shan was surprised to find anyone here, especially in a small spaceship like this one.

'Shut up and send me some food and I'll explain everything. I'm dying, haven't eaten in days,' the voice groaned.

'Is your transporter working?' Shan asked.

'Yes!' replied the voice.

'OK, I'll send a probe,' Shan said over the radio, at the same time preparing the probe using his mind. It was a simple torpedo-like device usually used for research.

An hour after receiving the supplies, the lost traveller replied, 'You saved my life. That porridge is not something my species can normally eat, but I don't have much choice.'

'Well, it gives the energy and nutrition you need. Drink some water. Tell me what happened,' Shan said.

'Can you fix my ship?'

'First, tell me what happened,' Shan demanded.

'My name is Sork.' The voice calmed down. 'I was sent here from Sector Three; our species built a wormhole generator. We could only send one spacecraft with a year's worth of food to check this galaxy for possible planets so my civilisation could escape the collision and wars. As I couldn't check the whole galaxy, before the mission our scientists selected five solar systems where they thought sufficiently advanced civilisations might live. I was to find a suitable solar system and then come back to bring the rest, or evolve myself.

'The plan worked until I discovered those systems nearby, the three stars. There is a vast orbit of wreckage around them, spacecraft from all over the place. I tried to dock to a few, and found one from our galaxy, incredibly old, but the computer was still functional. I found out a lot about the people here. Shan, they are warriors; they mostly kill and take over other planets and species. Their ships are powerful, but they haven't developed an LLTS drive yet. I couldn't fight them on my own; I only have basic defence systems.

'They discovered me and started shooting. I escaped using the light drive; I tried to use my LLTS, but they damaged it. Their spacecraft are not as fast as ours, even with light drives. Otherwise, I would be dead. You can download data about them from my computer. Basically, they kill everyone so it's better not to go near them. But how did you get here? How long did it take and why did you come?'

'What do you mean, evolve yourself? You're not the only one who wants to escape, and that's a story for another time. I'll fix your spacecraft, and give you a few months' worth of food. I'm afraid I can only offer this porridge. You explore half of this galaxy, and I'll do the other. We need to explore first and then bring everyone else here, so it makes sense if we do it that way. It'll be quicker, and if you find more wreckage like that, let me know.' *He mustn't find out about my improved LLTS. I'll tell him I came by a wormhole.*

'I'm Tencta. We don't have a set gender; it's fluid and can change depending on the situation. At the moment I'm your equivalent of a male, but that will change in a few years. Anyway, do you know the design of my spacecraft?' Sork asked. The Tencta species spent most of their lives underwater, so their spaceships were filled with it. Over millions of years their fins had evolved to be able to hold objects, and when their brains evolved too, they had quickly developed civilisation.

'I do. I'm an engineer. It will be tricky, but I'm sure I can figure something out, and from what I remember you have a hybrid loading bay where I can enter,' Shan replied, flying his ship closer to Sork's. He docked and greeted Sork in the loading bay, which was a tiny room between the docking system and a window where he could see the Tencta swimming.

'Nice ship you have here, I haven't seen a wormhole generator in years. I hope there's nothing seriously wrong with it,' said Shan. He'd brought his favourite toolbox; he was finally going to fix a spaceship.

'I thought I would die here. But wait, what do you mean you haven't seen a wormhole generator? How else would you have got here?' Sork challenged Shan.

'Oh, I meant I hadn't seen one in my garage. I'm an engineer; I fix spacecrafts,' Shan stammered, trying not to show that he was lying.

'It's my lucky day. I survived, and I've got a real engineer who can fix my drive.' Sork's mood brightened.

After checking the engine, Shan discovered that the wormhole generator ring wire was burned out. As it shared the coil rings with the LLTS, the same fault had broken the drive.

'I'll need access to your central computer to recalibrate the drive after I replace the coils.'

'Of course, anything.'

Shan went outside. It took him an hour to replace the wire, then he came back in.

'You are seriously lucky. If I hadn't had those parts, you would be in trouble,' Shan replied, connecting his tools to the console.

'So, where are you from exactly?' Sork wondered.

'Sector Two,' Shan replied, balancing the drives and wirelessly copying all Sork's data to his computer. *I know I shouldn't steal his data, but I'm curious.* Collecting data was his only addiction, and he was powerless to resist.

'I don't know much about your sector; I've spent most of my life training for this mission. They only selected the best.'

'It's an important mission, the most important. You must be the best,' Shan replied, starting to understand what kind of a guy Sork was.

'Of course, from hundreds of candidates, they selected me.'

Shan couldn't wait to leave, as Sork's constant bragging would get on anyone's nerves. He calibrated the spaceship's new coils, gave the Tencta a lot of food, and left.

From the data Shan had copied, including Sork's diary, he found out that Sork wasn't the ideal candidate for this mission as he had claimed to be. In truth, he was useless — crazy, and brave, but useless. Back on Sork's planet, he was an experienced test pilot, and he'd gone on missions almost as crazy as the one he was on now. He started as a teenager with blowing things up on the ground, then he moved to rockets, still blowing things up, but higher. After that, he was crazy enough to fly into space in his homemade rocket to blow up an asteroid, forgetting he had to return. When they rescued him, he was hired as a test pilot for secret missions. Specifically to evaluate the future wormhole spaceship and try not to blow it up. He was chosen as one of the candidates mostly because he was good at lying. He wanted to be on this mission so much he had changed his records and lied about the rest of his life, so they would select him. Once here, he had panicked after his instinct for blowing things up took over and someone from the trinary system attacked him. To hide this fact, he almost killed himself so nobody would find out how big a coward he was.

* * *

Shan flew to the ring of wreckage, though he knew he shouldn't. Sork urged him not to. The area around the three stars was full of trash, debris, scraps, rubble and dust from the smashed spaceships.

The three stars were still separated, but gravity was bringing them together, gradually making them more chaotic. Although it was not yet visible to the naked eye, simulations showed that they would collide in the far future, slowly becoming a huge three-body explosion — I mean, a problem. For now, King Tiranian's civilisation was thriving as the planets were not that far from each other, and even with their basic light drives people could travel between them in a reasonable amount of time.

Shan didn't realise it, but the main reason he had come here was because his subconscious had chosen it for him. His only addiction, collecting (mostly data and memorabilia), got out of control and took him over. There hadn't been much to collect in his garage, but here, with unlimited debris floating around, he couldn't control his impulses.

A quick scan revealed broken and trashed machines of every kind. A few were identifiable as being from Shan's galaxy, and others looked oddly familiar as well. *I guess physics is the same everywhere.* Seeing all this technology reminded Shan of Goe's brain augmentations. *I don't like them… but all that data.*

Seeing the possibility of getting data drives, Shan couldn't think rationally. He went to his room to get the box Goe had prepared for him, then sat down in the kitchen and opened it. The box held different skin pads with simple descriptions. He laid them all out on the table, then began applying them to his skin one by one. *You never know what's in those ships, or who.* He peeled off one of the pads and put it on his arm.

Within seconds, nanobots found a way to his brain, and he discovered a new sensation he hadn't known existed. First, the jolt hit his head and then, as Goe had explained it would, with each applied pad a new sense came to life. It was confusing at first. The feeling of virtually attaching a new nose, ears, eyes, touch, was indescribable. Something new started generating additional signals in his synapses, accompanied by tickling and pleasure in his brain.

Shan grew accustomed to the new feeling after the bots finished connecting all the relevant neurons. He drifted into the interfaces of his spaceship, into data banks, transfer lines, power conduits and radars but also his own mind. Bots under no one's command tinkered with his brain and attached

Shan's memory to the onboard computer, allowing him to surf his own memory banks.

* * *

He flew closer to one of the orbital rings, where the extensive collection of spaceships floated. *Let's start with the one that looks familiar.* It was roughly the size of his ship, and mostly covered in LLTS coils. An early prototype with giant rings and a massive hole ripped through the middle. This had not been used for the wormhole but made by some kind of weapon. *Someone shot at them.*

Shan left his ship and went exploring, wearing his spacesuit. There was no way to dock at the first ship, so he went in through the hole. The interior was simple, filled mostly with the engine, generator and batteries needed to power the wormhole drive. The spacecraft was old – ancient – and with objects and artefacts floating around it looked like a slow-spinning tornado inside a museum. Shan recognised it as a design that had been used after the second electrical revolution, which gave him some idea of how to make it work again. The batteries were long gone, but the generator should be working.

Even after all this time, the simple mechanical devices worked. That was something you couldn't say about modern inventions. The generator was precisely that, a simple device that collected electrons and shunted them forward. It was often called the harvester or pusher. Shan knew what had failed even before he looked at it. The collector was intact, but the wire wasn't, the most common problem. You would think that in such an advanced device, they would at least have installed proper cables. But at that time, the now long-gone system of money had been a problem, so everything was manufactured by whoever charged the least.

Shan just needed to power the central computer, which only required wires, a generator and no batteries. He spent the next few hours fiddling with it and going back and forth to his loading bay for connectors, before he finally got the computer to work. Goe's extension helped as nanobots connected to the main terminal while the translator was doing its job. It turned out the spacecraft had been made in what was now Sector One. The lonely pilot was long gone, but by copying all the data Shan made sure she would not be forgotten. *The early pioneer of intergalactic travels.* She hadn't been lucky: although the drive hadn't failed, her cryo-pod did, leaving her stranded between galaxies. *I couldn't have met her there.* After an almost two hundred and fifty year journey, when the pod failed, she went outside her spacecraft and stayed there. Turning on the autopilot, she told the spacecraft to keep going. Finally it had ended up here.

Shan attached his spaceship to a second wreck. It was made from metal, an early and primitive design, powered by combining oxygen and nitrogen, thus causing a controlled explosion. *No wonder they didn't get far,* Shan thought, but it was the first step into space for most species. An expensive and dangerous one, but in the long term worth it.

He opened one of the spaceship's doors. It was dark inside: no life forms and no power. Shan moved the scanner around until it picked up something sitting next to what looked like a data disk that was still plugged into the computer, next to the massive hole in the cockpit wall. He looked around and saw more floating tools, parts, clothes and even what looked like frozen food. He checked the other corridor and found it hadn't been destroyed, but it was dark, small and empty, with various different objects flying around. After taking the data drives, he moved to a newer wreck, again with a similar hole. He didn't have to dock as the hole was big enough to get inside. This time the power was running, but it wasn't enough for the whole ship. *Good, they're not that advanced, they mostly use electricity, the first generation.* It would be easy to find out how it worked and fix it.

He was just docking to the fifth spacecraft to get data when the people who had attacked Sork discovered him. He realised they'd come when he saw flashes and flying debris. He quickly went back to his ship, set his destination to the other side of the ring of wreckage, and disappeared.

* * *

A month later, he was still there, collecting data and parts. Shan couldn't stop; this was his paradise, a trap, and a drug. He wasn't sleeping; he wanted more and more: more data, parts, documents, paperwork, photographs, everything. It was dangerous; he weakened and became delusional and paranoid, seeing bodies and ghosts. *I need to stop... But one more spacecraft won't hurt.* He entered another piece of wreckage. It was new, modern, artistic and damaged. He had to break the docking port to enter.

This spacecraft was a piece of art, not only outside, but inside, too. *Some government official's vessel?* Carpets, paintings, photographs, gold plate, insignia, maps, ornately designed chairs, curves, ornaments, marble staircases, statues, coats of arms – it was beautiful. He moved further down the corridor and discovered more paintings, gold, carpets and photographs. Surprisingly, nothing was floating; somehow, everything was attached to the walls and the floor. Flying further along the corridor, Shan found cryocapsules, empty and broken, apart from one.

Inside, behind frosted glass, was a creature with many arms and thick skin. It looked like it had been made, not born. It had markings all over its skin, burned or pressed in; lines and circles a few millimetres deep. They weren't like the markings on the paintings and were definitely nothing Shan had seen before. *Why is everyone else gone and this one was left?* Shan's curiosity took over. He didn't want to open the pod before finding out something about the creature. After connecting himself to the onboard computer he managed to find something that looked like a status diagram of the spaceship. It was mostly bright colours indicating that something was wrong.

Shan was browsing the spacecraft's systems, not understanding much of what he saw, when messages started appearing. The vessel was waking up. All the little lights came on; doors tried closing, main lights began flickering. Shan felt a vibration, probably more doors slamming or engines starting up. A moment later, a continuous rhythmical thumping could be heard. *The alien.*

He tried to return to the back room where he had found the cryo-pod, but there was a loud bang, and the whole ship shook. The hostile aliens from three star systems had found him. Everything started spinning, flying and crashing into everything else, causing havoc. Shan felt the G-force.

This wasn't good. He had no idea where he was, and only thanks to another hit, did he end up near the cryo-pod containing the alien. The creature was trying to open the pod from inside but gradually realising that it wasn't possible. Seeing Shan, it pointed to a lever outside the pod. Shan, glued to the wall, pushed himself forward, trying to reach the handle, but his brain was slowly losing its blood supply. At the last moment, he managed to open the pod before losing consciousness.

The alien left the pod, and strangely the G-force and lack of air didn't affect it. Using one of its many arms it grabbed Shan and walked to the bridge, towing him along, casually ignoring all the debris, vacuum, and lack of gravity. The alien began pushing buttons on different screens, but they were damaged beyond repair. Then it ripped out a floor access panel and started moving levers and knobs, gradually slowing the spin of the spacecraft, which allowed Shan's brain to wake up. Shan stood up and, using his remote control, brought back his own vessel.

The junk flying around at high speed was smashing into it, but the quantum field protected it at the same time as helping to clear the garbage away. The alien showed that it needed air by pointing to what looked like a mouth. Shan pointed at his spacecraft, and they both climbed through the hole and waited for the flying cosmic junk to disappear. Shan slowly brought his ship closer to the hole, and they entered the loading bay. Then he sent his ship into sub-quantum space, automatically pressurising it and locking the doors. He took off his suit and tried to talk to the alien, but the creature only made noises that suggested it was breathing heavily.

'OK, we need to talk,' Shan said, but the alien only replied by looking at him, which at least meant it could hear. Shan touched one of the walls, and the console screen appeared. He turned on the improved translator in learning mode, and a big board appeared. *OK, we need to agree on some common meaningful words, some common language.* Shan tried to think of how to start a conversation with another intelligent biological species that had never heard his language, only made some noises of its own, but didn't seem aggressive. *Numbers. They are all common to all species, especially if they can travel across space and control a spacecraft.* That was the only thing Shan could assume about the alien. *I can draw numbers in my language or lines representing numbers, but the alien might interpret them as something else. We could probably invent some new language… Oh, fuck it.*

'Hey,' Shan said to the alien. 'Come over here,' he continued, waving his hand. UUGL – universe universal gesture language – usually worked. The alien walked over to the screen on his lower pair of legs, and Shan started drawing lines. One line, two lines, one under another, representing numbers from one to nine. *OK, now what… Oh, I know.* Shan took something easy to count and readily available, post-it notes. He put one next to one line, two next to two lines and so on until there were nine. *Why didn't I bring smaller ones?* He drew an addition sign next to one post-it note, and then he added another before drawing an equals sign and adding two more notes. He had only added a few more when the alien stopped him and finished the rest of the calculations.

'Now we're getting somewhere; you can count.' Shan was happy they'd found common ground. Next, Shan wrote numbers in his language on the left side of the lines. The alien was smart enough to draw the same numbers in an alien language, matching them with the lines and Shan's numbers. The robots' automatic translator did the rest, getting it almost but not quite right. *So, they have a written language… A seriously weird one, but who am I to complain? Now, do they speak?* Shan pointed to each number and said the word. The alien did the same… with its many arms.

'Great, so you speak using your hands,' said Shan. 'That makes things a bit more complicated… but maybe not.' He brought more equipment in on a floating trolley, connected it all, and indicated to the alien to speak again; this time the automatic translator was recording. The translator found similarities to other sign languages and did the rest, again almost right, but not quite. *Now to language.*

Shan wrote his name, pointed at it, said his name, and pointed at himself. The alien was quick to do the same, but again used its arms. After plenty more words describing various parts of the loading bay including chairs, benches, doors and all the bits Shan had collected from the ring of wreckage, the robots' translator had enough data, and it was ready to translate.

The first thing Shan said to the alien was not 'Greetings, take me to your leader,' but 'I seriously need some more body enhancements from Goe.'

'What's Goe?' the alien asked. That was a simple enough sentence to translate.

'She's a friend; it doesn't matter,' Shan replied. 'OK, who are you? What's your name? Why were you in that cryo-pod? How can you live in a vacuum? Why is your language so complex?' *Too many questions?* The translator was trying to display simulated arm movements.

'I need to sit down,' the alien replied and walked to the bench. Shan sat next to it, pulling the translator along with him on a floating trolley. The alien started talking again, and the translator immediately started work. It recorded the alien's movements and displayed translated words to Shan, and vice versa. At the same time, it was improving and learning more about the alien language.

'What is "she"?' the alien asked, clearly confused by Shan's translator.

'It's how we describe different genders. Do you have genders?' Shan asked, remembering some of the central government language grammar rules.

'We do, although in the past we could reproduce asexually, this ability is almost never used anymore. At this point in my life I am a female, and I'm happy to explain our customs later on. My short name is Qv^guk. Before you opened that pod, I checked the date on it. I was frozen for a hundred years. It was supposed to be much longer, but we had an accident,' Qv^guk explained.

'An accident? You call this an accident? You were attacked by those guys out there; me finding you was the accident. If it weren't for me, you would have been stuck there forever,' Shan exclaimed.

But the truth was, it was Qv^guk who had saved Shan.

'From the data I gathered before we left, I learned they killed the crew. They never take anyone alive. We had been on a diplomatic mission and were heading back to my planet, Aofneu from planet 2032. We were supposed to bring our two worlds together, to work together, to be stronger together. It takes us two hundred years to get from one planet to another, which is why we use pods.

'I live on a planet with little atmosphere, so nature gave us thick skin, hidden eyes and ears, telepathy for communication, large lungs and little need for oxygen. I can survive in a vacuum for quite some time, and if we must, my species can hibernate. This allows us to survive until conditions improve and we can wake up.' Qv^guk finished and took a deep slow breath.

'OK, my turn,' Shan started. 'Telepathy? It looks like you use your hands. And if you can travel between planets, you must have knowledge of other galaxies, right?'

'We use hands to communicate with those unfortunate enough to be born without telepathy, and with other species.'

Aeons of evolution had allowed Qv^guk's species to optimise the language to preserve their knowledge. They could write extraordinarily complex ideas using just a few signs; complicated signs, but very efficient ones. Their written language allowed them to rewire their brains in such a way that when they looked at the signs, they automatically saw all those complex ideas in their minds without actually reading them. It was like looking at an encrypted message and seeing the decrypted text.

'Yes, we've been observing the universe for a long time, and we have good maps. Where are you from?'

'I come from another galaxy, two and a half million light years away. I have the technology to travel that distance in about thirty of our days. I came here to find a new home for myself and everyone else. The main reason most people in my galaxy want to escape is that we have a civil war. Put the wars, the galaxies' collision and my crazy cousin together, and you get a good reason to escape,' Shan explained.

'I know about that collision – we saw the galaxies moving through our telescopes – but it's far off in the future. We never thought it was possible to travel faster than light. Crazy cousin?'

'Not important. I'm here to make some contacts and find a place where the species of our galaxy can move to. I think we can both help each other. I'll take you wherever you need to go, and you'll help me with my mission. What do you think?'

Having no other choice, Qv^guk agreed. Analysing the data from the broken ship, they found out that most of its crew had been killed. There was no explanation as to why

Qv^guk was spared. A mistake perhaps, or the attackers had just been in a hurry.

* * *

As the spacecraft left the ring of wreckage, its scanner picked up an energy source and two life forms. *Here? How is that possible? Maybe they need help, or maybe they came to kill the alien?* They were in a small shuttle, too small to get very far. *They must be trying to escape.*

'There's a small shuttle, too small to go anywhere or to fight. They look like they're trying to escape to me. What do you think?' Shan asked Qv^guk.

'I will not trust anyone from this place after what they did to us. We'd better leave now,' Qv^guk replied, not showing any emotions but no doubt feeling them.

'Normally I wouldn't trust them either, but the ring is too far from the planet. The shuttle is small, too small to fight anyone. Either they're escaping or they've ended up here as you did.'

Ignoring Qv^guk's gesticulations, Shan manoeuvred his spacecraft above the shuttle so he could see people inside, upside down through the window. He waved, they waved, Qv^guk waved. *They seemed friendly.*

'Qv^guk, do you know what frequency we can talk to them on, and in what language?'

'We learned their language from many transmissions we tapped into over the decades. Show them this frequency sign and say your "hello". By listening to their voices, you can program your translator.'

Shan showed the two survivors in the shuttle what Qv^guk had written, and they turned their radio on.

'Hello,' he said over the radio, then asked Qv^guk, 'How do you know this?'

'Before we went to the other planet, I had to learn everything I could about neighbouring systems,' Qv^guk replied before adding, 'Talk, say words, point and name stuff like we did earlier on.' Shan set the translator to learn mode. 'Maybe because of telepathy and the way our brains work, we can accumulate a lot of information in a relatively small amount of time,' Qv^guk said.

* * *

'Can we trust them? Maybe the king sent them,' the princess told the seller as they watched Shan and Qv^guk through the window.

'Here?' the seller replied. 'Come on; they can't know we're here, and if they did we would be dead already. You know the king; he shoots first then asks questions. These two are our only chance, and that one doesn't look like any species from our system. We can't go back, and we can't go forward – if we do, we're dead either way – but with them at least we have a chance.'

'But they know our language; they know the frequency we use.' A lifetime of worry had taught the princess to be paranoid.

'The weird looking one knows because this alien is there. I saw their species once on a poster; the king's police were looking for them. I don't see any other way. You've taken one risk already, and the only way is forward, from now on. Of course, no one saw me, I think, so I can still go back, but you…'

That convinced the princess. 'OK, you talk.'

'Well, it's not talking. He's just pointing at things and saying words.' The seller was baffled.

'I've seen this before when I had to learn other languages. I think we need to say the words for what she's pointing at so she can learn our language.'

After a few painful hours of entering sounds into the translator, the computer could finally say something meaningful.

'Hi, we come in peace,' Shan said first and thought, *now I feel like a real explorer.*

'Who are you? Can you help us?' the seller asked.

'I saved this guy, so I've got no reason not to help you. This place is too dangerous, and if you want to hitchhike, you're welcome to join us. Of course, if your oxygen requirements are the same as ours, that is.'

The seller sent Shan the details of the atmosphere inside his small shuttle. It wasn't that much different to the air in Shan's spacecraft, and let's be honest – most species need oxygen; the rest is only needed to keep the atmosphere from blowing up.

The docking port of the seller's shuttle was square, and Shan's docking port was round. Geometry defeated them, and Shan decided to use his loading bay to get the shuttle aboard. He positioned his spacecraft behind it, then opened the cargo bay and the seller flew inside, barely avoiding the parts that were lying all over the floor; objects Shan had collected from the ring of wreckage, and boxes of Tiranian gold.

His clothes are old and dirty, and she looks royal. An interesting combination, thought Shan. The princess was wearing a majestic floor-length ivory dress embellished with sparkling diamonds, now almost black from trailing through the dirt in the crashed spacecraft.

'Your ears are not where I thought they would be. Where are they?' Shan asked, looking at the seller and the princess, while the floating translator displayed hand movements for Qv^guk and spoke words for the newcomers.

'Everywhere, our whole bodies can hear. Why?' the princess asked.

'I've only seen a species similar to yours once before. Anyway, give me a minute to find some headphones. If your whole body can hear, normal headphones should work, too,' Shan said and rummaged through a box of cables and parts he'd found in a loading bay. A minute later, he gave both of them sets of wireless headphones and connected them to the floating translator.

'Why are you trying to escape, and who are you?' Shan asked first.

'I am Princess Alayna Hames, and this is Laaki. I am the wife of King Tiranian of the trinary star system Hilmbu, but I escaped, and Laaki helped me. Can you help us? Who are you? How did you get here? Who is that? Do you have any food and water?' The princess asked a lot of questions.

'Well, long story short: I am Shan. I came here from another galaxy and saved Qv^guk, who comes from Aofneu, a planet not far from here. I'm looking for a place to move to, Qv^guk is in the process of moving and you, I guess, want to move, too?'

'We just escaped King Tiranian's world. I suggest we leave as soon as possible because he will be looking for me,' Alayna warned him.

'Let's go to the bridge,' Shan said, pulling the scrap-built video translation unit along behind him. 'I seriously need to make this translator more portable. I'm sorry, but I'm not sure if you'll like the food I have.' Shan walked into the kitchen. They all sat down, tired and hungry, trying to adjust their bodies to chairs that had been designed for Shan.

'We can eat anything, as long as it's nutritious and contains proteins. Plants or meat,' Laaki replied.

'I can survive without food for another day, I just need water. I mostly eat plants, as you'll see when we get to my world,' Qv^guk explained.

'Fruity porridge for us, water for Qv^guk,' Shan replied, preparing the food.

'If you came here from another galaxy, why did you come to the three-star system and the rings of wreckage?' Alayna wondered, evidently suspecting something. Shan remembered a discussion with Goe about being more open. *Shit, my addiction started up again and only ended thanks to Qv^guk,*

Shan thought. *I was in the ring of wreckage for a whole month. I need help.*

'Well, to be honest, I don't like to talk about it, but as Qv^guk and you two saved my life, I think I owe you an explanation,' Shan started, but Qv^guk interrupted him.

'If you hadn't come, we would all be dead now. Well, a few millennia for me, but still. You saved our lives.'

'I have a weird addiction,' Shan continued. 'And till now, I've been able to control it. I like collecting things, especially old things: parts, computers, and all the data I can find. Where I come from this isn't a problem, as due to wars, we don't have much, but here this ring of wreckage is my paradise. Before I discovered you, I spent a whole month here. That's a long time. I wasn't sleeping, I started seeing ghosts, and now you know why my loading bay looks like it does. So I would like to say thank you for saving me.'

'We thank you for saving our lives,' Alayna said.

* * *

Before the robots' improvement program had taken hold, Shan's spaceship had been a sleek, silver, perfectly smooth piece of titanium fuselage. Now it was a not-so-smooth and not-so-titanium-based fuselage fifty metres long, ten metres wide and two levels high, with storage. It provided Shan with a perfect living space. The spacecraft was large enough for a full-sized bridge, kitchen, living room, four bedrooms, room for two shuttles and the cargo bay, which was now mostly filled with Tiranian gold, the princess's small shuttle and so much junk he had collected from the wreckage there was not much space left for anything else.

Shan assigned the room next to his own to Qv^guk, adjusting the oxygen level, and the rooms opposite to Princess Alayna and Seller Laaki. He set the course to Aofneu on LLTS 1 and, exhausted after their earlier adventures, everyone went to sleep. Although they had different sleep requirements, they all needed rest.

When they woke up the next day, garage time, Shan upped the speed to level two again, and after breakfast they entered the Aofneu system.

He saw a rocky, dark, atmosphere-less asteroid-like planet with only a few spaceships but many artificial satellites in orbit around it. After scanning all frequencies, Shan discovered various transmissions he couldn't understand, and Qv^guk confirmed the radio frequency for communications. Shan adjusted his transmission protocol to match Aofneu's as per Qv^guk's advice, and sent a message. After an hour a reply came with a confirmed invitation to Qv^guk's world, but the royal couple, as Shan had started to call Alayna and Laaki, decided to stay on the ship. For one thing, they didn't have any spacesuits, and secondly, they were afraid of the aliens working with the king.

Shan landed on what appeared to be a new landing pad, so new that it looked like a freshly flattened piece of soil. It was surrounded by gigantic shadows cast by sharp mountains, something Shan only saw on lifeless asteroids. Shan, pulling his floating translator, and Qv^guk, happy but seeming emotionless, left the ship and walked towards a cave in the side of a mountain.

An alien who looked similar to Qv^guk came out to greet them, wearing fabrics in bright shades of red, pink and white. Like Qv^guk, it was somehow perfectly fine without oxygen, at the same time as being bombarded by the harmful rays from the nearby star. By using arm movements the alien invited Shan and Qv^guk inside; and for the first time, Shan felt like a real explorer. It was the first time someone from another galaxy had come to these aliens' home planet. They entered a large round cave, which was twice as high as Shan, and after a few minutes' walk, the corridor started to get smaller, ending in a door.

Qv^guk's planet had lost its atmosphere aeons ago, but the molten core kept the temperature high enough to allow Qv^guk's species to evolve. Developing over millions of years from microscopic creatures, with almost no oxygen and often no water, they had built a civilisation. Specially evolved skin allowed their internal organs, including eyes, to be protected from pressure, radiation, and cold. Their vision moved to the right of the spectrum and enabled them to see perfectly in UV, X-rays and gamma rays but not so well in Shan's range and towards infrared. *That explains their clothes, spacecrafts and machines and the ridiculous decor.* It included bright red, pink, yellow and white fabrics, paintings and carpets, and all the furniture was made from hardened fungus, in similar colours.

The atmosphere inside the cave was different, but as far as Shan's body was concerned, it was a vacuum. Another alien came and started speaking to him, and the translation was displayed inside his helmet, transferring data from the floating trolley. When Shan himself spoke, the screen attached to the trolley showed moving hands, and when the alien spoke it showed words. The aliens did not use this technique among themselves, and Shan could see they were communicating telepathically.

'We welcome you with respect,' the alien said. 'This is the first time we have met someone from another galaxy. I am deeply sorry, but we weren't expecting diplomats from Planet 2032 for another hundred years, and we definitely weren't expecting anyone from another galaxy. Please forgive us that we are not able to offer you a place to stay, as we haven't built one yet, and our atmosphere is not suitable for you. Even deep underground where we normally live, you wouldn't be able to survive,' the alien said to Shan and with the translator's natural language option set to maximum, so that it added more words from its databanks.

'That's OK; we'll leave soon,' said Shan. 'As you are aware, I'm here to return a favour by taking you to 2032.

Who will come with us? Unfortunately, I can only take two of you.'

'We already discussed this,' Qv^guk replied. 'I'll be going, together with our diplomat Pe^Meno. We'll be taking gifts and apologies as the people of 2032 are not aware of what happened to their diplomats.'

'Do you want to spend some time here with your family first?' Shan asked.

'We have no concept of family as defined by your translator. It's a lot, but I can explain our culture on the way to 2032. We're already preparing food, clothes and other gear to take with us. We'll need it as we're going to spend many years on Planet 2032. It shouldn't take much space in your cargo bay.'

'Yeah… I should probably clean the cargo bay a bit first,' Shan commented.

* * *

After leaving Aofneu using the LLTS drive, they all arrived at the 2032 solar system. A scan revealed eleven planets and a number of spaceships with heavy weapons.

'Hey, Pe^Meno, we need to communicate with them. What's the frequency and the protocol?' Shan asked.

'You use this frequency,' said Pe^Meno, giving Shan a piece of paper, and continued, 'and this is the message in their language, together with the code. Without that code, they will shoot. They use the same transmission protocol as we have, so your computer is ready. I already programmed your translator to recognise their language,' Pe^Meno replied.

'Nice.'

Shan moved the spacecraft closer to the main planet and sent the message. The reply came a few hours later.

This is Adeanian planetary defence; we weren't expecting you for another hundred years. As you don't have the technology to travel faster than light, we cannot authorise you to land until further proof of your identity is provided.

'Well, they're right to be suspicious, and why they called Adeanian?' Shan said to Qv^guk and Pe^Meno, who were having a telepathic chat.

'Adeanian is the official name, 2032 is the catalogue number,' Pe^Meno explained.

'They're very touchy. They're going to kill us! All those years lost!' Qv^guk said, and he and Pe^Meno both started staring at each other again.

'I'll do this my way,' Shan replied and sent another message:

Greetings. My name is Shan. While I was travelling, I saved Qv^guk from wreckage in the Hilmbu three-star system and took Pe^Meno from Aofneu. They are both here with me and have shared with me the whole story of communication between your two species. The spacecraft that was going to Aofneu was destroyed, and only one cryo-pod survived, with Qv^guk in it. To prove this I will be sending you data I collected from damaged spacecraft. I am not here to cause trouble, only to help, and I need your help and advice in return. I will explain everything if you allow us to land on your planet.

Qv^guk and Pe^Meno went to their room to sleep, since in Shan's oxygen-rich atmosphere their bodies needed to slow down. The royal couple stayed on the bridge with Shan awaiting a reply from 2032.

'Sorry about the clothes, I only have these.' Shan apologised as he offered garments for Laaki and Alayna to change into. 'What's your plan, you two? You can't go back.'

'No, we can't,' Laaki agreed.

'We don't know what to do,' Alayna added.

'You can stay here; it looks like their planet has a typical atmosphere. Well, reasonably typical; you'll survive, and after some years your body will adapt. The people of 2032 have already seen Qv^guk and Pe^Meno, so they shouldn't be that surprised by your looks. There's no point going back with me as we'll have to return here at some point anyway.'

'We'll ask them if we can stay, at least for now. We can help them in their diplomacy with Hilmbu, and maybe one day we can come back. Maybe bring our families,' Alayna replied.

'I wouldn't go that far. If our military comes here there won't be anything left of Hilmbu, I'm afraid.'

'My family is there,' Alayna said.

'I have no one there, and I don't want to be a seller again. I used to be a pilot before the king took over my world,' Laaki replied.

'Sounds like the king makes everyone's lives miserable. Where is your family, exactly? How many people are there?' Walking towards the console map, Shan wondered if he was asking too many questions, too fast.

'My three parents and my brother. They're probably in prison now. He's going to kill them.'

'Don't say that,' Laaki said.

'Why not? It's true.'

'We can free them.' Shan spoke quickly without thinking about the possible danger. 'Where are they exactly?'

'Probably on the Crunidef colony,' Laaki said.

'How do you know that?' Alayna asked, surprised.

'I work in a market. It's the best place for information, and my friend used to fly to Crunidef. It's not a place you'd want to go to,' Laaki explained.

'Show me Crunidef on a map.' Shan opened the map, and Laaki pointed at a small planet the size of a moon.

'It's heavily guarded and difficult to get to. It's where all the criminals are sent for execution. The king punishes all criminals with death. Some people tried to bring in rehabilitation programmes instead, but he killed them, too,' Laaki explained.

'He sounds like a really nice guy. OK, the plan is: we talk to the Adeanians first, and maybe we can get them to help you. But even if not, I will get your family out of there,' Shan said to Alayna.

* * *

When the message from Adeanian planetary defence came back, it read:

The data you sent matches the data we hold. You are authorised to land. Take up orbit around the second planet. Another spacecraft will escort you to the surface. The confirmation code is attached.

'OK, listen up,' Shan said, walking up the stairs from the loading bay. 'I made the floating translator smaller and portable. We'll have to wear these helmets all the time.' He gave everyone simple helmets with built-in-camera, speakers, headphones, microphone and screen. 'We'll use both shuttles, and I'll set the main ship to autopilot. I don't want to risk it being destroyed down there,' he explained.

'Sounds like a plan,' Alayna replied, walking to the loading bay.

Once they were in orbit around the planet, a small spaceship approached them. Through the window of the shuttles, they briefly saw Adeanians, who looked normal by Shan's standards. The Adeanians confirmed Qv^guk and Pe^Meno's identity by looking at them, and indicated with what Shan called UUGL – universal universe gesture language – that the four visitors should follow them.

'The planet looks nice, but a bit like a desert,' Alayna said, looking through the window.

'It does. Look at those canyons, they're enormous,' the seller replied, and pointed at vast canyons that looked like cracks in a dried-up river. Seen from high above, the planet wasn't green, blue, or even red but yellowish.

'Looks like that's where we're going, and there's nothing else apart from those canyons anyway,' Shan said, steering his spacecraft to follow the Adeanians. As they approached cracks, they appeared bigger and bigger, finally showing themselves to be so immense that they contained cities. The Adeanian spacecraft went to one of the canyons and landed on a small pad with markings in Adeanian language. There was another pad next to it with flashing lights, and that was where Shan and Laaki decided to land.

'The atmosphere looks good enough for all of us apart from the aliens, but I guess they'll survive that,' Shan said, studying the composition of the air outside.

'Look,' Alayna said, pointing at two Adeanians carrying something that looked like a spacesuit with multiple arms.

'What's that? We don't need that,' Shan replied, surprised.

'We do,' Qv^guk replied. 'I designed and built them many years ago so that we could survive during our stay here.'

'That explains a lot. Let's go then,' replied Shan and opened the shuttle door.

Qv^guk and Pe^Meno went outside and bowed – movement that was similar to retracting their bodies like a telescopic pole. The Adeanians bowed, too. Shan just nodded slightly.

* * *

The Adeanians' bodies were all somehow different from one another. Their torsos were wide and flat with two legs that had four toes on each foot; two arms with two thumbs and four fingers on each hand; a flat head like a hammerhead shark's with two big blue eyes on each side; and what Shan assumed to be multiple mouths and nostrils on the torso between their arms. Each Adeanian had a different mouth, head, and eyes, and each had a unique hairstyle on top of their heads, with some wearing hats.

'Greetings. I'm Shan. I was the one who sent the message. You know Qv^guk and Pe^Meno from Aofneu, and this is Princess Alayna and Seller Laaki from the Hilmbu trinary system.'

'Thank you for helping, Shan. Our presidents need to speak to you. This way.' *They're a bit direct, taking us straight to the presidents. I guess I'm important now.*

Being at the bottom of the largest canyon they'd ever seen made them feel small, like ants. The entrance was a narrow opening below an enormous carved circle with seven lines and seven rings at the end of each line. At the entrance of the underground building, hundreds of small Adeanians wearing beautiful colourful clothes greeted them, some of them running out from inside like headless cosmic chickens. *It looks like they weren't prepared for our visit.* After a short walk deep inside the cave, they saw seven presidents, each of whom looked the same. *Clones? Their hats are the same, too; what appears to be makeup is the same; their clothes, even their wrinkles and the black dots on their skin are the same.* They were sitting in a half-circle on what appeared to be thrones, and one of them spoke.

'We are happy to see you. I hope you forgive us for not being prepared for your visit. It was very unexpected.'

'We are honoured,' Qv^guk replied. One of the presidents moved his arm, and everyone left the cave, leaving only Shan's delegation, the presidents and a few advisors standing behind them.

Qv^guk continued speaking using his hands. The presidents had already learned Aofneu's hand language, so the translator was only needed for Shan's party. 'As you know, we want to continue to collaborate with you for peace and mutual growth. We would like to stay here, have a cultural exchange and set up trade routes as we initially agreed. Princess Alayna and Seller Laaki would like to ask for asylum to stay here and to help with the killers from Hilmbu. Shan?' Qv^guk said and pointed to Shan to speak.

'I come from another galaxy, much more advanced than yours. I can travel between them in thirty days, but for you, it would take millions of years. The reason I came is that our galaxy is in danger. It's on a collision course with our satellite galaxies and is having a civil war, and everyone wants to escape. I will not lie to you; I will be very honest. When we all come here, your lives will change. You even might be destroyed. Most species in this galaxy might; we are so advanced that Hilmbu, who are a threat to you, are nothing to us. It's as simple as that. We can travel fast, we can destroy planets and black holes, but the technology we have didn't save us from war and destruction. What I want to do is to prepare you and help you, and hopefully you can help us. Whoever comes here first will colonise your planet, and this galaxy and, trust me, you want that guy to be me,' Shan explained.

'That's impossible, breaking the light barrier is impossible; this is all lies!' one of the Adeanian advisors who was standing behind the presidents shouted, but the presidents all just looked at the advisor.

'You are correct,' said Shan. 'The light barrier cannot be broken, but I didn't break it. The speed of light is a limit in this frame of reference, but I can travel in a kind of separate frame of reference, or another dimension if that's easier for you to understand, even if there are no dimensions.'

'You seem not to give us a choice. We will have to accept your offer,' one of the presidents said.

'I do give you a choice. Just say the word, and I will leave now, and you won't see me again. But I genuinely want to help. Without me, you will lose this battle and believe me, I don't want that.'

'When will this happen? Your galaxy colliding with another. And why doesn't it affect us?' another president asked.

'I don't know how long you've been observing our galaxy, but yours is on a collision course with us, too. The difference is your collision is billions of years into the future. My galaxy will collide with our satellite galaxies in about fifty years. Let me show you.' Shan set a small holographic device on the floor and projected the simulation.

'How does that projection work?' one of the advisors asked.

'That doesn't matter at the moment. This is a simulation of the collision; we need to leave now, or start leaving. We have wars and millions die, most of them innocent people who are just trying to escape a war they didn't want. We seek help like those two.' He pointed at Alayna and Laaki. 'Many are trying to escape the small wars and battles. Everyone just wants a peaceful life. I seek help for myself and everyone there, and I want to help you. I don't want to see another species being wiped out. We are too small in this universe for that.' Shan sat down, then all the presidents stood up and started to walk in circles. It was an odd ceremony, and after a few minutes they sat down again, but this time each on a different chair.

'You see, Shan, we used to live in chaos,' the first president from the right started.

'We still do,' said the third president.

'Yes, but now it's another kind of chaos,' said the fifth president. 'Each of us comes from a different background. We used to be divided into countries with borders, with problems.'

'Sometimes, we wish to be like King Tiranian. Just one decision and it's done, but we know that in the long term that doesn't work. Even Tiranian knows that,' the first president said.

'Every race on this planet wanted something different to the others, and they all wanted what was best for themselves,' offered the sixth.

'They were all racists a long time ago. Now we finally understand that we need to work together to achieve something. Especially peace,' returned the first.

'We had those problems for millennia,' said the seventh. 'Every leader, that one single unit who is in charge of a country, wanted one thing: power. Countries and borders only spell destruction. They are the reason for wars, but what everyone wants is a simple, nice life, as you said. You see, after the endless wars our ancestors fought, those who survived met here in this very cave and decided to end all that. What they did was very radical, but at that time, it was the only way forward in a world destroyed by wars where even borders had lost their meaning. They created a country; a union called Adeanian. Yes, the same name as our planet. No borders, no countries, anyone could go anywhere. They created new laws, new rules, and there were seven of them, our ancestors. They became the rulers of this planet.'

'The presidents,' continued the fourth. 'Not rulers of the countries but of the whole planet. No, it wasn't perfect, but the wars ended. That's where we come from. We are all descendants of those seven presidents. We are chosen by the most intelligent, who knows what is best for everyone. Not everyone is allowed to vote, but everyone is allowed to have an opinion, and we listen to them before making logical decisions. Yes, again it's not perfect, but we have no wars, no hunger and everyone lives a peaceful life.'

'We are very prosperous, our science is advanced, and now we are going to collaborate with you and Aofneu,' said the first president. 'We've even colonised a nearby planet. It's not easy, but it's worth it for everyone. It's another chapter in our evolution. You all can stay here for the time being as long as you accept our laws and rules. Please enjoy our world. We will meet here again tomorrow. Shan, we need to discuss your offer.'

One of the Adeanians asked Shan's delegation to leave.

* * *

'Do you think we can trust them?' Alayna asked Shan over the radio. They were now in the two shuttles, following the Adeanian spacecraft.

'I think so, why?' Shan replied.

'They don't seem to be happy to have us, and weirdly they all look the same in spite of coming from different backgrounds.' Alayna suspected something was wrong with the presidents.

'I know, I thought the same thing, but for now I don't want to be involved in their internal affairs. On the other hand, you need to understand that this is not easy for them. Look at us from their point of view. We all come from different planets; I come from another galaxy. It's difficult to believe in, let alone be open with aliens. I think they are incredibly open, anyway. They live in peace, and I don't believe they have any issues with us, they're just trying to be careful. If they wanted, they could arrest us right now. Also, their decision now will affect their whole civilisation. It's not easy, trust me; my planet has been there. Your king probably killed all the aliens or kept them separate behind walls, so you never had this problem. On the world I came from we have hundreds of different species from all over the galaxy; imagine that. So, to me, everyone looks normal.'

'We do have issues with other species on our planets, and they only come from our neighbouring worlds, so I guess you're right. How you deal with it?'

'We don't. There's nothing to deal with. We all live in the same universe, and just because others look different, why treat them differently? It's pointless. As long as they don't cause problems, they're welcome.'

'What if they do?'

'That depends. There are some species whose nature is to kill and be stupid, but they don't get far developing an economy and technology. Those who live in hate, who hate other species, and work, and everything; they live in a constant state of war and poverty and never get anywhere. Those who live in peace and acceptance thrive, it's as simple as that. We used to have countries, too, and with that came problems and wars, and our planets were divided, but with time we realised it was pointless. We became united, educated ourselves, and those who truly didn't want to integrate, we had to put in jail or remove. Then it came to another war, and everything started again. Look,' Shan pointed out of the shuttle window at the view of the city.

'I can't find words to describe it,' Alayna replied, looking at the incredible view. They were above the planet's surface, looking down at a building standing at the junction point of three canyons. A beautiful, majestic structure with towers, glass domes, greenhouses, trees, grass and flowers everywhere, but none of the actual structures rose above ground level. This building had bridges everywhere, between towers, between small buildings, and between canyon walls connecting everything.

The shuttles landed on some pads set on the side of one of the middle towers. An Adeanian came out, Qv^guk and Pe^Meno bowed, and they all took the bridge-walk from the landing pad to the main building. Inside, lots of sunshine came through the window, and there were benches and plants. There were also many Adeanians not looking at Shan's party, which was weird for many reasons. Members of three different species had just landed in the Adeanians' city, and no one cared. *Odd.*

Shan saw a flying robot cleaning the glass dome. The robot didn't seem to have any ropes or engines, but somehow it was floating. *How does it work?* Shan's engineering mind was wondering. After a few minutes' walk, looking at everything, one of the Adeanians showed each of them to a room.

The first thing Shan did was go over to look out of the glassless window, and he was amazed. Shan spent a few minutes in silence watching the lively city below. Robots and Adeanians flying their small shuttles, walking and doing various other things. The building Shan was in was made of stone, but the other buildings were wooden. They were colourful, with flowers growing from every cranny, and wooden bridges and ropes connecting buildings and canyon walls. Some had small lifts on cables going up and down; some newer ones had lifts powered by some kind of engine. Shan couldn't see the base of the city as all the bridges blocked the view. He thought, *we are so advanced, but this is beautiful and incredible. The difference is, they don't have a war on. Looking at all this, art and science are probably thriving here.*

After some time standing in the sun and watching the life of the city, Shan, being from a species that sweated, needed a shower. He entered the bathroom and… *Yeah… I know they have a different anatomy from mine, but I hope they take showers here.* This was either a seriously advanced bathroom, or a very primitive one, or it wasn't a bathroom at all. Pipes emerged from every wall, the ceiling and the floor, and they pointed in all directions. *OK, I get it, each pipe washes something different. Those are for your mouth, those are for feet, and those are for your head, and I don't want to know where this one goes, but let's try.* Shan stood up in the middle of all those pipes, and the shower started. Water started coming from all the pipes, under considerable pressure – too much for Shan's body to take. He jumped out and used a nearby bucket to wash.

* * *

In the morning, after sleeping in a not-so-comfortable bed and eating a not-so-tasty breakfast, Shan went outside to talk to Alayna. She was standing next to the window in her room that had no door.

'Hi,' Shan started while the translator was doing its job.

'Hi. This place is nothing like our system. Much more culturally advanced. We have no culture; we used to, but it's all been destroyed. The king only cares about weapons and technology, but I love art so much. Also, I need to ask them for some water in a bucket, that shower almost deafened me,' Alayna replied, looking outside.

'You can be an artist here. And I know, that shower almost took my skin off.'

'I always liked to make things. Not painting, but maybe sculpture or engineering. My parents are artists, and they still try even if it's forbidden. I wanted to learn, but I was taken away to the king.'

'Look at that.' Shan pointed to a robot who was cleaning the tallest pillars he'd ever seen. 'You could build one of those.'

'I like robots. The ones we have aren't that advanced. They can barely mimic us. They're extremely basic. They don't think on their own, they're remote-controlled and can walk, kind of. They have built-in radar and stuff, but it's nothing like these. So yes, I would like to work with them. Do you want to go down to the bottom?' Alayna asked.

'Are we allowed? Must be dark down there; all those bridges block all the light. And what about Laaki?'

'I checked his room when I woke up. He said he slept better than he had in years, and he was planning to stay in bed. Besides, he can join us later, they say to enjoy the city, so yes, I guess, and if not, someone will tell us.'

They went out into the main corridor and Alayna pointed out a tiny room. It looked like a lift without doors.

They went inside. *I seriously need to ask someone why they don't use doors. No buttons, so maybe it's not a lift then?* One Adeanian saw them and told them they both needed a wristband. Wristbands were used to control many things in the city. The Adeanian pointed them to a console built into the wall opposite the lift, where they could get the wristband installed.

'So... how does it work?' Shan asked Alayna as they stood next to the wristband-dispensing machine, not knowing what to do.

'I think you need to put your hand here.' She pointed at what looked like the right place. The only problem was that Adeanians' hands were rather different, rounder than Shan's or Alayna's.

'Let me try.' Shan put his hand in, and the machine wrapped a band around his wrist. It was made of leather, with metal locks, buttons, and a little green screen.

'Just press some buttons and we'll see what happens,' Alayna replied, getting her wristband connected.

They walked back to the lift, and the screens in their wristbands lit up with the lift information. *OK, so that looks like navigation.*

'You see, this is the kind of stuff I want to make,' Alayna said to Shan, showing her wristband.

'I think this is awesome; I want to keep it, and maybe I can use it on my ship.'

Shan selected floor zero, which was hopefully the ground from what he understood on the screen, and pressed another button to confirm. It worked; the lift moved. *No doors? This is dangerous, put your head out there and you lose it.* They didn't know how many floors it was to the bottom, as they couldn't read Adeanian language, but it was a long way. When the lift halted they couldn't stop staring, and for a moment they didn't say a word.

'Are we still on the same planet?' Shan asked.

'I know. Come on. Let's walk,' Alayna replied.

The city was completely different down here, and they couldn't take their eyes off it. Dark, colourful, but metallic, golden and wooden with screens everywhere, and the sky was blocked out overhead. They were below the many bridges, lifts, buildings, plants and trees they'd seen from above. It was like being under all those spaceships in the wreckage city with streets, shops and streetlights.

* * *

They started to walk down a long street that was lined with small shops on each side. Each shop was a shipping container with one of its longer sides removed. It was dark, and the only light came from the shops and streetlamps. In one of the stores, they sold shoes; another container was filled with green screens, another had tables and another had chairs. Each shop sold a specific kind of item – flooring, appliances, doors, cups, fans, belts, hats, tents and water pumps.

'What's that?' Alayna pointed at someone, or more like something, that was shaking like a vibration table for concrete moulds.

'It's a robot, I think,' Shan replied, coming closer to a shop that was filled with robots of varied sizes and shapes. Small, big, looking like Adeanians or completely different. Most had engines for flight, and arms, but only one had a wheel. Parts were everywhere, but the shop was mostly clean and perfectly stacked. *It looks like the robot seller has OCD*, thought Shan.

'Oh, hello,' the seller said in a sleepy voice.

'Are you selling robots?' Alayna asked.

'Fixing, selling, building,' the seller replied, completely ignoring the fact that Shan and Alayna were aliens and were using helmets to communicate.

'They're great,' Alayna replied with amazement.

'She's looking for something to do. Could you hire her?' Shan asked the seller.

'I didn't ask you to find me a job,' Alayna said to Shan, a little embarrassed.

'Hire?' the seller asked, surprised.

'I mean, help you so she can learn about robots. You'll have to start working here some time, so it might as well be now,' Shan told Alayna.

'No one is interested in robots anymore,' the seller replied.

'Why?' Alayna asked. 'They're everywhere.'

'It's a dying trade,' the shop owner said, sitting back down in a chair.

'What about those cleaning robots? Or the flying robots, and those.' Shan pointed to the more specialised ones. 'I'm sure you need them.'

'We *used* to need them. That's the difference.' The seller stood up again and walked outside. 'Look at this place.' The seller pointed at the street. 'This used to be a clean and most beautiful city. Now it's dark thanks to all those bridges. What

I would give to live up there, or even on the surface! I love nature, but here, to survive, I have to build robots. It's better if she goes to the craftsman who makes green screens, or up to the top.'

'I would like to help you and learn. Can I? I love robots, and I don't mind being down here.' Alayna was getting overexcited.

'You love robots? Why?' The seller was surprised.

'I don't know; there's just something about them. It's a combination of art, science and maths, three of my favourite subjects.'

'Well, I can teach you, but unfortunately, I only make enough to survive. I can't pay you.'

'That's OK; I'll figure something out.'

'Sorry for asking, but are you and everyone here really not interested in us?' Shan asked.

'Interested?' The seller looked confused.

'We look different, we don't speak the same language as you, we use these helmets to communicate, and we haven't seen anyone else who looks different, so how come no one is interested? No one asks questions: where we're from, what we're doing here. Why?'

'Oh, that. We already know all about you. The news is spreading quickly, and we're used to different species. We have many visitors from other planets, they've been coming for years, but they never stay,' the seller explained.

'Why do they never stay?' Alayna asked.

'Because this planet is not in perfect condition, as you're probably aware,' the seller answered.

'Is it dying? What are you talking about? No one told us anything,' Shan replied, surprised. *I have some form with dying planets recently*, he thought.

'Yes, and everything is green and clean and pretty up there, so how is it dying?' Alayna asked.

'It's worse than I thought then. We used to live on the surface. Long before my time, centuries ago. But the surface became dry as the temperature increased. We had to move to the canyons to be close to water and survive. Now the temperature is increasing again, water is drying up, and slowly we will perish. Come back tomorrow for work,' the seller told Alayna and went back to the store.

'So you have a job.' Shan was pleased for Alayna. 'How awesome is that? Apart from the dying planet.'

'Yes, and thank you, but what about this planet? You heard what the robot seller said, and in that case, we can't stay here.'

'Something's not right. I mean, it's not that hot, and what about all those flowers and trees at the top? The surface isn't that dry, I've seen rivers up there. Maybe he's spent too much time down here,' Shan said, walking next to Alayna.

'Yes, something isn't right...'

'Look out!' Shan shouted, pushing Alayna away, but it was too late. Two flying robots swooped in and caught both of them in a net. Then they flew into some tunnels, to an empty container deep underground.

* * *

Shan woke up to a series of demands.

'Who are you? Why are you here? You look different to us. Give us information, or we'll kill you. Wake up.' Bewildered, he tried to stand, but was held down in his chair by a robot.

'What's going on? Who are you? Why am I here? Let me out!' Shan was trying to break free.

'Are you here to take over our planet like the rest of them?' one of the Adeanian kidnappers demanded.

'What? No! Who are you? What's going on? I don't know what you're talking about!' Shan angrily tried to force his way out of the chair.

Alayna was struggling, too. 'Let us go; we're not here to steal your planet!'

'She speaks their language; we need to kill her before it's too late,' another kidnapper said.

'What? No! She escaped from the king; she's looking for asylum. What do you mean, she speaks their language? Tell us what's going on,' Shan demanded.

'The king is in talks with our presidents to take over our world. The king wants to expand; he wants to rule more and more planets. He's conquering everyone. He's too powerful for us, but we will fight!' the kidnapper shouted.

'What about that seller who told us the planet is dying?' Alayna asked.

'That's propaganda from the presidents, those idiots believe it all. Radio and TV controlled by the government are brainwashing everyone to get rid of us, to get rid of everyone, to control everyone so the presidents can get all the power from the king. But we know he won't give them any power. He'll kill us all.'

'We've got nothing to do with it. Set us free,' Shan protested.

'You're different; you talk funny, and she speaks the king's language. Throw them in the cell,' the kidnapper told a robot and left.

The cell was the size of one container shop, with a metal door that would not open from the inside.

The first day and night Shan and Alayna mostly spent banging the metal walls in case anyone could hear, although they also spent a lot of time talking, staring at walls, and trying to open the door. But the container was too deep underground for anyone to hear them, or for Shan to summon his spacecraft using thought control. The door was not sealed, which allowed them to breathe some fresh air; they needed it – maybe not yet, but soon. Sleeping on the metal floor was less than ideal, but for now, it was their bed.

The morning came and went. Their bodies demanded food, water and removal of the previous day's food. Yes, they needed fresh air, but they needed food and water even more.

The day passed with no events, apart from some more talking and trying to drink their saliva, in almost perpetual motion, but not quite. At the end of the second day, their bodies went into survival mode. Dehydration took over. The headaches were the worst, but the tiredness wasn't pleasant either, and along with the dryness in their mouths it sent them into depression. They knew that Shan would never find his grandfather now, or Alayna her family.

On the third day, as they were almost unconscious, feverish, fighting the stench, someone opened the door. The metallic sound of a lock scraping woke Shan from his trance. He was lying on the floor, unable to move, with Alayna next to him. She woke up, too, but couldn't move either. As the Adeanian kidnapper opened the container door, his nose was hit by such a terrific smell the alien almost vomited through his multiple mouths.

'What is that smell? What have you been doing in here?' he roared, covering his nostrils.

'Food! Water! We are dying here…' Shan was trying to speak, but he was so weak that his hand fell from his leg to the floor like a dead pigeon. The Adeanian kidnapper pulled them both out of the container and gave them water and something to eat. Neither Shan nor Alayna could tell what it was, but at this point their bodies needed energy, and this stuff would provide it. They could only eat lying on the floor; after three days without any food they were too weak to stand.

'We didn't know you need to eat that often,' the Adeanian kidnapper said, looking at them in wonder at the weakness of their species.

'We were in there for three days without water! We need to eat every day; we need to drink every day; we need to defecate every day. We are not you; our bodies are different,' Shan explained after a few minutes of eating and drinking, still lying on the floor.

'Oh...' said the first Adeanian kidnapper, looking at another of them.

An hour later, Shan and Alayna managed to sit up, and the kidnappers joined them in the underground room.

'We have news,' one of the kidnappers said, 'but first, how did you land here?'

'We used two shuttles, one mine, one hers. There are more of us, two more aliens and her friend,' Shan answered, nodding at Alayna.

'Both shuttles were confiscated by the presidents. You are now enemies of the state, the same as we are.'

'What? What do you mean, enemies of the state? We didn't do anything. The presidents told us to enjoy the city, so why we are the enemy now?' Alayna tried to shout, but she was still too weak.

'Did they tell you their little story about their ancestors and seven presidents and a big war?' the Adeanian kidnapper asked.

'Yes, why?' Shan asked.

'Our planet is not a happy place, but it's not dying. It's not so simple to destroy a planet that has been here for billions of years. If anything, the planet might destroy us. There is some truth in their story, though. We had wars; we had seven presidents, those first leaders who ended the war. The problem started when one of them wanted all the power. This president started eliminating other presidents and creating clones of himself. Himself?' the Adeanian kidnapper wondered. 'Your translator seems to have our gender system mixed up. I guess "himself" will do for now.

'After centuries and generations of propaganda, normal Adeanians believe in the presidents so much they can't accept the truth anymore. They call us crazy, paranoid; they don't want to help us to fight the cloned presidents, they are so blind and stupid. The presidents have destroyed this world, turning it from a prosperous planet into a dying desert. The clones shifted the system from democracy towards totalitarianism. They started slowly, first by taking more and more power for themselves, confusing everyone and accusing them of crimes, then eventually removing the boundaries between state and religion, and then the entire judicial system. The longer you do this, the more everyone will believe you, and by giving just enough to keep everyone happy you retain power. They secretly destroyed the water pumps and convinced everyone that moving to the king's planet was the only choice. Only for some, though; the rest would have to sacrifice themselves for the greater good. They didn't stop there; they asked everyone to come, especially high-ranking officials from other planets who they then handed over to the king. They would most likely torture you until you told them the location of your planet, so the king could invade it,' the kidnapper explained.

'Yeah… Good luck with that. Hold on a second…' Shan was thinking. 'I can help you fight them. And who are you anyway? What are your names?'

'We are the Adeanian underground, and we keep our identities secret, so it's better if you don't know our names. It's fine to call us aliens. We are fighting to restore our lost freedom, to destroy the presidents and King Tiranian.'

'Seriously, no one likes this guy,' Shan said.

Another kidnapper came over, bringing a green screen, and said, 'It's too late to fight the king. We lost. Our spy close to the presidents told us the king's army is already on its way here. We are soldiers, we train, but most of our members are normal Adeanians who just want to help. If the king is coming here, we have no chance; his army is enormous. We would have to go to his palace and kill him.'

'He's right,' Alayna said. 'The king is the king, he's got total power. The only way to win is to kill him. I can show you where he is.'

'How do you know that?' one of the kidnappers demanded, standing up.

'I am the king's wife. I spent some time preparing for that role until I escaped.'

'So you are the king's spy!' the kidnapper shouted.

'No! She escaped, together with Laaki, who is probably now in prison,' Shan replied.

'I'm not a spy; I hate the king!' Alayna shouted.

'Let's say I believe you, for now. We can't get to the king's palace anyway, it's far away, and it would take us a long time to get there. Their spacecraft are faster. It's also the most protected place, and according to our spies he's got an underground bunker.'

'This might be your lucky day then. I have a ship capable of reaching the king undetected,' Shan explained.

'Take us there!'

'I'm not a soldier; I'm an engineer and a pilot, you have to understand that. And what will happen when you kill him?'

'We've already found descendants of the original presidents, and they are ready to step in. Once the king is dead, we will replace the current presidents, and the Hilmbu resistance already has a new king who is ready to step in.'

'My ship is in orbit. I can remotely bring it here, but we need to go up, to the surface or somewhere outside. Also, I think we need some kind of proof that what you are saying is true. After all, you just kidnapped us.' Shan was suspicious.

'We can't get to the surface, but we can use the tunnels to go to the edge. It's an old robotic railway, not officially used anymore. It was built a long time ago before the surface was in ruins, and it stretches around the whole planet. We use it to get resources. We can be at the edge in a few hours. Proof? We could have left you in this container to die, but we didn't. After we heard about you becoming enemies of the state, we needed to find out who you really are. If you still want to see the proof, look at the screen.'

'Tomorrow. Right now, we're too weak even to stand,' Shan replied and put his head on the table.

'This is the terminal connected to our network. Use it to find the truth,' the Adeanian kidnapper said and left them alone, locking the door after him.

After reading it for some time, eating and drinking, Alayna spoke.

'Looks like they're telling the truth. If we'd stayed in our rooms, the presidents would have captured us too, like they captured Laaki,' she said, watching the presidents discuss catching a spy.

'Yes, what do we do now?' Shan asked.

'We have to help them; we don't have much choice.'

'We always have a choice. We can escape.' *Didn't I affect them too much already?*

'What about Laaki? I would be dead without him, and if we don't help them, the people here, they're all going to die. I spent enough time living in fear, trying to be passive about the king, until that day I met Laaki. It's time to do something about the king before he kills everyone. You are the Adeanians' only chance; no one else has your technology,' Alayna explained.

'Where I come from, we have a law that forbids us from helping less developed civilisations, although I and everyone else have broken that law many times over many years. It's a very tough moral and philosophical problem.'

'Really? Three planets have already been conquered, and you're talking about morals? Now you can make it right. If we don't help them now, they'll vanish.'

'I never liked that law anyway.'

* * *

Shan and Alayna greeted the Adeanians as they brought breakfast, a massive bowl of unrecognisable meat and vegetables. It wasn't what Shan had had in mind, but in his state, he would eat anything.

'We have information from our spy that the king's army is already on the way. They'll be here in two days. The presidents are hiding all the radar stations, and they've destroyed all publicly accessible radars. We need to kill him before that. Are you going to help us?' one of the kidnappers asked.

'Yes, I will, but will you help me?'

'With what?'

'My civilisation needs help. We have to move here at some point, and we'll need a planet, or a few planets.'

'When you help us to save our planet, we'll help you find a new home. Now eat a lot; the road outside is not an easy one.'

* * *

The flat that belonged to the Adeanian underground army was located deep within the densely populated structures of the inner city. The flats, houses and businesses, including weapons dealers were as illegal as you can get, and kept secret by those who had joined the underground army. The outer city, on the other hand, was bursting with legal life although plants would have had a tough time growing there. Natural light was something only the richest could afford, living high above the bridges.

Walking through the crowded streets of the outer city towards the railway line was out of the question. The presidents' spies were everywhere, and even ordinary Adeanians would report enemies of the state to the police if they saw them. The massive network of intercity walkways provided access to all places, and Shan and Alayna had to use it to reach the railway. It wasn't fun; it was the opposite of fun. Centuries of neglect and building work carried out without permission had turned the inner city into a maze of corridors. They were damp and filled with pipes, wires, furniture and rubbish but also businesses: bakers, hair salons, doctors, dentists, offices, electricians, plumbers, post offices, butchers, sellers, artisans, workshops, casinos and brothels.

'Well, that was intense, seriously,' Shan said, after almost vomiting into the darkness at the smell of some dead Adeanian rats. After walking through the alleys and corridors, and finally taking an old cargo lift deep underground, they arrived in one of the railway stations.

'This is it,' one of the kidnappers said to Shan and Alayna. They were both at the bottom of the canyon at a long-forgotten vacuum railway station. The platform, tracks, and carriages were old but beautiful. The Adeanians' love for art had made this station, the tunnels and the carriages a work of art, now slowly falling into disrepair. One of the aliens waved towards the control tower, where another Adeanian was standing, and moved one of the trains into a platform. The tunnel was round, the carriage was round, and the Adeanians were round too. The door opened, and they all entered before sitting down on round seats, designed for Adeanians' anatomy.

The Adeanians, more accustomed to higher G-forces, weren't uncomfortable in the moving train. But Shan and Alayna felt as if they were on a roller coaster, pushed back into their seats by the enormous pressure of the atmosphere. The speed of the train allowed them to travel hundreds of miles in minutes.

'Not all lines are operational; some have been destroyed by natural forces or by the presidents' army. Other lines are maintained by us,' one of the Adeanians explained.

When they got to the edge, it was precisely that, the edge.

'And they said there is no water on this planet...' remarked Shan. He and Alayna couldn't believe their eyes. They were standing on a vacuum railway platform looking at what appeared to be the largest waterfall they'd ever seen.

'There is water, it's just that we don't have access to it. Claiming there's no water is just the presidents' propaganda to keep everyone slaves, blindly believing in their rule of law.

The building you see in the middle is the old pump station, but it was destroyed to keep everyone under control,' the Adeanian replied.

'Where is your ship? We don't have much time for stories; we have an invasion to stop,' another alien said, unhappy about the slow progress of the mission.

Shan used his mind to bring down the ship; it had been in sub-quantum space and then suddenly appeared just behind them, pushing sand and water in all directions.

'It doesn't look like a warship. It doesn't have any weapons.' The Adeanians looked over the almost featureless spaceship.

'It's not a warship, but it's completely invisible. I can take you wherever you want. Directly to the king's palace. Kind of, close to it. It depends on where he's hiding, but I'll check that once we board.'

'What about Laaki? We need to save him,' Alayna insisted.

'Once we help the Adeanians, all the prisoners will be freed, and if we don't, we'll all be captured. We'll come back for him, don't worry,' Shan replied.

Two of the aliens, along with Shan and Alayna, went to the spacecraft. Shan opened the map and the Adeanians pointed him to the main planet where the king was located.

'That's not where he is,' Alayna protested.

'How do you know? We have this information from our spies,' the Adeanian replied.

'The king is smart, but he also makes mistakes. I am one of those mistakes. Your spies got the information the king wanted them to have, sending them to the wrong place.'

'So where is he?' Shan asked.

'In the safest place in this system, the same place my parents are,' she said, pointing at the small insignificant planet.

* * *

Crunidef colony wasn't a paradise – in fact, it was hell by many standards – but ironically the temperature was very pleasant. The colony was located on a small planet far from the habitable zone of the star. It was covered in a thick, easily combustible acidic atmosphere, and the only place to survive was deep below ground.

'That's the weirdest spacecraft I've ever seen,' Shan said, looking through the window after arriving at the ring of wreckage.

'As I explained earlier, that's the only way in,' Alayna replied, watching the spacecraft through the window.

The only way to get into the colony was by using specially designed butterfly-type spacecraft. The vessel itself could have been mistaken for an art installation. It consisted of two butterfly-like wings, each one set at one hundred and forty degrees to the other, perfectly smooth and covered with a protective black tar-like substance with holes everywhere. It was designed to withstand the harsh environment and to keep the acid and combustion in balance.

The idea was that the spacecraft would descend gently through the atmosphere to maintain its low temperature, and the acid would flow harmlessly around the hull. This was important as I'm sure the last thing you need is to be burned and dissolved alive at the same time. Spacecraft like this one were only built for that one purpose, to transfer criminals, goods and of course the king, and the only way to get one was to steal or to find it. That was the plan, to find one of those vessels and get from it data about the colony. After Shan's addiction adventure in the ring of wreckage, he had scans of all the ships, and one of them had been a butterfly. *Now, how do you get inside?* he thought. From his earlier experience, he knew that these guys used big guns, and those guns made big holes. *Bingo!* There was a hole right through the butterfly ship.

'Well, I'm the only one who has a spacesuit so wish me luck,' Shan said to Alayna and the Adeanians, walking down to the loading bay.

'How are you going to power this up?' one Adeanian asked.

'I don't know yet, I'll figure something out,' Shan replied and walked off down the stairs.

The butterfly spacecraft was in front of him, floating and rotating around the star, together with thousands of other broken spaceships. Shan flew through the big hole in its stern and looked towards the bridge, but apart from seats on each side the corridor was empty. He flew to the cabin and saw one of the pilots was still wearing a suit, a dry and wrinkled skin was visible.

The simplicity of the ship didn't leave much room for advanced computers, and what Shan found was a simple binary system, similar to those he had encountered before. He found a power source using his scanner, and replaced it with one of his own batteries. The computer booted up, and the spacecraft's lights came on. Shan, already having the Tiranians' language in his translator, connected himself to the onboard computer using one of Goe's extensions. He knew he didn't have much time until they discovered him, so instead of trying to find the data he needed, he copied everything, including the computer's memory itself, to his spacecraft.

'OK, I think we have what we need,' Shan said, walking to the bridge. 'Look here,' he told everyone while browsing the file system he had transferred earlier. 'I didn't have time to look through it all, so I brought it here. Now I can use my virtual garage simulator to run it.'

'What?' Alayna asked, looking at the Adeanians, who hadn't understood a word.

'I can run their computer here, without being in the spacecraft. I use this in my garage to test the new firmware in a separate virtual environment. The first time it took me weeks to boot up a similar one in the floating wreckage.' Shan was watching all the systems coming up with countless errors after they failed to detect the rest of the spacecraft. Browsing the files, he found a list of the prisoners and a map of all the cells.

'Alayna, search for your parents,' Shan said, giving her access to the console.

'Found them,' she replied a few minutes later. 'They're in Cell 5483. Can you transfer that map to my wristband?'

'Not to that one, but I'll give you another screen to mount on your arm,' Shan replied and walked to the loading bay. 'OK, how we are going to do this?' he asked, walking back with the arm screens.

The Crunidef colony was a simple planet covered in caves and tunnels, but the hidden cave of the king had been removed from the plans. Shan found it on his sub-quantum radar.

'We'll have to use their butterfly ship, that's the only thing that can get through the atmosphere and bypass security. They need to think it's one of theirs,' Alayna replied, looking at the plans.

'It will take too long to fix it,' Shan replied. 'There's a big hole in its hull, we haven't got parts for it, and from what I've seen that spacecraft doesn't have any bolts, it's like one big 3D-printed part. If we start patching it, acid can get into the hull, and we'll die.'

'We need another solution. We can't just fly there. What about other spacecraft? What if we hide in one of their leaf ships?' one of the Adeanians suggested.

'Hide? When there's barely space for the crew and prisoners? This spacecraft is as flat as a leaf; there's no room. We would have to be one of the prisoners, and I'm not doing it,' Alayna replied. 'They're killing everyone, they've got my family and friends, and that colony needs to be freed. We can't leave the people there; he's going to kill them.'

'Easy enough to say. My quantum field could protect the spacecraft from the acid atmosphere, but we wouldn't be able to get to the caves anyway,' Shan replied.

'We can't go through the planet, so we need to find a way,' said one of the Adeanians.

'Well, since you mention it, we actually can. How big is the main cave?' Shan went to the hologram of the planet, took the projection of his vessel and inserted it into the largest cave. 'My spacecraft fits perfectly.'

Everyone looked at Shan, wondering what was going on.

'And how are you going to get inside?' one of the Adeanians asked.

'Well, that's exactly what LLTS does, the drive that powers my ship. When you travel using LLTS, you're not here; you're below the level we exist on. You are deep below atoms, in quantum space, so you can, in theory, travel through planets. At least, I tested that theory some time ago, and it worked.'

'The cave is as big as your spacecraft, but what are you suggesting?' Alayna asked. 'I don't understand.'

'Well, everyone will tell you not to do it, not to travel through planets or stars or black holes. There's a reason for that. The denser the planet, the more gravity, and the more things can go wrong. Going through stars and black holes is completely forbidden. Not even forbidden, but unless you can sink deeper into sub-quantum space, you will simply die if you go into the star or a black hole.'

'So, in theory, we could simply appear in that cave?' one of the Adeanians asked.

'With a big bang, and we could kill everyone there.'

'Why kill them?' Alayna wondered.

'Well, if we simply appear in that cave, the air which is in there now will have to move somewhere else to make space for our spacecraft, and that somewhere is… somewhere.' Shan was looking at the diagram of the colony. 'The planet is big enough; the cave system is big enough; the air should move to the other parts of the planet. If this can make all of them unconscious for a little while, we'll have time to find your family and the king.'

* * *

Shan used his onboard sub-quantum radar to find the king's secret chamber and map the tunnels. He entered the plans into the computer, and the robots' improved algorithm did the simulation. It showed the pressure going through the roof, but that shouldn't affect the planet's integrity; something that couldn't be said about its inhabitants. He moved the spacecraft ten minutes' flight time on LLTS 1 away from the planet and orientated it perfectly with the cave.

'This is it. If you're not sure about this, we can still go back,' Shan told Alayna and the Adeanians while putting on a bulletproof suit and preparing the guns they'd bought in a dark alley in the inner city.

'The more we think, the worse it gets, so let's do it before I change my mind,' Alayna replied.

Shan rechecked the data and activated the LLTS drive; the clock was ticking. When they were five minutes from the cave, they all went to the loading bay and strapped themselves into the seats.

Five… four… three… two… one… Bang!

'Shit! This was loud,' said Shan, unfastening his seatbelt.

'And now it's strangely quiet,' Alayna added.

A moment later everything began to shake when falling rocks started hitting the spacecraft's quantum force. Shan's screen went red with warnings, but with the help of bots the self-healing technology would take care of most issues.

Shan opened the loading bay door, and they all crept to the edge, not knowing what to expect. The bodies of Crunidef guards were lying everywhere. The guards had two main legs, two main arms, and additional smaller arms and legs. They were wearing shabby, dirty clothes with no armour.

'Are they dead?' Alayna asked Shan, leaving the spacecraft.

'Some of them, probably. That change in pressure damaged their bodies, and they were slammed against the walls.' Something dropped on Shan and he looked up as the cave shook.

'Quake?' Alayna asked, covering her head.

'I think the bang damaged the integrity of this place,' Shan replied.

'I don't like the sound of that damaged integrity,' Alayna said, looking at the screen on her arm.

'I mean we don't have much time till this thing collapses, and they wake up. Adeanians, you know what to do. We'll need the floating trolley for Alayna's parents if they're unconscious.'

The Adeanians ran to the king's chamber, and Shan and Alayna ran towards the cell where her parents were being held, taking the floating trolley. As they jumped over the bodies of the guards, Shan and Alayna knew they were fighting with time. It wasn't easy going; the stairs were carved into slippery wet rock. *A couple more floors.* Shan was tired.

'Fourth floor, one more,' he said to Alayna. There they found the small and damp Cell 5483. It had two beds on each side, but no light, no table or even a toilet, proving even further what a tyrant the king was. Two of Alayna's parents were lying unconscious on the floor, wearing the same clothes as she remembered, now muddy and unwashed.

'Can you open the door?' Shan asked.

'Not without the terminal. It's next to the stairs. I'll go,' Alayna said, but Shan stopped her.

'No time. Let me try.' He shot the lock off the door. It wasn't pretty but worked.

'My dad is missing,' said Alayna. 'There should be three of them in there. We need to get the latest data from the terminal. You take them to the ship; I'll find the computer. Talk to me via the wristapp.' And she began moving them onto the floating trolley.

Shan was running, pulling the trolley behind him, and then it started. Hell. Bullets were flying like sideways rain in the forbidden forest. He hid behind a wall, shooting at the guards, trying to keep the trolley hidden behind him. *They're so stupid, their aim is even worse than mine*, he thought.

'Alayna, where are you? I'm surrounded,' Shan asked over the wristapp.

'I'm at the terminal, I found my dad and my brother in a cell on the tenth floor. The list of prisoners from the spacecraft was quite old. I'm going to get him.'

'I'm at the bottom with your other two parents. I'll help you when I get them to the ship.'

At this point, a huge explosion took out part of the wall Shan was hiding behind. Once the smoke cleared and the dust settled, he saw two Adeanians.

'What the hell are you doing here? You're supposed to be finding the king. And what did you do to this wall?' Shan shouted, covering his nose.

'Both tunnels were destroyed. We cannot get through, and it looks like you need our help.'

'OK, you go to the tenth floor and help Alayna, and we'll get those two to my ship.'

'We're coming!' Shan and the Adeanian left the spacecraft after strapping Alayna's parents inside. They needed to run up ten floors, but Shan had to stop on the fifth for a break. *I seriously need to exercise more.*

One of the guards attacked Shan from behind, but an Adeanian was quick enough to kill it. Adeanians were three times the size of the guards and had combat training. By comparison, the guards were useless mutated little rats who clearly didn't know how to use modern weapons. More guards started shooting in all directions, and Shan stupidly pointed the gun at one of the pillars – and half the ceiling came down. *I shouldn't be doing this. OK, let's run. Floor seven, floor eight, no more stairs?* They went down with the pillar. *I'm stupid! The lift!* What Shan called a lift was a cage on a rope that was powered by pulling the rope. On the tenth floor, he saw Alayna in Cell 947 talking to a prisoner.

'Hey, we have no time to talk! Let's go!'

'That's my friend, I'm taking her with me. And that's my dad and my brother. My dad said he's not leaving without his stolen stuff.'

'What stuff? We're all going to die if he doesn't come now!' Shan replied, dodging bullets.

'They're back in the other cell.'

'Arrrggh!' Shan hit the wall in frustration. 'Let's go to the lift. You four, get down.' He pointed at Alayna, her friend, her brother and her dad. 'We shoot!' Shan pushed them to the floor, and with the Adeanian alien started firing. Shan hadn't seen that much blood and that many body parts since his youth. When they arrived at Cell 5483 Alayna's dad pointed to a large trunk.

'It's heavy! Grab the handle and pull. We'll cover you,' Shan said, and he and the Adeanians started shooting the guards. The guards were more furious than intelligent, and as their guns were bigger than their bodies, they couldn't control their aim. They were effective against prisoners but not against Shan's team.

After mostly sliding down the slippery stairs from the fifth floor, Shan opened the loading bay remotely, and they all ran to the spacecraft. He closed the hatch and activated a preprogrammed escape sequence, causing the spacecraft to appear just outside the atmosphere.

'What do you mean, the tunnels were blocked?' Shan asked the Adeanians, wiping sweat and blood off his face.

'Completely blocked, destroyed. We need to find another way, but this atmosphere is not helping,' an Adeanian replied, pacing. 'We haven't got much time!'

'Well… I have an idea,' Shan said, walking to the console.

'Is it as crazy as going through the planet?' Alayna asked.

'Crazier… the king's chamber is too small to get the ship inside. I have something in my cargo bay that might help, but we need to do this now. The king is probably aware of what happened in the prison; he might try to escape. I'm sure they all felt the quake.'

'What's in your cargo bay?' one of the Adeanians asked.

Shan just looked at him and replied, 'OK, the plan is we launch the contents of my cargo bay out into the atmosphere, and we'll see what happens. Sorry I can't tell you what it is, but it's yellow, and it'll help.' Shan entered the details of the atmosphere and the Tiranian gold into the computer to simulate the explosion.

His plan was to remove the atmosphere, which would take one big box or three small boxes of gold. The problem was that the gold needed to be halfway up the lower strata of the atmosphere. 'OK, I was wrong, that idea involves us going down to the planet, but it should be fine,' Shan explained, watching the simulation. 'The boxes will be fine for the time we need to put them there, and we still should have enough time to escape.'

'You want to remove the atmosphere? From a planet? That's impossible,' one of the Adeanians said, watching the simulation and following Shan to the loading bay.

'Flying through the planet wasn't impossible enough?' Shan remarked.

'What's that?' another Adeanian asked, looking at the sticky yellow powder inside the box that Shan was opening.

'Try a bit. It tastes like oranges. Not sure about calories though,' Shan said and opened three smaller, empty, boxes.

'If we can eat it, how will that help us?' Alayna asked, confused.

'It's an enormously powerful weapon, and you'll be better off without it, trust me. It's already caused far too much chaos where I come from. And don't eat too much of it,' Shan warned, looking at one of the Adeanians, whose mouth was turning yellow. He started scooping up the gold in his hands and moving it from one big box to three smaller boxes. 'Help me move the gold.'

After a few minutes of everyone helping, Shan closed the now-full three boxes.

'Shan, your radar is showing movement on the surface.' Alayna was watching the console nervously. 'If the king escapes, he'll destroy everything. We need to do this now.'

'Shit...' Shan said, thinking he wouldn't have the time to put his suit on now. In his mind, he gave the maintenance bot instructions to come to the loading bay.

'The bot will mount the boxes outside. Let's go. We need to let the bot out,' Shan told everyone while the bot waited patiently for the loading bay to open. It took one box at the time and attached them to the outside hull, ready to be deployed at the right moment. Once the bot was back inside, Shan flew his ship into the atmosphere, going slowly enough to not cause much friction. He deployed the first box, then after a minute the second one. Just before he deployed the third box, the grey atmosphere turned fire yellow before disappearing and leaving only the planet's grey surface.

'You saw that? We should be dead!' Shan almost screamed, not understanding what had happened. 'It took huge power to destroy the atmosphere, and we didn't even feel anything. The same thing happened to me in the mine.'

'Look!' one of the Adeanians pointed at the window. They saw a burning royal butterfly ship falling down to the planet.

'The king is dead,' Alayna said, looking at a zoomed-in onscreen image of the spacecraft.

'Long live the queen!'

CHAPTER SIX

It was a hot day, so hot that it was quiet; there was no wind and not a single sound. There was also no water, no grass, no trees and no animals. It was a very hot day.

There wouldn't have been anything wrong with that, except that it was like this every day. It had been for the last few hundred years, at least. Welcome to the greatest desert of… Well, this desert had lost its name a long time ago, and the planet had lost its name, too. Anyway, beings lived in this desert. They had learned that water and cooler temperatures were to be found deep below the ground, so they dug and mostly lived underground in natural caves. They hated the race who lived on the other side of the planet.

It was a cold day, so cold that it was quiet; there was no wind and not a single sound. There was also no water, no grass, no trees and no animals. It was a very cold day.

There wouldn't have been anything wrong with that, except that it was like this every day. It had been for the last few hundred years, at least. Welcome to the greatest desert of… Well, this desert had lost its name a long time ago, and the planet had lost its name, too. Anyway, beings lived in this desert. They had learned that water and warmer temperatures were to be found deep below the ground, so they dug and mostly lived underground in natural caves. Did I mention that they hated the race who lived on the other side of the planet?

One side of this planet, located near the centre of the galaxy, was hot, and the other side was cold, and that was the main reason the two races hated each other. It had used to be an average planet with full rotation, but then the planet became locked on one side of the star. Extreme temperatures destroyed most civilisation, and only those who moved underground or lived on the poles survived.

A long time ago, on the cold side of this planet, a girl had been born. She seldom saw the sun as her species had to live deep below the surface. The girl was naturally curious, and from a very early age she wanted to know everything, especially about how things worked. To the surprise of her parents, she disassembled everything she could find in their cave. Starting from books when she was little to radios, computers and the air-conditioning system when she was older. After she had read all there was to read in her own and neighbouring caves, she sought out everything published in their internal cave computer network. Years later, after finishing school and university as the best student in the history of the newly divided world, she became bored and wanted to explore further. She set her sights on what lay beyond her planet.

Escaping the planet wasn't easy, as her family lived almost exactly in the middle of the frozen equator, deep underground, and spaceships only came to the north and south poles where temperatures were still bearable. But she was so determined to explore and to change her life that on the pretext of going to another school, she crossed the whole planet to get to the spaceport. On the way, she worked and stayed in odd caves, trying to survive, until finally, three years later, she arrived at the south pole.

Cargo ships came in every week, but passenger spaceships were rare due to the danger of black holes, wars and pirates. She managed to get a place on a cargo ship in exchange for her skills. Before she left, she sent a message to her family about her trip and promised she would come back one day, but she never did.

When she finally arrived at the cargo terminal of a neighbouring planet, she found herself with nowhere to go. The management of the terminal offered her a job, but she wanted to keep going. She knew science was her strongest point, but here, science was almost non-existent. She slept in the terminal with other travellers, and learned again how to survive. The opportunity she wanted came with another small cargo ship that arrived from a planet-sized mining platform, where she was hired as a technician, after she became famous on the spaceport for repairing the primary navigation system. Four years later, she left with another girl to learn more about the physics of the universe. Ten years later, after improving LLTS drive technology and becoming a hero, she was on a scientific ship to a bar where nothing worked, where she would spend another ten years researching with no results.

Now, she was in the middle of the largest construction site in the galaxy, building a wormhole generator to replace a star.

'Yes, I do need a place to stay, and I do need to sleep,' Eli explained to the robots as they tried to leave her on the landing pad after Shan had gone. 'Where can I live? Do you have any hotels here?' she asked one of the robots, who came back, not knowing what to do with her luggage.

Hearing the word 'hotel', together with other words, the robot's quantum brain calculated the proper response and took Eli's luggage to the nearby spacecraft. They arrived in front of a hotel where the attendant robot opened the door and let them in. 'Thank you,' she said, but the robot didn't reply, only bowed in a floaty sort of way. 'That's a tall building, I have to say,' Eli said, looking up.

'The tallest in the city,' the luggage-carrying robot replied. 'Please follow me to the reception area,' it added while opening the door.

'Wow.' Eli didn't know what to say. The hotel was modern, and with a twist. It was named the Sky Hotel, and formerly it had had a remarkably high reception hall with the sky painted on the ceiling, creating a feeling of being outside. Then the robots took their improvement efforts to the next level, and instead of painting the sky, they actually created it inside the hotel. During the day there were floating clouds and a blue sky, and during the night there were stars, planets and even galaxies. It was recreated so perfectly that you could bring your telescope and you wouldn't see the difference. Eli went to the reception area, where a robot receptionist asked her which room she would like.

'The best you have.' *Might as well try*, she thought.

'It's all done. A robot will take you to your room,' the receptionist replied.

'So, do I get a key or a card? Or how do I open the door?' Eli asked.

'The door will open for you automatically,' the receptionist answered.

'Can you wake me up tomorrow at seven am please?' she requested.

'Yes, the wake-up call is now scheduled,' the receptionist replied.

Eli followed one of the robots, and her luggage floated along on a trolley behind her. The hotel room turned out to be very peaceful, and after having spent all day with Shan, she quickly fell asleep. The next day, she woke up to the ringing phone.

'Hello?' she said, trying to rouse herself.

'Good morning. This is your wake-up call as requested,' said the voice on the line.

'Is it seven am?' she asked.

'Yes, it is. Breakfast will be ready on the top floor,' the voice replied.

'Thank you,' Eli replied. She put the phone down and, still lying in bed, looked out of the window.

Her room had the most magnificent view of all the hotels in the city. The bathroom with a big bath had a view of the mountains, and from the other rooms you could see the park, palm trees, the promenade and, of course, the ocean.

Eli got up, walked to the window, and was looking at the ocean, the waves and the sun when suddenly she yawned. She stretched and went into the bathroom. The shower looked ordinary but… there was no soap, no shower gel and most importantly no tap or any other way to turn the water on. *Maybe it's automatic.* She went closer. The shower door automatically opened, she entered, and part of the wall turned into a screen. It displayed her body with all the details about her shower preferences detected from her mind. Water pressure, temperature, pH, shower gel and shampoo ingredients were adjusted for her skin and hair. Two options appeared: Bot Water and Quantum. *Quantum? Bot water until I find out what the quantum shower does. At least it's got 'water' in the name.* She touched the bot-water option. The screen changed to show her head, and bots began gently washing her hair with a mix of water and shampoo. After that, the screen switched to displaying her body again. Water, at the perfect temperature, combined with shower-gel bots, started cleaning her body. (Shampoo and shower-gel bots are nano copies of bigger robots, and they are designed to clean your body instead of a sponge. They not only clean but also repair and improve hair and skin.) After her shower, the door opened onto a heated floor, and a towel was waiting for her. The towel was not for drying herself with, as that was also a job for nanobots, but to gently cover her body. *Wow, she thought, that's what I call a shower, not that thing I have.*

Today was the first day of seeing the robots at work, designing the wormhole generator. Having had few occasions to wear something special at the bar, today Eli wanted to wear something nice. Opening the wardrobe, she saw on the right all the clothes she brought with her – perfectly sorted – and on the left the latest in robot fashion, including an outfit selected for today. Eli pulled out some of the clothes to take a closer look. Some dresses and trousers were very colourful from top to bottom, some were made of a single atom stretched to cover your body, and some took their design from an improved version of abstractionist modern art. Very efficient for keeping you safe and dry but not something Eli wanted to wear, probably ever. She decided to wear her clothes without all the attachments she'd had to use at the bar, and went outside. The floor lit up, showing her how to get to the restaurant, and she followed the path. Breakfast was on a roof terrace covered with improved glass to protect diners from the improved weather. One of the robot waiters came to greet Eli and showed her the table, right next to the open window where she could enjoy the fresh air.

'Thank you,' said Eli. She sat down, and watched robots coming for breakfast and others already eating. The food, or its energy, was somehow transferred to the robots wirelessly or in some cases via cables that led in and out of the plates themselves. *An energy source?* She ordered what the menu called 'Breakfast for Eli', listed as containing hard-boiled eggs, bread and butter, tomatoes, salad, cheese and coffee. The robot waiter, with a towel on one of its arms, brought the food on the floating tray and left, wishing her bon appetite. 'Thank you again,' Eli said, studying her plate. It was remarkably similar to the ones the robots had, but without wires.

'Excuse me,' she said to a robot waiter.

'How can I help?' the robot answered, trying not to drop the plates it was holding.

'Can I have salt and pepper, please?' she asked.

'The amount of salt and pepper in your breakfast equals the amount your body needs until lunch. This breakfast is specially designed for you,' the robot waiter replied.

'OK. How do you know how much salt my body needs?' Eli asked, trying to think when they had checked her body.

'The shower you took this morning did a complete mind and body check.'

'What kind of check?'

'It checks your skin and adjusts the water pH, the shower gel ingredients and the operations of the bots. Additionally, it checks your DNA and mind for food preferences, and your body fat, weight and height. Then it adjusts the ingredients of your meals for perfect nutrition throughout the day,' the robot waiter explained.

'OK, so what does the quantum shower do?'

'The quantum shower remodels your body and at the same time removes all the dirt and dead skin, regenerates your organs, improves what can be improved and fixes all the damage you might have to your body, including DNA,' the robot replied.

'So you send me into sub-quantum space and then change my body on a quantum level?' Eli asked.

'Yes,' the robot confirmed.

'So it's like teleportation?'

'Similar,' the robot agreed.

'So you're telling me you can teleport objects and organic matter, but you're using it as an advanced shower?' Eli asked, puzzled.

'Yes,' the robot confirmed again.

'OK. Can I have some salt and pepper, please?'

The robot brought her what she had asked for.

After she had finished breakfast and also eaten some improved-looking fruit, she went to her room to brush her teeth and freshen up. The toothbrush she found in the bathroom was a bit different to her own. When she took it in her hand a screen appeared above it with two options: Quantum and Bot. *Quantum teeth cleaning? Oh, what the hell.* She selected Quantum. Immediately all her teeth were removed, together with half her jaw, sent to sub-quantum space for cleaning and repair, and put back faster than light can travel. More precisely, with LLTS speed. Although she didn't feel anything at first, quantum cleaning left her with a refreshing mint taste. *Nice!*

* * *

Eli was on her way downstairs when one of the robots appeared and took her up again to the landing pad on the roof. From there, it took her to the research centre where the wormhole generator was being designed. The spacecraft was small with a seat perfectly modelled to Eli's body, and all the controls were in her language. It was yellow and didn't look like it had been created by robots. It was too sleek, and robots were too rectangular.

'This spacecraft is designed for you,' said the robot. 'You can use those two joysticks to control it. You can also control it with your mind.'

'Let me try with joysticks first,' said Eli, sitting in the pilot's chair next to a robot.

Eli knew how to fly various different types of spacecraft, so she quickly learned the simple controls. The improved map built into the dashboard wasn't very convenient, but the holographic projection on the front of the spacecraft showed her where to go.

The former space research centre where robots were designing the wormhole generator was located on a hill about ten kilometres north of the city centre. Eli ignored the route for now, and went to see the ocean and the beach again, listening to the cries of the birds. She arrived at the space centre an hour later, landed on the roof marked with a big sign and went inside, following the robot. The door opened, the floor lit up, and she was guided to the main room through the telelift. The research centre hadn't looked big from above, but what she saw inside was an enormous room with no end in sight. Robots were everywhere, most of them, to her surprise, still using pencil and paper. *Why do they use paper if they're so advanced?* In the middle of it all, the holographic animation displayed both solar systems with a rough design of the generators. A robot came over to her.

'Hello, Eli. You will need this.' The robot showed her a little pill it was holding in its hand.

'What is it?' she asked.

'It's a device which will allow you to understand our language and connect directly to our computers, and it will allow us to use your brain as computing power. Nanobots in this pill will integrate with your brain and replace some of your neurons with more advanced ones,' the robot explained.

'You want to use my brain like a calculator? Wait, what do you mean, replace my neurons?' Eli asked, surprised

'Yes, your brain is very powerful, and we can use it to calculate simple things faster, without sending them to the sub-quantum computers. Your neurons are fast, but we can improve them by replacing them with LLTS neurons to transfer data faster,' the robot explained.

'Am I going to feel anything? Will this do anything to the extension I already have?' Eli asked, trying to swallow the pill.

'Your extension is old and not compatible with our systems, and it will be replaced. You should feel a little jolt in your head, and we will use some parts of your brain dynamically adjusting it, so we will only use the part of your brain that we can, not all of it,' the robot answered.

After swallowing the pill, Eli felt the jolt. Slowly, she started understanding the robots' internal communication system, plus she saw and felt more in general. She looked at the holographic simulation, and it all came to life. She was connected to it. She could change it, and her imagination took over and started projecting her thoughts. At some point, one of the robots had to stop her.

'You can go to that room…' the robot pointed at a door, '…to learn how to use the new features.'

'Sorry, I didn't used to project my thoughts at random,' she explained.

Eli went into the room, the door closed, and everything inside changed to her house. Not the wreckage city, but the caves on her home planet. She was a child again; she saw her parents and all the books she'd read. She saw her siblings, her friends and all the neighbours. After a few moments just feeling dazed, she sat down and started crying. 'I haven't seen my parents in years,' she said.

She started to run through the caves, and the image changed as she went. She was running through the whole planet's cave system to the spacecraft, then she left her world, went to the spaceports, to Shan's garage and finally, the bar. The projection was like a dream, but a very real one. *What am I doing? Pull yourself together… You are strong…* She stopped and started projecting the wormholes again.

'I'm ready,' she said to one of the robots, after leaving the room. The wormhole design projected in the middle of the room, where robots were working, showed a smaller completed version of both systems with added interactive layers. The wormhole generators were of circular construction, rings with a radius almost the size of the star. The robots had started construction already by moving millions of asteroids closer to the star to be mined for resources. Both generators would be built in both places: at the dying star of the robots' planet, and at the star that was going to replace it. Eli's idea was to just remove the dying star and replace it with one from another system. The robots changed that plan and made it more complicated, deciding to swap two stars. They didn't want to annihilate the source solar system even though it was lifeless.

In theory, it was easy. The three-way process would take one hundred and twenty-five milliseconds in total. Firstly, the dying star would be transferred into position below the source star. Secondly, the replacement star would be transported to the place where the dying star had been. Thirdly, the source planets would adjust to the gravity of the new star.

The robots didn't really need Eli's help, and apart from her brain being used as a calculator she spent most of her days learning, understanding and transferring the robots' knowledge to her own mind. OK, that's a lie. The pill allowed her to instantly understand everything she saw. Any printed text was automatically transferred into her mind without reading. Eli understood it all; starting from the oldest entries about artificial comets hitting the planet and starting life, to when the whole civilisation had to leave, to one of the last survivors sent to find the place where comets came from, Shan's grandfather. The whole history of the robots made sense to Eli apart from the last two orders they had been given. The first one was to never try to recreate their kind, and the second was to improve. But she couldn't find any details of either.

* * *

Eli was lying on the grass, so still she might have been dead. She lay on top of the highest hill, not far from the research centre. Her eyes were closed, her heart was pumping blood, and her lungs were pumping oxygen. It was a perfect day to lie on the grass and enjoy the improved greenery. But that was not what Eli was doing. She wasn't there. She was in heaven. Her improved LLTS neurons were transferring data faster than light, allowing her to browse and learn all the vast knowledge of the robots. In her mind, she was flying across regions of the universe unknown to her, that had been discovered by the robots. From the local group of galaxies to clusters to superclusters to attractors to undiscovered blackness beyond.

Thirty days later, with her improved body getting energy without needing to eat, she was still on the same hill. The city was still spread out below, the grass was growing, the birds were flying, and the robots were, well, improving. Eli spent most of the days on this hill as even with improved neurons, her consciousness couldn't absorb all the knowledge of the robots at once. She had to go through it gradually. Reluctantly she woke up, feeling confused. *I want to live forever, I want to go there, to all those places, all those galaxies, meet all those species, know everything, go beyond the universe. See, and experience, everything no one has seen before.*

After all that time spent gathering knowledge, she had forgotten about the nature problem until one day improved poo from an improved bird fell from the improved tree onto Eli's improved hair. That swiftly reminded her, and she accessed the robots' data about it. The first entry displayed a rose bush with its DNA and RNA strands. The robots' long history and experience with genetics allowed them to understand each and every gene, strand, cell, molecule, chromosome, acid, protein, bond and base. With that knowledge, the robots had started to improve rose bushes.

'Hey, robot,' Eli addressed one of them over the LLTS network in virtual sub-quantum chat. 'Am I understanding this correctly?' She displayed the internal structure of the rose plant. 'You moved the colour wavelength of the rose petals, so the bees could see it better. You made the rose smell more strongly, so it could be detected for miles around. You made the pollen tastier and stickier. You improved the plant's water and mineral management.'

'Yes,' the robot replied logically.

'Some other garden robots were still complaining that their roses couldn't grow taller or have more leaves and super-sharp thorns. In response to that request, you injected nano AI bots into the already improved rose to understand what else could be done.' Eli displayed the nanobots and the inner workings of the rose.

'Yes,' the robot replied logically.

'So the nanobots connected to your planet's knowledge network helped the roses to evolve and improve even more. They improved roots so they could absorb new minerals from the soil. The improved soil contained all sorts of minerals and atoms that gave the rose access to all sorts of new building blocks. Cells evolved to use them, and built nano-factories to produce other materials: titanium, steel, fabrics, glass, gases, carbon, aluminium and magnesium. This is ridiculous! There's a whole new rose civilisation out there. That rose is now tall, colourful and indestructible,' Eli finished, trying to digest it all.

'Not only roses, all the plants and animals,' the robot happily replied.

'What?' Eli started searching other improved plants. Super-green grasses, colourful tulips, cacti with indestructible spines that could be used as interplanetary rockets. Oceans of intelligent mosses, spinach that gives you superpowers, tomatoes, potatoes, super-tall and super-strong trees, corals the size of cities, seaweeds covering oceans, and every other plant there was. 'So, this all evolved because of that one bee that collected pollen from an improved rose?' Eli asked.

'Yes,' the robot replied logically.

'Animals?' Eli asked, but she had already started to imagine the improved fauna. 'A tiger with the power to break steel? A cheetah that can run faster than sound, dinosaurs, elephants… and seriously, what the hell happened to the giraffe?' Eli asked, looking at all the animals. She was still amazed when the presentation switched to insects and fish. 'Those are no longer animals. How do they eat if everything in their food chain is indestructible?'

'All the animals can use photosynthesis to get part of the energy they need. They can also produce their own food, and they've learned to use weapons to catch it.'

'This is not an improvement. You have to reverse these changes. The animals need to go back to their original state, how they were before you improved the rose,' Eli explained, but the robot was quiet. Based on earlier experience, she knew it was thinking. Ten minutes later it replied.

'Yes, we can go back. The restore process is in progress.'

'What restore process? You can't simply restore the old order, you have to slowly bring in the original animals and then reprogram those nanobots, so they can work backwards.'

'Our IT department's improved backup and restore process can restore anything to a specific point in time,' the robot explained, and Eli started seeing the restore process in progress. Nature entirely disappeared from the planet, and was replaced by a version taken from a backup copy made before the rose had been improved.

Eli couldn't do this any longer. She disconnected from the virtual network, jumped into her yellow spacecraft which was parked nearby and started flying, somewhere, anywhere, fast, crying as she went.

The improved compass needle was almost spinning as Eli flew in all directions around the planet. Her world had collapsed, the world of knowledge, a world where she was the master, where she knew everything, where she was always a step ahead. Now she was far behind, as the robots' scientific knowledge was beyond anything she had ever imagined.

On her home planet there wasn't much to do. Science wasn't getting anywhere. Her species were deeply divided by civil war and another war in the galaxy meant they had to put all their effort into defences. Her life path had been set since she was born, as had everyone else's. Schools were teaching only the basics to get you through life and towards a military academy that wasn't designed for someone with anxiety. Eli wasn't shy, but the military academy required something she couldn't do; many things actually. From living together in an open-plan dormitory to running for miles with heavy equipment to finally becoming a killing machine. She had a mental block about killing, a barrier she couldn't cross. She wasn't even able to hold a gun. The only military training she attended helped her with self-defence. She was good at it, but only because she was smart and understood she would need it at some point in life. Eventually she escaped, and science became her weapon and a way to deal with everything, including emotions.

After flying around the robots' planet, she slowed down the spacecraft and stopped crying. *What's going on with me? Slow down, start again, don't think too much, take your time...* She had stopped above the now-blue ocean when her spacecraft pointed her to the nearest popular tourist spots. She looked at one of them and recognised it as the place where the comets had fallen. *That's the thing they know least about. Interesting.* Eli's mood changed: finally here was something robots didn't know. Guided by her vessel's built-in map, she flew towards the comet museum and landed on a floating platform.

Eli left the spacecraft, followed the guidelines displayed on the floor and entered the telelift. She was quickly transported to the bottom of the ocean where the enormous improved glass domes contained the perfectly round cores of two comets.

'Hello, Eli, welcome to the comet museum. The current depth is twenty kilometres, and the pressure outside is 1981.36 atmospheres. Please follow the arrows to collect your ticket,' the guide robot explained.

'Great, I'm sure knowing that won't stress me out about that glass dome breaking,' Eli replied, although she knew that it wouldn't happen. She followed the arrows, looking nervously at the ocean behind the glass, which was dark, powerful and sometimes even colourful, lit by improved bulbs and many monstrous bioluminescent fish.

'Hello, Eli,' another guide robot said. 'We will start with the discovery of the comets. A long time ago, with our improved scanning and mapping techniques, we started exploring the oceans. During that time, we explored, mapped, and documented every single atom of the ocean floor and the ocean itself. We found many shipwrecks, guns, gold, buildings and artefacts, but the most important discovery was made here,' the robot guide explained.

'Just show me the comets, please. I know the story,' Eli said, annoyed.

'This way,' the robot replied, opening the door.

'Wow!' Eli said, looking at the comets. They were suspended right in the middle of the museum complex, surrounded by moving viewing platforms. 'Those aren't real comets, are they? I mean, comets don't look like this.' What Eli was seeing were two perfectly round comet nuclei, ten metres in diameter.

'Originally, they were about ten kilometres in diameter, but when they entered the atmosphere, the surrounding rock was destroyed, leaving these,' the robot explained and pointed at the comets.

'What are those markings? What are they made of? What's inside? How can that glass withstand the pressure?' Eli asked a lot of questions, forgetting she already knew the answers.

'We were unable to decipher the markings, we never determined the material those comets are made of, and the glass is made from a mix of transparent titanium, carbon and graphene,' the robot replied.

Eli's curiosity took over like a drug. She controlled the viewing platform, moving her hands and fingers over the strange shapes. She could feel them, metallic and unchanged for millions of years. Some of the symbols were like nothing she'd seen before. At first sight, they were randomly placed all over the comets. Some were just dots, squares or symbols of any shape you could imagine, and others seemed to represent flowers, animals, machines, devices, stars, galaxies, aliens, plants, trees and fish. Eli accessed all the robots' knowledge about the comets, and found out that all attempts to understand or destroy them had been unsuccessful, even in sub-quantum space. Whatever they were, whoever had built them was more powerful than the robots. She couldn't find anything in the robots' knowledge base that could help; she was on her own. *Finally*.

The robots had tried to find patterns they recognised, but had found nothing, and after only a brief period of research built this museum. Eli looked at one of the shapes; it wasn't big, maybe an inch across, but scored so deeply into the surface that you couldn't see the bottom. One thing she did find was the highly accurate scan of the comets the robots had made. From a normal point of view, it was nothing exciting, but a closer look revealed that each shape was only an atom thick, and behind each atom-thick shape was another shape, which was also an atom thick and divided by a few atoms, and so on. More interesting was the fact that each figure had precisely the thickness of an atom. That meant, Eli calculated, that there were at least ninety-four billion and three hundred and fifty million layers.

'Hey, robot,' Eli said to one of the guides.

'Yes?' it replied, waiting for further instructions.

'Do you have a torch or some light?'

'No,' the robot replied logically, not having any.

'Can you bring me some?' Eli asked, irritated.

'Yes.' The robot did so. It was a small keyring torch from the museum shop.

'That will do for now. Wow! It's powerful.' Eli tested the keyring, and she almost blinded herself with the light.

'Yes, we improved the LED, cooling and power source in this keyring,' the robot explained.

'I can *see* that,' Eli replied and aimed the light into one of the shapes carved into the comet. There turned out be nothing of interest in there. Next, she projected the scan of the comets next to the real one to see all the shapes, but the room was a bit too small for all the billions of layers. She went outside to her ship and flew high above the ocean, projecting the comet's scanned structure. The projection was a 3D image of endless spheres stretching from the ocean's surface all the way to space. It was enormous, and only when she adjusted the projection to the size of the planet itself could she see a few layers so she could fly between shapes as if between planets. *It's a map?* Eli thought, and for the next few weeks, she ran comparisons of each shape against all the constellations and planets known to the robots. The results returned absolutely nothing... or, more precisely, absolutely everything. The vast number of shapes gave too many results, and after a few more weeks, Eli gave up. She decided to travel for a while, and for the next few weeks, she visited every part of the robots' planet, as well as all the colonies, learning the robots' knowledge as she went. Nature went back to normal, and the robots kept on improving other things.

* * *

After spending weeks travelling, sightseeing, trekking, thinking, and enjoying herself, she finally found a place that seemed too perfect to be true. The house she rented was located on the most beautifully improved lake, half the planet away from the city where she and Shan had first arrived. It was there she discovered the meaning of the 'improve' command that had been given to the robots.

'Hi, robot. Why don't you fix this building?' Eli asked one of the robots who were cleaning the street next to a tumbledown house.

'Fix?' The robot was a bit confused.

'Yes, fix, improve, you know. Fix that hole in the wall, repair the roof, that kind of stuff,' Eli tried to explain logically.

'We've already improved that building.'

'It doesn't look improved to me. It's completely derelict, almost falling down.' Now Eli was even more confused.

The robot pointed at the remaining part of a half-collapsed wall. 'We improved all the edges, dust, holes and bricks in this wall, and now it looks more derelict. We improved the derelict building to look improved-derelict.'

'OK, does the same apply to that hole in the road?' Eli asked, pointing at it.

'Yes, we improved the hole so it's more like a proper hole.'

'Grass, rubbish, jobs, paint, the light, too?'

'We improved all those.'

'So that's why you never fix stuff, but come to Shan instead. You can only improve things.'

'Yes,' the robot confirmed.

Now she understood that the robots had taken their final order entirely literally. So they were not only improving technology, but every job there was, including sellers, cleaners, receptionists, scientists, politicians, baristas, farmers, soldiers, pilots and even hotel guests. But that wasn't all: when they saw a hole in the street, they didn't fix it, they improved it. They found a balance between the hole and the road itself, which shouldn't really have had a hole in it, but that wasn't their way of thinking. Repairing that hole in the road wasn't an improvement for them: making the hole more hole-y, that was an improvement. With perfect roads, you don't need to improve cars, but with perfect holes, you could drive a car with the robots' improved suspension through a minefield, and you wouldn't feel a thing. They improved dust, rubbish, water, rain, snow, flowers, holes, cracks, graffiti, prisons, tables, radios, TVs, music, music festivals, fashion, glass, grass, lawnmowers, cameras, photography, wars, weddings, funerals, cables, wires, seas, oceans and every single thing they could find, even the coal and oil deep inside the mines.

* * *

Eli was lying on her bed feeling bored, refusing to think about her home planet, or robots. She tried to watch improved films and TV series, but soon gave up on that and turned her thoughts to Shan. He was now in another galaxy; he was living her dream, travelling and meeting other species. Ironically, she was living her other dream, improving the knowledge in her brain beyond her understanding.

She followed Shan's progress on a projected map, as she still couldn't get used to seeing things directly in her mind. The galaxy he had gone to was beautiful, with stars and rings and planets and... *Wait a fucking minute...* Eli stood up as quickly as her improved muscles allowed, zoomed out of the galaxy, and then she saw it. Multiple stars in an almost circular shape. *This could just be a coincidence. It's unusual... but what if it isn't a coincidence?* She began talking to herself and quickly started a second scan to compare all the shapes from the comets with all known galaxies, using improved input parameters. *Too much data... I need to focus on one, maybe two shapes... OK, the circle, let's start simple.* She ran a comparison between all the circles on the comets to the circle of stars in Shan's galaxy. *Yes!* This time she had the right number of results to work with: precisely one.

Now this place. Eli projected the map of her own galaxy, but it contained no significant shapes. She checked the brightness of the stars that made the circle shape in Shan's galaxy, and discovered they were almost identical. She checked for stars in her galaxy with the same intensity: nothing.

She kept changing the brightness until she found stars arranged in the right shape. Both galaxies were on the same comet shape layer, next to each other. Next, she tried to run the algorithm in the sub-quantum computer, but lack of synthesis between her brain and the robots' computer resulted in too much data again. She had to become one with it.

The idea was simple, and the connection was simple too, but the risk was huge. Goe connecting her brain to a regular computer was one thing; Eli's LLTS neurons directly linking to the fabric of the universe was another. Her curiosity took over again, and she asked the nanobots to join one of her neurons directly to the sub-quantum computer – the location of which was oddly unknown even to the robots, but the connection was established. One neuron wasn't enough to calculate all that data in a reasonable amount of time, so she instructed the nanobots to connect all her body's neurons, nerves, cells, and everything else that could be linked. *Well, what could possibly go wro…*

At this point, her senses stopped working. She would have appeared dead to someone checking her pulse. She wasn't here, she was there, on the other side; she had connected herself to the universe and become a sub-quantum ghost. Her vision changed; she didn't have eyes anymore, or a nose, arms, body, or organs. All normality disappeared. Physically she was still in her room, but she couldn't see it anymore. She couldn't see the bed, the carpet, the lake or even the house, but particles, atoms of the gases that made up the air, forces, radio waves and the house's old-style improved Wi-Fi. She became an atom, a quark, a sub-quantum particle; she became the fabric of the universe itself. She was enjoying it, she was finally in her heaven, her paradise where she was the goddess, the goddess of knowledge and science; she saw everything. She flew far above the galaxy, seeing the unseen, the pure energy the universe was built on, the stars, the black holes, the planets, the dark matter, everything.

After a while, she reminded herself why she was doing this. She projected the map from one of the comets, resizing it to the original scale, mapping it onto the two galaxies she knew and the shapes she'd found. The map matched perfectly. Now she was flying towards the centre of the comets' nuclei at incredible speeds – when she felt her body's senses again, and woke up in shock. Suspended in an anti-gravity ring in the space centre, she started screaming.

'Where am I? Why have you disconnected me?' Eli demanded of the robots when her consciousness returned to normality.

'You were using too much power. The further you go, the more power you need to keep connected. If you get disconnected, you will stay as a ghost forever,' one of the robots replied.

'Take me down!' Eli demanded.

The robots took Eli down to the floor, and she ran to the roof to pick up her ship, calling it as she went. She flew high into the air again, projecting the maps from the first comet onto the map of known galaxies. It fitted perfectly, but the second comet didn't fit any galaxies. *I need to go there, to Shan's galaxy, to find more comets. I think they were sent to all these places. It's all some kind of puzzle map; the second one must show another part of the universe. I need to go to the centre.*

* * *

A month later, Eli was standing in the design room, checking the robots' data. She was kind of bored at this stage as the robots were mostly busy building the generators, and she was browsing their knowledge base. She didn't want to enter the sub-quantum universe at this point without learning more, as deep down in her mind she was scared. Only when she had come back from being a ghost did she realise what she had done, and that she had almost died. Now she needed to find more comets, but the only things she could do were think and wait. She was browsing the robots' gallery of simulations, just out of curiosity when she found the section on the forthcoming collision of galaxies. She turned it on, sped it up, and then something unexpected happened.

'What is that?' a confused Eli suddenly asked a robot that was flying to one of the generator construction rooms, almost making it fall out of the air.

'It's a simulation of the galaxies colliding,' the robot replied.

'I can see that, but why is the collision not happening in your simulation?'

That confused the robot even more, but it replied, 'The collision will not happen.'

'Yes, it will. Look, those are our calculations and our simulation,' Eli switched the simulation to the one everyone was familiar with, projected from her brain.

'Those calculations are wrong,' the robot replied after quickly confirming the maths.

Eli was really annoyed, almost angry, now. She closed her eyes, took a deep breath, and said: 'WHERE?'

'You are missing one parameter,' the robot said.

'Every single civilisation in this galaxy has checked those calculations, and everyone knows the collision is going to happen. What parameter?'

'The bar,' said robot.

'The *bar*?' echoed Eli.

'The bar,' repeated the robot.

'Aghhhh! Where is the bar on your simulation, and why would I need it anyway?'

'The bar planet is in the path of the collision, and as nothing works at the bar, the collision won't work.'

'So your theory is based purely on that? Seriously?' Eli demanded.

'Yes.'

'Do you know who built this bar?' Eli was now completely lost.

'We did.'

Hearing that, Eli almost collapsed. '*You did?*'

'We did.'

'Why?' Eli replied, trying not to throw something at the robot.

'To stop the collision,' it answered, logically.

'Seriously! I'm going to jump out of this window,' Eli closed her eyes and took a deep breath, trying to calm down.

'Why are you going to jump out of this window? You cannot open this window, but the windows on the floors above you can. If you jump from the floors above, the chances of your survi…' said the robot, but Eli interrupted.

'OK, robot, tell me who built the bar and why, and tell me its whole history.'

'Our creators knew about the collision a long time ago, before they created us. At that time, the collision was millions of years into the future, and no one had the technology to escape or to stop it. Once our creators invented sub-quantum technology and made us, they built the bar to stop the collision. You can read its full history in our database,' the robot explained.

'Well, I kind of ignored the collision and the bar in your database because I thought I knew everything about them. Anyway, how will the bar stop the collision?'

'The bar was designed to extend the "won't work" field further the closer it gets to the centre of the collision. When the galaxies get close enough to enter the field, they will be directed away from each other,' the robot replied.

'The "won't work" field? What kind of scientific name is that?'

'Our creators called it that because they didn't know how the "won't work" field works. It was created accidentally.'

'So all those thousands of years of wars and killing could have been prevented? The war could have been stopped a long time ago? I spent ten years of my life in that bar, and you're telling me this now? Fuck me, I need a break.'

Eli went for a walk, projecting some of her thoughts in front of her as she pondered the latest revelation. Should she say anything to Shan? Should she say anything to anyone?

With this simple piece of news, she could fix at least some problems and hopefully stop the wars.

But as with the LLTS drive, it was a moment and instinct to tell everyone, this time it felt different, more serious. She was sitting on a beach listening to the ocean and watching the sunset. A robot came and offered her a cold cocktail with a little paper umbrella in it. Another robot came to give her a massage, another to take her on a trip. More robots were lying on the sand simulating sunbathing and enjoying the sunset or sailing around in boats like their creators.

A couple of hours later she woke from a nap. The ocean was still there, and some robots, too. It was dark and calm here, with the sound of robots enjoying the music at a nearby bar. She was in paradise, far away from the wars and killings. Then she reminded herself of the stories about how the galaxy had been a paradise before the wars. Now it could be again. *Shan will be here soon. I need to tell him, I need him...*

CHAPTER SEVEN

Eli watched the robots' building work from orbit high above the star. She was feeling absent again; not that she was connected to the universe, but since she'd found out that the collision wouldn't happen, her mind had been somewhere else. That knowledge was scary, mostly because to keep such a secret from the entire population of a couple of galaxies was a huge burden. *Once this is done, I will visit my parents; life is too short not to see them again.* A million thoughts were running through her head; life, family, the bar, the galaxy, the collision, Shan. She was thinking about him more often now, not just as a friend anymore. Now there was another idea. With the robots' technology and her knowledge, she could realise her dream, and a new goal, or at least part of it. To travel to the farthest places in the universe, not just a single galaxy or local group. To the centre of the universe, to the centre where the comets had come from, and maybe not alone. *Perhaps Shan would join me?*

Seeing Shan's spacecraft docking at the robots' station, Eli closed her eyes, trying to clear her mind. Thanks to the pill the robots had given her, she could do it quite literally.

A few moments later, Shan entered the room. 'So, this is it,' he said.

'Hello, stranger. Long time, no see. How was the trip?' Eli turned towards Shan and tried to smile.

'It was…' Shan paused for a moment, 'interesting. I don't recommend living in my spacecraft for thirty days. I had to stop once just to see some stars.' He came closer to the window, stood next to Eli, and they both looked at the generator. 'The other galaxy is suitable for us, for everyone really. I met Sork there.'

'Sork?' Eli wondered if she was supposed to know this person.

'A guy, tencta, from our Sector Three. He's still in the other galaxy, exploring it. He was sent there as a sole explorer from his species. I partially explored the first and second sectors there, and he's doing the rest. I came because I didn't want to miss what's happening here. It's quite a circle,' Shan was admiring the machinery the robots had built.

'It is. I still can't believe we're doing it. Replacing a star, who would have thought?' Eli paused for a moment. 'Tell me more about the other galaxy.' She needed to take her mind off the collision, and they both sat down on a sofa opposite the window.

'I learned a lot, not only about the galaxy but about myself, too. It's weird; the more you're alone, the more you know about yourself. If you know what I mean?'

'I do. My time here taught me something about myself, too. I've learned more in a few months than I did in ten years in the wreckage city,' Eli replied, still deep in thought.

'Can't wait to hear all about it. The other galaxy is like ours, but only half the size, and we've already divided it into four sectors and layers. It's full of life, full of beautiful planets and species. Not as advanced as we are, but advanced enough to know and to understand the universe. Some species are too primitive, and I haven't visited them much, only a few times to get some fresh air and clean organic water. I even found coffee! Hopefully, they didn't see me in those fields,' said Shan.

'You shouldn't be doing this. They don't have galactic wars so… they're still protected,' Eli replied, slowly shifting her thoughts to the new topic.

'Yeah, about that… Wait till you hear more.' Shan smiled hugely.

'I don't think I like that smile. Something happened, right?' Eli asked, remembering Shan's earlier adventures.

'Well, the short version is that I kind of helped with a revolution and removed a few presidents and one king and managed to get loads of data from some wreckage I found. My love of old ships and stuff almost killed me.'

'Removed some presidents and a king? Well, that's the "no involvement" policy out of the window. And the data?'

'That's how I've learned about the place, about lots of different species in that galaxy. I collected so many data disks I lost count. I know about so many species, their technologies, their lives, and struggles, it's amazing. I'd love to collect all of it and put it in some museum.'

'I know,' Eli said.

'After all that travelling I want more. To travel more, see more. We're living in an infinite universe. This was just the next galaxy; imagine the whole universe! Imagine all those data drives and artefacts I can collect.' Shan was extremely excited, describing his journeys. Clearly, he'd caught the travel bug. 'I've no idea how I spent all those years in the garage.'

'The robots are starting,' Eli told Shan when she received the data from the robots, sent directly into her mind. They both walked to the window, and one of the robots asked Eli to check if everything was correct as per her request.

'They ask you for advice? Do you think they got all the calculations right?' Shan asked, wondering how robots could be wrong.

'One thing I've learned here is that they have no instincts. So I asked them to ask me before they start, just in case. It looks good to my instincts and to me,' Eli told the robot after quickly glancing at the data.

'Are we going to see anything?' Shan asked, watching the generator.

'Not much. It will take a hundred and twenty-five milliseconds to complete. I'm recording the whole thing. I want to see it in slow motion,' Eli said, trying not to blink. She was watching the generator work with her eyes, and at the same time trying to keep the projection running together with another view in her mind. Since she'd got the pill, she'd been training her mind to do more than one thing at once.

'Look,' Shan pointed at the generator, which was starting to light up.

Eli began projecting status messages onto the panoramic window.

- Raising MC shields,
- CPLD is powering up,
- EMP is loading,
- Transfer in progress,
- Lowering MC shields,
- Transfer complete.

'Aaaand it's done. I'm a bit disappointed, I must say,' Eli replied, then added, 'Good job I have it all recorded.'

'Sorry, but if you want more excitement, we'll have to go back to the old days of space wormholes. Back then, it was a trade.' Shan's fondness for history took over his thoughts for a moment. 'People did it as a family business. Passing knowledge from generation to generation. There weren't many people left doing it after LLTS, and your improvement killed the rest.'

'Very funny, and I know, but they're still there. We still use wormholes, but they have issues, and they're dangerous, but to be honest, every innovative technology brings that. Every industrial revolution we've ever had caused disruption to the economy, to people's lives and to everything else. Remember what the second electrical revolution did? That's life,' Eli replied, then added, walking back to the sofa, 'There's nothing more to see, now they'll dismantle the generator and recycle it. They'll take us down to the surface now.'

'How is it all possible? Well, I know how, but it's still amazing,' Shan said, following Eli.

'You know how with chemical rockets and a light drive you're pushing yourself forward, kind of?'

'Yes,' Shan replied, already knowing the answer.

'LLTS doesn't work like that. You're using enormous energy to get into the sub-quantum levels, and then the universe pushes you around like an ocean current, but by squeezing you. You only need energy to get there; once you're inside, you can easily control your path. If you want to go faster, you need to go deeper, but it gets kind of easier once you're there. That's why you can't travel slowly or control your speed at will. You have to go as fast as the current, which is why we have speeds of one, two, three, and so on, corresponding to a specific sub-quantum level. The deeper you get, the faster you go.'

'Yes, I know exactly how LLTS drives work. I've been fixing them for years. I meant this.' He pointed at the generator.

'Sorry, I know, I just needed to add LLTS context first. 'Wormhole' is a bit of a misleading term, anyway. A long time ago, before we actually tried to use one, a wormhole was thought to be like a tunnel. Only after further research, and attempts to build one, did we find that the tunnel wasn't there at all. The wormhole generator doesn't create holes or tunnels. It bends space, kind of. What we're doing here is using LLTS with wormhole technology. That was the improvement the robots made, because my idea was to use only wormholes.

'I understand how this works, but it's so extreme and ridiculous that it's not easy to explain. I can see it in my mind, all the calculations, and it's still difficult. I mean, using wormholes inside sub-quantum space, it's just beyond imagination, but it works. Anyway, we have a single ring above each star. First, we move the generators to sub-quantum space using LLTS. To keep it stationary we have to use enormous energy, that's why the generators are so big, not because they have to be bigger than the star. Keeping them stationary in sub-quantum space is what puzzles me most; somehow the robots were able to keep this enormous machine stationary against the sub-quantum forces. Once they are in sub-quantum space, the wormhole part takes over, bending the sub-quantum space and moving the star to the other system. Meanwhile, the second generator is moving the other star back here. The universe is bending together with the star in sub-quantum, so from the star's point of view, nothing is happening. Like when you're in your spacecraft: you're actually moving, but not relative to the ship.' The more she talked about her favourite subject, the less she was thinking about the collision.

'Makes sense,' Shan replied, understanding the concept, 'but tell me about the robots. You've spent some time here, and I'm sure it was an interesting experience.' Shan wanted to hear everything as, apart from his previous visit to this planet, his interaction with robots had mostly consisted of fixing their ships.

'There's a lot to tell,' Eli replied, hoping he would say yes, so she could continue concentrating on something other than the collision.

'We have time, and that sofa is super comfortable.'

'They're easy to control. Just tell the robots something is or isn't an improvement and they will do it or not do it. That's how I told them to remove the nanobots they'd implanted in nature, and it's fine now.'

'So nature is fixed?'

'Yes, but not how you might think it would be. I had to explain to them that improving nature in that way is not actually an improvement,' Eli replied, then after a pause continued, 'Their knowledge goes well beyond moving stars, Shan. This is much bigger than any revolution we've had, even bigger than the second electrical revolution. I tried to use our mathematics to move this star, but it gets so complicated that our maths isn't enough to even comprehend it, let alone do it. The robots have improved maths to a point where it's not maths as we know it anymore. They don't have numbers or signs or even calculations. They don't just compute, they somehow send the raw data into the fabric of the universe using not quantum, but sub-quantum computers. The universe is like a giant AI supercomputer and they've hacked into it.

'They implanted nanobots and LLTS wires in my brain to help me communicate with them, and that opened a floodgate of information into my mind. Shan, I saw things, I saw so much, experienced so much, failed to understand so much and understood everything... I can't explain it. My mind simply can't comprehend it. Sub-quantum space is vibrating, it's creating, it's destroying, it's beautiful, and scary. We and everything else are being created and destroyed at the same time, constantly, even now. Atom by atom, quark by quark, force by force.

'What I also found out is that we may not go deeper into the universe but to the other side of it, to an anti-universe. Something we used to believe in, then we rejected it, and now we may find out it's true. Whatever that even means – the other side. The robots can go well below all the forces, particles, quarks, and everything we know. I tried to understand all of it, but it's so difficult. It's like old theories: we used to think we could go deeper, to the lower dimensions, but we proved a long time ago that they don't exist. They used to be part of our everyday physics, and lectures, and maths, and equations, and all kids would learn

224

about them, but they don't exist. I mean, mathematically they do, but they are no longer useful for understanding the universe.

'The robots' technology operates at a level of complexity way beyond that. Their knowledge far transcends our understanding of the universe. It goes beyond particles, dimensions, non-existent time, everything. They can travel deep in sub-quantum space, they have radar in sub-quantum, they can build stars and planets, they can move stars in sub-quantum space using LLTS and wormholes. Somehow, they've plugged themselves into the universe, into its very fabric and even lower, into the interface of the universe itself. How fucked up is that? Tell me, please, am I so stupid? Are we all so stupid we don't understand? You have no idea how many times I've thought about becoming a robot to understand it all. I even dived into the fabric of the universe, I almost flew to the centre of something, some universe. I almost became a ghost forever but the robots brought me back. I personally saw sub-quantum particles, quarks, atoms, forces, waves and the fabric of the universe itself, for fuck's sake.' Eli didn't want to stop talking, and in frustration, she put her head between her hands and bent over to rest them on her knees.

'Eli, it's OK.' Shan hugged her. 'I'm sure we'll understand this at some point.'

'What's the purpose of a fridge?' Eli asked quietly, seemingly at random.

'What? To keep food fresh? It isn't that difficult. The fridge, I mean,' he replied sarcastically.

'Yes, I know, but what would make the perfect fridge?'

'I don't know. I guess the one that can freeze to absolute zero?'

'That would be a perfect freezer.'

'Right. And?' Shan was trying to understand the meaning of that conversation.

'Well, this is one of many things that surprised me on the robots' planet. The improved fridge.'

'I'm listening.'

'Are you ready for this?' Shan nodded and Eli went on, 'OK... The perfect fridge would be the one that can stop time inside it. That way you could keep the food indefinitely. But now you're thinking about time. Time doesn't exist, so how is that possible? Well, yes, time doesn't exist, or the flow of time, but what the robots did is something unexpected. They replaced the pump inside the fridge with a fucking black hole. Again, I'm sorry for swearing. Actually, I'm not sorry, because this is ridiculous,' Eli explained, closing her eyes again.

'What? That's impossible.'

'Yes, you heard me. Basically, rather than stopping time, the small black hole prevents the food from going bad by stopping its molecules, atoms and everything else from moving. That's how the fridge in your ship works,' Eli explained.

'Does it? It looks normal, and I don't see any difference. Anyway, I can somewhat understand this, but how do you get food to and from it? How do you trap the black hole inside? As far as I know, there's a limit to how small black holes can be.' Shan had not seen a black hole in his ship.

'Well, the time and the flow of time itself don't exist. But you, and I, and atoms and quarks and metal and air and forces and quantum space do. You can touch these things, measure them, but time, you can't. There is no past and future; there is no such thing. Only now exists, and movement, and the vibrations of particles, which we experience as time,' Eli explained. 'I mean, it's easier if I show you the fridge later, or if you take that pill with nanobots. Oh, and changing the subject, I did get ill there, once. It was just a cold and a headache, nothing serious, but it helped me to learn about their doctors. It's simple: you just go to the doctor, who is a robot with some kind of active skin that can change to a medical outfit. He or she – well, they don't really have genders, although actually they do, but that's a long discussion… Anyway, so the robot doctor checked my lungs and my temperature, like a normal doctor, nothing advanced really. I could have gone to that advanced shower and been cured, but I wanted to see their doctors. The robot doctor gave me some pills and a nose spray. I asked about the shower, and the robot said the shower would cure me straight away of any diseases I had.'

'So why didn't they just tell you to have a shower?' Shan asked.

'Because the shower is an improvement for a bathroom, not medicine. The original pills cured you in eight days, so they kept them. The improvements to the pills are that there are no side effects, and nanobots do all the work, plus they can actually tell you why you have a headache. So you see, they have a shower that can cure you, but they give you pills anyway.

'The robots copied their creators, doing everything they did, just an improved version of it. I saw them sunbathing. They sell drinks and ice cream and can even give you a massage. You've seen the coffee shops; they go to work, and they do their work. All the shops are open, all the businesses. Transport, cars, planes, spaceships, mines, and they even fish. I took a train, a real train, imagine that. It goes all around the world. A seriously improved train, but still; and it's all operated by robots. They copied their government too, but it's an improved version with improved arguments, and improved logical thinking to work out what's really best for everyone. They have no wars, no hunger and no disease. Well, they actually have wars and all that, but I would have to show you what they entail for you to believe it. Because they've even improved suffering, pain, and happiness.

'I know they're not biological and don't need food, but they've found a way to produce food without destroying the planet, and they've found a cure for every single disease there is. They only use natural energy sources. No pollution, and they've removed CO2 and cleaned the air and recycled all the rubbish on their planet, including nuclear waste and plastic. The funny thing is, they improved the recycling process, but they didn't stop producing rubbish. They carry on so they can use those recycling machines. They produce CO2 so they can use machines to remove it.

'They've explored the deepest caves, the volcanoes and the deepest places in the oceans. Their maps are so perfectly detailed and accurate that there is no possibility of getting lost. Their GPS system can actually tell you exactly where the needle in the haystack is. They know everything there is to know about their solar system, this galaxy and many more galaxies. They live as if nothing has changed: you could put them in their creators' skin and you wouldn't see the difference. They are explorers, travellers, scientists, bakers, owners, politicians, soldiers, peacemakers, brewers, cooks, farmers, office workers, and everyone else. You see, if there's a hole in something, they don't fix it, they improve the hole. That's their way of thinking. They use pens and paper. Why? Because they've improved pens and paper and the writing system. For them replacing paper or fixing a hole is not an improvement.

'There was a building in a pretty bad condition. Instead of fixing it they improved it by demolishing even more of it. I was going to explain that to them, but I've already changed the galaxy too much with LLTS, so I don't want to interfere with other species. They've invented teleportation, and you know what they use it for? For an advanced fucking shower, and I used that shower. You know what it did? I saw a report; I may live forever actually. They've fixed everything there was to fix in my body, every single cell, every single DNA strand, every organ, and even every single neuron has been checked, and most of them actually replaced. I have nanobots and improved motor proteins in my body that are constantly fixing it and helping with DNA and cell replication. How seriously fucked up is that? Sorry for my swearing, but it's just incredible.'

'So we might both live forever then. The robots improved my shower too, it's the same one.'

'How? I didn't see it when I was on your ship.'

'Because I asked them to keep one ordinary shower, the one in your room. I sometimes need old-style water. Also, you just helped me to make a decision.'

'Oh, OK. What decision?'

'About rebuilding the robots' original civilisation,' Shan replied. 'I can't recreate them here. It's the robots' planet now, I need to find a new world for my kind.'

* * *

The spacecraft Eli and Shan had flown in to see the star replacement process landed on top of the space centre. Eli stood up and said, 'Let's go, I have something important to show you.' Her face turned grave.

'Should I be worried?'

Eli just smiled at him. The kind of expression people use when the situation is too serious for smiling, but they have to do it anyway.

The space centre was a glossy-looking building, with windows and walls that supplied the energy to run everything. Inside, robots were busy with another project and with general improvement programs. Eli took Shan's hand and pulled him into one of the rooms, where she had initially learned to project her thoughts.

'There's something I need to tell you. And I'm sorry, but there's no easy way to explain it, so I'll just show you. It's a bigger surprise than what you told me about the bar, and the LLTS drive,' Eli told Shan, closing the door.

'Now I'm worried.'

'It's not bad news, it's actually amazingly great news.'

'I don't understand.'

'Look, this is our collision simulation.' Eli projected the simulation from her mind into the room.

'Looks normal to me.'

'Yes. Now look, this is the simulation created by the robots.' In fast-forward mode, the simulation showed galaxies failing to collide with each other.

'That doesn't look normal,' Shan said, surprised. He walked around the projected image wondering at it.

'Why do you think the robots don't want to escape? Why they don't care? Why in all the negotiations they said no and wanted to stay?'

'You're starting to worry me now,' said Shan. The idea that the collision might not happen appeared in some of his neurons deep inside his brain.

'There will be no collision, Shan! They knew that all along.' Eli started to walk around again. 'I heard rumours it might not happen, but those were just stories told by crazy guys. But it's true!'

'I heard those stories too, but how is everyone else wrong and the robots right?' Shan asked, remembering doing the calculations himself.

'Because they will prevent it! They built a device to stop it.'

'Where is it? It would have to be pretty big to stop all those galaxies.'

'The bar,' Eli said, calling up a hologram of it.

'The bar?' Shan said, surprised.

'The bar,' replied Eli. 'Yes, the bar where I spent the last ten years of my life, trying to work out its purpose. The planet where it's located crosses the path of the galaxies during the collision, and its "won't work" field will expand, thus deflecting the galaxies. The robots built the bar for that purpose.'

Shan was looking at Eli with an inscrutable expression, something like sarcastic confusion.

'Now you know how I felt when you told me about moving a star and other surprises,' Eli said.

'So, we don't have to move, we can stop all the wars and suffering. If you'd told me that before I wouldn't have had to spend all that time in the other galaxy. Sork is still there exploring for no reason, and his species used most of their resources to send him there. Why didn't you tell me or anyone? We have to tell everyone!' Shan was both happy and a bit angry at the same time.

'Yes, we do, but not yet. We need to think about this and decide what to do, and I need your help with it. This one revelation will change this galaxy forever. For now, let's celebrate; we did move two stars and stopped some galaxies from colliding today. That's enough impossible things to do before dinner,' Eli replied, and walked out of the room.

* * *

The replacement of the star was that night celebrated on all the robots' planets and colonies, for many reasons. For the robots, the most important was the restoration of nature and the replacement of the star that had been a threat to their existence. For Eli and Shan it was the averted collision. At Eli's request the robots started possibly the largest party in the galaxy. They drank, danced, sang and launched significantly improved fireworks for the whole night, with Eli and Shan as guests of honour. The next day, they woke up without a hangover on the big bed in the best apartment on the top floor of the best hotel in the city.

'We might not stop all the wars, but averting the collision might help a bit. You said you wanted to travel more,' Eli said to Shan as she lay next to him. 'I have a plan for that if you'd like to join me.'

'Tell me.'

'There isn't much for me to do here anymore, and with the robots' technology, I can partially realise my dream.'

'And that dream is?'

'To explore the universe.'

'Explore the universe. Sounds easy,' Shan said with a hint of sarcasm.

'I'm serious,' Eli said and stood up. 'We need a spaceship, a big one. I used the robots' computers to design it and calculate everything, and they actually started building it from all those resources left after disassembled generators. I even found another speed for LLTS – six – but I'm not sure if the robots can achieve that. I asked them, though. I don't even know what speed six would be in light years.' Eli started explaining, talking about her favourite subject again. 'Mathematically it's correct, but I don't think it's really possible. It would mean going to an even lower level of the universe, and I don't know if there are any lower levels. At LLTS 5, we could easily explore our local group. In one quantum year, we can travel over one gigaparsecs, and our local group of galaxies is a fraction of that. Imagine the possibilities! We could even go to the centre of the universe, wherever that might be.' Eli was extremely excited.

Shan was still lying in bed, trying to follow. 'And what's the size of the universe? What would we live on for all that time? The centre of the universe? How far is that? What's a quantum year?'

'Quantum year? Over one gigaparsec at LLTS 5. I just came up with it. Anyway, we would install cryo-pods, and take a couple of robots to manage everything. Thanks to those showers, we may already live forever anyway. To the centre? No idea. Can be twenty thousand parsecs under the quarks or any other number. The universe is too big to explore, but it's a start, and I've discovered something even robots don't know. You see how awesome I am?'

'What is it?'

'Your grandfather told you about comets that started a life here, remember?'

'Yes.'

'I found them. There are two of them.' Eli projected the comets into the air of the hotel room. 'Ten metres in diameter, each with different shapes embedded in them. It's a map!' Eli couldn't hide her excitement. 'Shan, it's a map! A map of all the galaxies, the map that precisely fits this galaxy, and the one you went to, and many others.' Eli focused on the second comet. 'The shapes on the other comet don't fit any galaxies we know, but I think it's part of a puzzle and we need to find more comets. I found the location of another system in the galaxy you went to, where we might find them. We need to go there,' Eli explained, projecting the map of the other galaxy while Shan got up from the bed to look at it more closely.

'I'll come. But there's one more thing we need to do; well, two things. Actually, three or maybe even four,' Shan said, thinking.

'What do you mean?'

'We have to tell everyone about the collision. That's the first thing.'

'Yes, we have to. Otherwise, everyone will keep killing each other. There's no point to that, we've had too many wars, and too many worlds have been destroyed already – and for what? Look at us, we sleep here in this wonderful place on a nice bed, we have everything we want. When I was born, I had nothing, we had nothing. Some people on my home planet still have nothing. It's a terrible place. I'm terrible, too; I haven't been there for years, I mean my home planet. No, I'm not terrible, well I am, a bit, but compared to others I'm OK.'

'It's OK, Eli, we all have little wars inside ourselves. It's OK to have one,' Shan said, trying to cheer her up.

'Anyway, we can't stop all the wars, but at least we can stop a few. Everyone should understand how small we are: one quantum year, over one gigaparsecs, and still this is nothing, completely nothing. Compared to the universe we are nothing, so what's the point of all that killing? The only point is in exploring, to find where the universe goes, how big it is, and to find everything, and now we can.'

'OK, first, we tell everyone about the not happening collision, and the bar, then we go to the garage. Goe needs to take over and send someone here to the robots so they can build their own garage planet. I can't close the garage, it's people's jobs, and a new garage planet will give jobs to millions. It will help fix all those damaged spacecrafts. Then we'll go to see my family and yours. After that, we'll go exploring.'

'Sounds like a plan,' Eli replied, smiling. 'What's the other thing you wanted to tell me?'

'Yes, that's important, too. I still want to find my grandfather, so if we travel in the direction he went, I'll be happy.'

'I read about him. And you're pretty awesome as a robot prototype.'

'Thanks, but I'll also need your help with the project to regenerate the robots' creators. Let's have breakfast, and I'll explain. But first, the quantum shower,' Shan said, walking towards the bathroom.

'No, old-fashioned water, please.'

'One last thing. Are you going to broadcast the plans for a new LLTS drive again?'

'I've been thinking about that for a long time, and no. I think this place needs to sort out its own problems first before they go exploring the universe.'

* * *

Shan and Eli arrived at the orbit of the robots' planet. The robots directed them to a new spaceship they had built for them.

'Isn't it slightly too big?' Shan asked Eli, looking at the vast spacecraft.

'The robots built it according to my requirements,' Eli replied.

'I don't think we'll need a flying city,' Shan replied, watching the dock from the windows of his spacecraft.

'Come on, it's not that big. Anyway, you'll have lots of room for your space museum, which should be on the upper deck as far as I remember.'

'Really? You incorporated a museum into it?'

'Those are the plans.' Eli transferred them into the console Shan was using.

'Your spacecraft is ready. Please provide a name,' a robot said over the radio, testing it at the same time.

'Name? What for?' Shan asked.

'A name for the spacecraft,' the robot replied.

'I thought no one did that anymore. But I like that tradition, although I never named my ship. It's kind of important, and we forgot to find a name for the first spacecraft to travel the universe.'

'So what's it going to be?' Eli asked.

'*Adventure*? *Discovery*? It's your dream, Eli, I think you need to decide.'

'It's our dream now, so let's call it the *Dream*. A mysterious dream, like the universe itself,' Eli replied.

The *Dream* spacecraft was designed with the robots' latest improved features: built-in flexible quantum teleportation and morphing technology so the spaceship could change and adjust, LLTS 5, and obviously sub-quantum showers and black-hole fridges. At the last moment, due to the ship's size, Shan decided to take more robots, as the five initially planned would have a hard task managing everything.

Shan easily parked his ship inside the *Dream*, and they both got out and walked across the dark, shiny, pristine hangar floor towards the bridge. The enormous hangar could be easily mistaken for an empty factory as with built-in morphing technology everything could easily be made from the hull itself. After walking through many corridors admiring all the rooms, they entered the bridge with its colourful walls, rainbow floors, and consoles. Shan asked, 'Did you design the colour palette?'

'Very funny, and no. This is the robots' improved colour palette.' Eli replied, finding the details in her knowledge base. 'Anyway, we can change it later.'

'Are you ready?' Shan asked. He was looking at the console displaying the message they had written earlier, for broadcast now.

'Yes, let's do it,' Eli replied, and Shan pressed the send button. The message explaining the bar and the collision was broadcast to everyone, together with additional messages to Shan's garage and his and Eli's parents. After that, incoming messages flooded their inboxes, they could only read the ones from Goe, their families, the bar itself and of course Sork, who wasn't happy and was calling Shan to tell him so.

When Shan finally answered, Sork said, 'You're telling me this now, when I've almost finished exploring this galaxy? I'll look like an idiot; we spent all those resources on my trip for nothing!'

'Sorry about your disappointment that the galaxies will not collide, and the war will end,' Shan replied over the sub-quantum radio.

'I know. Sorry. Anyway, I found something if you want for spare parts for your garage. A spacecraft, I think,' Sork replied.

'You think?' Shan asked, trying to understand how you could fail to recognise a spacecraft in space.

'Well, it's not really a spacecraft; it looks like it's been detached from some bigger ship or a space station. Basically, it's a huge satellite dish. Probably left over after some battle,' Sork said.

'Is it working? Do you have it?' Shan asked, trying to locate Sork in the other galaxy.

'It's floating around my ship at the moment. One of the stars caught it, and it was going to be destroyed, so I thought maybe you'd want it instead.'

'Sure, be there in a minute. Can you calculate where it came from?'

'It looks like it's been flying around for quite a while. I'll transfer the data when you get here. I need to talk to my boss because I have no idea what to do here anymore.'

While trying to plot his course, Shan was disturbed by an incoming emergency call from the general. His finger hovered above the answer button for a moment before pressing it. He expected the general to be wrathful about the many things Shan had kept secret from him, but in the end, it was again Shad who stole the show.

'Shan, I have no other choice but to thank you.' the general said casually.

'You mean for stopping the collision?' Shan replied, assuming the obvious.

'No, but that, too. Your cousin told me to thank you. He also mentioned that he'll see you soon.'

'Thank me for what? What did he do this time? I thought you'd forbidden him from coming anywhere close to you?'

'Well, we were in the middle of negotiations with those guys from the original monstrosity ship when Shad's army kidnapped them. At the same time, he sent us all a message saying to thank you and that he won't be coming back.'

'Interesting. He stole that ship?'

'Yes, which means that he solved two problems for me. Them and himself.'

'Thank you for letting me know, general.'

'If you meet him, make sure he doesn't come back here.' And the general disconnected.

'Shad did steal that ship, look,' Eli said to Shan, projecting the map of the galaxy, which was marked with Shad's stolen ship. 'He's doing LLTS 3.'

'Can you calculate where he's going?'

'Shit, he's heading for the planet where the comets are. How does he know about them? We need to stop him.'

'Maybe he found something on their ship. Does LLTS 5 work here, or is it still experimental?'

'It was always fine, the robots put on that warning as they had to follow their own improved procedures,' Eli explained.

'So I could have been using it all this time? Seriously. Anyway, now we have LLTS 5, we have time. Let's pick up that ship from Sork and then we'll chase Shad.'

* * *

The *Dream* suddenly appeared next to Sork's tiny ship, causing a bit of a quake on his radar.

'What the hell, was that you? Where did you get this huge spacecraft from?' Sork was a bit surprised, to say the least.

'Is that the ship?' Shan asked Sork over the radio, and pointed to an object orbiting Sork's vessel.

'Yes, take it; I'm not sure how long I'll be here. You can transfer all the data about it from my computer.'

Shan used the tractor beam to bring the dish into the loading bay, transferring all of Sork's data from its computer.

'What's that?' Shan asked Eli as they both walked to the loading bay. The spacecraft was standing on the raised floor of the bay with its satellite dish pointing up. Other bits were pointing in all directions, mostly rods with different attachments.

'Looks like a satellite dish to me,' Eli replied, walking around it. 'Most likely part of some bigger spacecraft or a space station,' she added.

'I don't think so,' replied Shan, standing on the other side of the dish.

'A data disk of some kind?' Eli asked, looking at what Shan had found attached to the side of the probe below the satellite dish.

'It's round and yellow.'

'And it's got some markings on it,' Eli replied, moving her fingers across the disk.

'There must be some data on it.'

'If there is, I'm going to find it.' Eli took the challenge and started removing the plate.

'OK, be careful with it. I'll check the information Sork gathered about it,' Shan replied, leaving the loading bay.

A few hours later, Eli came to Shan on the main bridge.

'OK, got it. It took me a while. There were two discs inside this case, and each disc was inside another aluminium case, together with a small device to play it.' Eli projected a holographic representation of the discs. 'I suspect those long lines and those dots represent the location where the probe came from, and those show us how to decode whatever is encoded on those discs,' Eli explained, pointing at various markings.

'How is it encoded?'

'Look here.' Eli zoomed in on one side of the first disc. 'You're supposed to use the small reading device they provided to get the data, but with our technology, I don't have to. Whoever built it was very clever and creative. I mean, this technology is older than ancient for us. We used to have it too, but I think I understand why they used it. With their technology, it was the only way to store data for a long time. You see, whatever powered that probe is long gone, but physically engraving the data allowed it to survive for all that time. I scanned the grooves, and digitally stored them in our computer. That shape there,' she pointed at the wavy line engraved on the case, 'shows how to play it.'

'You can play it?' Shan asked, raising his eyebrows.

'It's digitally stored now; the computer did the rest. Do you want to see it? I only watched the first few frames,' Eli asked.

'Yes, please!' Shan replied with a huge grin.

It took them over five hours to listen and watch all the messages encoded in the disk: photographs, music and spoken words.

'What a beautiful planet.' Shan was almost crying. He didn't want to miss anything, and he tried not to blink.

'It won't be if Shad gets there.'

'Looks like we have no choice. We have a crazy cousin to stop and two comets to pick up,' Shan said, plotting their course.

ABOUT THE AUTHOR

Adam Grzesiczak is an IT professional and fiction writer. He spends his free time writing, traveling, taking photos, playing video and tabletop games, and learning new things.

Learn more at https://adamg.studio/

The Bar Where Nothing Works
Paperback edition ISBN: 978-1-5272-7879-0
Electronic edition ISBN: 978-1-5272-7722-9

This book was first published on
November 5, 2020.

This novel is entirely a work of fiction.
The names, characters and incidents portrayed in it are the work
of the author's imagination.
Any resemblance to actual persons, living or dead, events or
localities is entirely coincidental.

Copy editor: Anna Bowles
Proof-reader: Amanda Rutter
Cover design: Matthew Revert

Version: 1.1
London 2020

Published by Adam Grzesiczak

Printed in Great Britain
by Amazon